damn straight

damn straight

A LILLIAN BYRD
CRIME STORY

ELIZABETH SIMS

alyson books
los angeles

MANUFACTURED IN THE UNITED STATES OF AMERICA.

THIS TRADE PAPERBACK ORIGINAL IS PUBLISHED BY ALYSON PUBLICATIONS,
P.O. BOX 4371, LOS ANGELES, CALIFORNIA 90078-4371.
DISTRIBUTION IN THE UNITED KINGDOM BY TURNAROUND PUBLISHER SERVICES LTD.,
UNIT 3, OLYMPIA TRADING ESTATE, COBURG ROAD, WOOD GREEN,
LONDON N22 6TZ ENGLAND.

FIRST EDITION: JUNE 2003

03 04 05 06 07 a 10 9 8 7 6 5 4 3 2 1

ISBN 1-55583-786-7

LIBRARY OF CONGRESS CATALOGING-IN-PUBLICATION DATA
SIMS, ELIZABETH, 1957–
    DAMN STRAIGHT : A LILLIAN BYRD CRIME STORY / ELIZABETH SIMS.—1ST RD.
    ISBN 1-55583-786-7
        1. PALM SPRINGS (CALIF.)—FICTION. 2. WOMEN JOURNALISTS—FICTION.
3. LESBIANS—FICTION. I. TITLE.
PS3619.I564D36 2003
813'.6—DC21   2003040446

ACKNOWLEDGMENTS

My undying thanks to my family and my friends for their support and belief. (You know who you are.)

Also, I thank the thousands of readers who actually bought and read my first book, *Holy Hell*. Knowing you're there keeps me from a life of wantonness and despair.

I'm grateful to the booksellers, especially Suzanne Corson of Boadecia's (Kensington, California); the women of Mama Bears (Oakland, California); and my many friends at Borders Books and Music.

Special thanks to the people of the Kraft Nabisco Championship and Mission Hills Country Club.

I'm indebted to Joy Glover for sharing her medical expertise; Angela "Sensible" Brown for her good advice and encouragement; and Marcia, for everything.

1

The power struggled back up for about ten seconds—ten brown little seconds—then failed again. I shivered at the moaning, primeval sound it made and tugged down the cuffs of my sweater.

It was March, it was darker than a stack of black cats, and wind-lashed sleet was dragging down utility lines from Monroe to Saginaw. This winter had been a long and sorry one, and spring was supposed to be coming. Most people vent their winter rage on February, but how easy it is to forget treacherous March until it rolls around. You're anticipating spring, you're remembering a bygone balmy March thaw, and your reservoir of strength and cheer against cold and trouble is low. You long to be restored by the sight of a crocus poking its brave yellow petals through a patch of snow—just one goddamn crocus is all you ask—but it doesn't come.

I put on another sweater, my red lamb's-wool one, over my turtleneck, which overlaid my polypropylene long johns; then I pulled on one more pair of socks, overlapping the cuffs of my corduroys, and lumbered into the kitchen. The water was ready, bubbling above the gas flame. I poured in the macaroni. It was a good night for my specialty, macaroni and cheese primavera, a dish I relied on in times of uncertainty. I got out the frozen mixed vegetables, poured them in after a few minutes, and snipped the foil cheese pouch.

Todd and I dined by candlelight, sitting together on the floor. He was happy enough with his carrot top and a handful of bunny chow. I stroked his fur and gave some more thought to my plan to kill Mrs. Gagnon's dog.

Most dogs are wonderful by nature, but this particular one was terrible, vicious to the core. Monty. He'd almost murdered Todd last summer, twice. And Mrs. Gagnon thought it was *funny*. It got so that whenever I took Todd outside, she'd let Monty out to rocket across the street, snarling and snapping. The first close call, I'd had Todd more or less corralled inside the coiled garden hose as I washed my car, and had to dive for him, shielding him from Monty's jaws with my back. My T-shirt got shredded.

The next time, I hadn't even put Todd on the ground when Monty made for us as if we were the last spaceship out of Detroit. He tried to rip Todd from my arms, puncturing my wrist with one of his fangs. Only a kick to the nuts with all my strength made him back off.

It's not right to want to kill someone's pet. But it made me feel better to fantasize about it. What if I left a package of hot dogs to rot for a month, then fed them to him? If he didn't die, at least maybe he'd get good and sick.

Whenever Monty was out, Mrs. Gagnon sat on her porch and cackled. "Monty! Ha! Monty!" I'd moved into the neighborhood before she and Monty had, so I was doubly indignant.

What if I could give him a noseful of cayenne somehow? That was a thought.

Ever since the first snow flew, I'd been thinking about this. One day spring would come, and Todd and I would want to breathe some free air.

A tentative tap sounded at the door.

My landlady, Mrs. McVittie, stood holding a lighted candle and a small plate. "I thought you might like this pork chop, dear." In the candlelight her upper teeth glowed translucent. "When you eat, you stay warmer, you know."

She should talk. I'm sure she weighed less than me, which is saying something, although she was closing in on her seventy-fifth birthday, so you'd expect her appetite to be on the wane.

I'd gone downstairs to check on her when the power went out for the first time, late in the afternoon. She'd already brought in an armload of wood and gotten a fire going using half a roll of toilet paper as tinder. I brought another two armloads in for her. I didn't have a fireplace upstairs, but my flat received spill-up heat from below, so I wasn't worried about myself.

I loved Mrs. McVittie, who'd made her husband come crawling to me for forgiveness after he'd evicted me some few years ago. I was indirectly involved with some property damage; there had been a little matter of a blood-soaked ceiling, pesky police officers, TV cameras. She'd grown fond of me, I guess, even though I hadn't lived there very long. I was grateful to get my place back.

This week Mr. McVittie wasn't home, having gone on an ice-fishing safari in the Upper Peninsula with his sons. The McVitties took turns going up north for various reasons, the chief one being to get away from each other. When the weather was good, Mrs. McVittie liked to pedal her big old three-wheeler around the neighborhood and talk to anybody who was out.

I thanked her for the food. "I'll have it for breakfast. How's your wood holding out?" Until the power came back on it was wood or nothing. "And have you started your faucets dripping?"

"Oh, do you think the pipes will freeze?"

"They could."

She let me bring in more wood for her. As I turned to go, she asked, "What are you doing this evening, dear?"

"Trying to work out a foolproof plan to keep Monty away from Todd. Come spring."

"Oh, I hate that dog. He's a terrible dog."

I was surprised. She was such a tenderheart.

"Well," I said, "I guess it's not really the dog; it's that Mrs. Gagnon doesn't control him."

"Oh, no, dear, it's not just that." Her voice was pure and sweet. "Of course, if she kept him in her backyard, he couldn't hurt your rabbit, but it's not just that...he's a very nasty dog. A nasty personality."

"I agree but thought it best not to be the first to say it. I asked Animal Control to come and talk to her after Monty bit me, and they did, but I'm afraid he'll be right back at it when the weather turns nice." We peered out the stairwell window at the relentless sleet. "Actually," I went on, "I'm trying to come up with a way to kill him—uh, without really killing him, you know?"

"I understand. Well, I'll think about it too, dear."

"Thank you, Mrs. McVittie. Thank you very much."

"Good night, dear."

The phone was ringing as I opened my door, ringing out from the shadows in the dining room. "Hello?"

"Hey, Starmate. You have to come to L.A."

My best friend always just started talking when I picked up the phone, whether it'd been an hour or a year since we'd last spoken.

"Truby! What is it?"

"You have to come for a visit right now. I can't handle anything but yes." Her voice was oddly tight, oddly desperate, oddly something. "I need you. Lillian. Listen. I really. Really. Really. Need you. You've been talking about coming for another visit for three years now, and you haven't, and writing letters is great, and Dallas was fun, but I really need to talk to you." I heard a little gulp and knew what that meant.

"Truby, don't cry—"

A huge sob drowned me out.

"Never mind," I said. "Let it out. Let it out."

The only thing worse than having somebody lose it on you is having her do it over the phone. You can't put your arm around her; you can't go get her a drink of water; you can't search her face for a clue as to what the hell's going on. How serious is it? You can't really know.

"Hon, tell me what's wrong."

"Oh, God, I can't. Not over the phone."

"How come? You sound like you're in pain."

"Oh, God. Oh, God." She made an audible effort to catch

her breath. "I've never faced something like this. I'm so scared. Lillian, can't you *just come?* I really can't get into it. All I want is to hang up the phone knowing you're going to be on the next flight. Are you in the middle of an assignment?"

"No." In fact, I'd had a lean winter. A lean few years, to come right out with it. Since launching my freelance career with a big juicy story for the *Motor City Journal* about a series of murders that I more or less helped solve, work had been spotty. I was able to get a few more big assignments from the *Journal,* but not many other magazines took to my style of reporting. Not the ones that paid, anyhow. I made ends meet freelancing as a tech writer and doing a little busking with my mandolin down in Greektown in the summer.

Reading the tone of my monosyllable, she said, "Wolf at the door?"

"Oh, no, not that bad!" You know, lighthearted-like, which she also read.

"Then I'll pay for your ticket and—"

"*No.* Absolutely not. I'm *coming.*"

"Thank you. Thank you. God, I don't know what to do."

I'd never heard her like this. She'd always been so stoic, so capable, ever since our days together as undergraduates at Wayne State. We both went through some hard times then. Primarily, hers were boyfriend troubles, mine girlfriend troubles, with regular financial crises thrown in. She'd been there for me.

"The thing is, Trube, we're in the middle of an ice storm here, the power's down, and I don't think anything's going out from Metro tonight. If anything *was* going, I'm not sure I'd want to be on it."

"Oh."

"Is it warm there?"

"It is warm, Lillian. It's warm as hell."

"Plus I have to see if Billie can take Todd."

"Make it tomorrow, then. Bring Todd. Bring your mandolin. Bring everything."

I thought about Los Angeles. The warm pavement beneath your feet wherever you walked, the warm smog, the warm tar in the tar pits. Warm. I thought of my friend, sitting in her lovely apartment, traumatized by something.

"All right. I'll be there."

2

The next afternoon I was wedged in a middle seat, bookended by a couple of district manager types pawing the keys on their laptops. The plane was on the taxiway undergoing de-icing, that most claustrophobic of all air travel experiences: the hammering of the thick goo against the wings and fuselage, the oozy darkness moving creepily around the plane, the heavy chemical smell pouring in through the ventilation system. You're glad somebody invented this process—yes, you're glad they're doing it—but you can't help the dread that rises in you.

The storm had let up, allowing me at the wheel of my aging Chevrolet Caprice to follow a salt truck across town on Eight Mile. Then we more or less slithered down Middlebelt to the airport. My Navy surplus pea coat and my leather gloves kept me warm, and I looked forward to shedding them in California. As soon as I got off the parking shuttle at the terminal, it started to snow.

Holding Todd in his carrying case, I waited for the cheapest standby spot I could get. The district managers thought they were going to have a nice empty seat between them until I showed up just before they closed the door, toting my rabbit and mandolin as carry-ons.

"Hate to do this to you," I muttered to their sagging faces. They both immediately rammed their elbows onto the center arm rests.

I made sure Todd was all right in his case, switched on my reading light, and settled in with my paperback copy of *Valparaiso Farewell,* the latest Calico Jones adventure. I'm embarrassed to confess it, but I'd gotten hooked on Calico Jones. People say those books are trashy: just soft-core porn mixed with violence, and of course the books are never reviewed in respectable publications, but hot damn they're fun.

I'd picked up a used copy of the first one, *Incident at McMurdo Station,* at John King in Detroit and just stood there reading it from page one—couldn't put it down.

It isn't that the plots are so terribly plausible. But who could resist falling in love with Calico Jones, the dashing sleuth? She's rich, gorgeous, smart—everything. There's always these ravishing women and men falling all over themselves to get into bed with her. She trots the globe solving impossible crimes, getting into these totally deadly cliff-hanging situations, yet she manages to solve the crime and save her own skin, usually in one breathtaking move. She carries a big honking .45-caliber semiautomatic, and she never misses and never regrets it.

I just marvel at the author of these books. I never can remember her name, though.

In *Valparaiso Farewell,* I'd gotten to the point where the phony viscount had been murdered by mistake, and Calico Jones is tied up in the ambassador's wife's dressing room, and she's just regaining consciousness when the ambassador's wife, a stunningly sexy and very discontented-with-her-husband former movie star, opens the door.

So I picked up with it there, but after a few minutes even Calico Jones couldn't hold my attention. My mind started to roam. What could it be? What could be upsetting Truby Mills so terribly?

Our friendship spanned decades now, beginning when we were classmates at Wayne State University in Detroit. Both of us were from the wrong side of the tracks, from different parts of the state. Truby was rural poor; I was a city urchin. Both of us had Polish blood; both of us were half-assed Catholics. Both of us were scholarship girls. We gravitated to each other like twin planets.

And since Wayne State was the Sorbonne of wrong-side-of-the-tracks universities, we felt more or less at home.

I pictured students at richer schools strolling beside splashing fountains in cobbled squares, lounging in paneled seminar rooms with good heat and beautiful windows, thumbing volumes in well-endowed libraries with clean washrooms, their educations falling into their hands like ripe fruit.

By contrast, the students at Wayne State dodged drunk drivers on Warren Avenue, held down two jobs, caught sleep in unused classrooms, patiently added our names to waiting lists for books, assistantships, student loans, subsidized housing. It was a matter of digging our education out of the asphalt.

To be sure, there were some wonderful professors, but an unfortunate number were there by default, having failed to impress the search committees at better-endowed schools in prettier towns.

But I suppose we only resented things about ten percent of the time. We were, after all, on our own, free, free to make our own choices. Crappy choices, most of them were, but they were ours.

The de-icing dribbled to a stop; we took off to Chicago O'Hare, thence to LAX. My seatmates changed in Chicago and were just as charming as the first two. As the plane crossed time zones and mountain ranges, I continued to review Truby's and my school days.

Eventually, we pooled our resources and moved into an apartment on Prentis Street, where I encountered for the first time the most hideous emblem of the low-rent environment: the window frame with grit painted onto it. You know, where somebody paints over a filthy surface, over the scratchy grit that collects on city windowsills. No sanding, no cleaning. *So that the grit merges right into the paint,* becomes part of the resultant surface, like a lacquered emery board. You couldn't lean a naked elbow on it without recoiling. An uncleanable surface. I recall the visceral repugnance I felt when I encountered it for the first time; I assumed it was an unfortunate aberration. But I soon found how typical the painted-in-grit windowsill was. I tried to imagine the mind of a person who would do such a poor, careless job, or who would pay for it to be done. I couldn't.

This, more than rats in the alleys, more than roaches in the kitchens and clothes closets, more than leaky roofs and axle-busting chuckholes in the streets, was what signified to me where I came from. In the drafty classrooms and lecture halls of the university, I found clues as to where I wanted to go.

Truby and I battled the disappointments of life by calling our apartment "The Star." We were, then, Starmates. The Star was ship-like, low-ceilinged, and as cozy as we could make it with Indian print throws and spray-painted bookcases. We decided what course The Star would take during any given evening or weekend, who would be allowed on board, and who would eventually be driven off. We began with a schoolgirls' alliance and gradually moved into a semblance of maturity.

Truby had had an impressive string of boyfriends, grown men with cars and histories of adventure and loss. She spoke their language—she wasn't intimidated by them. Both of us were short on looks, but there was a special spark to her, the way she moved and laughed, and men adored her. She very much wanted me to approve of her boyfriends; knowing this, I was usually able to work up some enthusiasm. But men bored me, except for my Uncle Guff and Jacques Cousteau. I dedicated my extracurricular time to learning all about wonderful women.

Then college was over and we went our own ways—she to study French and art, managing years in Europe on God knew how thin a shoestring; I to a motley series of jobs in Detroit, eventually making my way to writing for money.

For the past, oh, two years, I thought, Truby had been seeing a guy named Theo, a chef at a fancy restaurant in Beverly Hills or someplace. Boyfriend trouble? She'd never settled down with anyone. I hadn't either, at least for very long. I doubted any guy could vex Truby very much. She never relied deeply on her boyfriends. When the chips were down, she called on her sisters or me.

Money trouble? She had a good job in the art department at Paramount. Drugs? Trouble with the law? Back in Detroit she'd revealed a slight streak of kleptomania, but I thought she must have left that behind with the poverty.

No, from her tone this wasn't some off-the-shelf crisis. I stared at the tops of the clouds.

Maybe she'd come across some secret, one she wasn't supposed to know. Maybe a stranger had approached her with a cryptic message, and she realized she's been mistaken for some underworld go-between, and the stranger keeps coming around asking for Ramon or Misha or Nam Thi or Eddie, and won't believe she isn't who she says she isn't, and things are getting tense.

Maybe, while doing research for a new movie, she was looking through some vintage architectural plans and found that the governor's mansion in Sacramento had been designed with a series of tunnels linking it to the nearby Romanian embassy, where a mysterious long-ago kidnapping had soured relations between the United States and certain factions of Eastern Europe, which had led to World War II, and she blurted something to somebody, and now the feds know she knows, and they don't want her knowing, and things are getting tense.

Maybe somebody's dead. My heart lurched: Maybe *she* killed somebody. Maybe Theo started slapping her around one night, and she brained him with a casserole, and now he's lying in the bathtub covered in plastic and formaldehyde, and she can't bring herself to go to the police. And things are getting tense.

The plane touched down in Los Angeles before I had a chance to speculate about satanic ritual abuse or alien abduction. A gust of warmth hit my face through a gap in the Jetway—welcome to L.A., baby. The breeze was half jet fuel, but it was warm. I searched for Truby's face as I hauled Todd and my stuff to the baggage claim.

There she was, arms folded, leaning against a pillar, looking pale. Her eyes were like embers. We hugged and cried just a little, then joined the throng around the carousel.

I said, "Can you tell me anything about it now?"

"No." She walked along looking straight ahead.

In her car on the way to Santa Monica she said, "Forgive me, Lillian, for being like this. You'll understand soon. Tell me about your trip, how was it?"

As we walked into her apartment I loved it all over again, mainly for its view of the vast Pacific Ocean. There was just a trace of indigo left in the sky; stars were pricking through, and the water was shining black. The apartment, a contemporary one, had beautifully smooth walls, parquet floors, and thin windowsills of extremely clean polished wood. Truby had decorated it simply and chicly, with an awesome old Persian rug and a few low tables and chairs. Great coffee table—the top of it looked like the cabin door from a racing yacht.

As I mentioned, she made good money at Paramount, much of which she'd spent on paintings. She wasn't rich enough to buy a slew of Agnes Martins, or Wayne Thiebauds, or Susan Rothenbergs, but she had a collection of paintings by up-and-coming artists whose qualities sort of reminded you of Agnes Martin, Wayne Thiebaud, and Susan Rothenberg. I liked them.

"Your room is nice and fresh," she said. "Veronica changed all the linens yesterday."

"Veronica? Oh." She had a cleaner.

Todd thumped in his case, reminding me of my first order of business. I took him out and let him look around. "He'll be good."

"I'm not worried."

I dropped our stuff in our room, then cleaned his case and got it ready for the night. Truby had thoughtfully left a stack of newspapers handy.

Always a calm rabbit, Todd had a high threshold for novelty. He bumped slowly around the living room. I could tell he was tired. I stroked his cheeks to relax him, gave him some water and chow, and closed him in our room, making sure to show him the newspapers I'd put down in every corner. Sometimes rabbits will mark a new place. I didn't want to close him in his case all night, but left it open for him to climb into when he was ready—rabbits being nocturnal and all. Tomorrow he'd have more freedom.

As Truby watched us, I tried to watch her a little. She looked gaunt in the face. And certainly pale. Her face was wide and active, easy to read, usually. Her upper body was small, and her hips flared out into strong big legs, which she usually tried to hide, but which I envied. She was moving all right. She looked stressed but not sick.

She'd put out a bracing assortment of snacks on the coffee table: a hunk of Camembert, a bowl of pears, a dish of walnut meats, a few celery sticks. There was a slim baguette and a bottle of Bordeaux that even I could tell cost above the ten-dollar range. Truby always had the gift of putting food together, no matter what odds and ends faced you in the cupboard: salami and popcorn, marshmallows and mangoes, Raisin Bran and beer. Really.

"God, I'm glad to see you," I told her.

"I know you can help me," she said simply.

We settled down to talk and eat.

I was beginning to feel very nervous. Given the enormity of her trouble, how could I help? Why turn to me? Yes, I was a trusted friend, but what could I offer her? I had no money, no influence—political or otherwise. I wasn't a black belt in any martial art; I didn't know much about law; I wasn't wise. However, I did have a reckless streak. I could act like a jerk. Hey, lady, need any jerky stuff done?—you got the right person.

She poured the wine. We turned to each other across the corner of the coffee table, raised our glasses silently, and drank.

I waited.

My friend grew paler still, if that was possible. She cleared her throat and tapped the cheese knife on the cutting board for a few minutes. *Minutes.* I ate a nutmeat and watched a tendon in her wrist jump. Then she grew very calm, composed her face, and met my eyes.

"I think I'm gay," she said.

3

I waited. There had to be more. What was the crisis?

Truby sat there expectantly, tragically.

At last I said, "That's it?"

She nodded, her eyes welling.

"Truby. What I'm asking you is, *is that it?* You think you're gay?"

"Yes."

"You got me all the way out here from Detroit just to tell me you think you're *gay?*"

The tears burst forth. "Lillian," she cried, "this is important! This is my life!"

"Oh, hon." I scooted over and held her as she sobbed. She really cried—man, she did some serious crying there.

When she could talk again, she said, "Well—wasn't it

important for you? And upsetting? When you—you know, came out?"

"Well, yes, but the thing is—Jesus. You're not. You're no more a lesbian than you are an albino." I took a slug of Bordeaux, scanned the room for a box of tissues, then fished a handkerchief from my pocket and handed it to her. "I mean, if somebody asked me which of my friends is the most hetero, I'd say you. My God. What happened with Theo?"

"Lillian." She said this reproachfully, around the folds of the handkerchief.

"I'm sorry. I thought that was a logical question. Okay. Why do you think you're a lesbian?"

Her tears at bay for the moment, she crossed her legs tailor-style on her cushion. "I've been reexamining my whole life. I realized I've done nothing but run from one relationship to the next, always looking for a guy I could really give my *self* to, my real self. A guy who could satisfy me by not acting constantly like a butthead. And I had to honestly admit that I'd never found one."

"I'm sure you know that's not unusual."

"Don't get smug on me. Theo—all right, Theo broke it off between us. He said something that made me go *unhh*—she sat straight up and clutched her fists to her chest as if receiving a hard-thrown football—he said, 'The word *frigid* has gone out of fashion, but they should revive it to describe you.' He called me *frigid*. And a bitch. And a latent lesbian."

"He stopped making you come?"

"God, on the nose. It wasn't as if anything really changed. Well, maybe it did change. I think he was starting to get impatient with my sexual needs. We'd been having problems for months."

"That's too bad. Maybe he was the frigid one. Why

don't you eat a little?" I chopped out a bit of cheese and handed it to her on a crust of bread.

"Thank you. He wasn't fucking frigid. He was just— look, the point here isn't Theo. After he left I was sitting in the bathtub thinking about everything, men, women, everything. And I suddenly thought, gee, it's hard for women to get abortions. Then I suddenly thought, gee, men rape women. And this big enormous bell went off, and I realized how it really is for women. I mean, how it is and why it is."

"Yes."

"I thought, well, maybe I've been blind to the obvious. I always just took for granted being straight." She chewed and swallowed. "But it's only brought me—well, at best it's only brought me temporary happiness. All my happiness, my whole life, relationship-wise, has been temporary. Maybe I've been fooling myself. Maybe I've been missing something."

I bit into a pear. "Have you ever been in love with a woman?"

"Well, God, years ago I think I was in love with Barb Speas—"

"*Barb Speas?* You were in love with Barb Speas?" She was our next-door neighbor in the building on Prentis Street, an education major who was always inviting herself over to rummage through our refrigerator in search of leftover pizza.

"Well, I remember looking at her a few times and going to myself, *Yes, she's appealing.*"

"Ugh. Ugh. Anybody else? I mean, didn't your heart race over any of our profs, or somebody at work? One of those movie stars that are always coming and going? Or even longer ago, like in high school? Tell me about your formative years, Miz Mills."

I sipped some more wine. It tasted deep and rich on my tongue.

"Come to think of it," she said, "I had one girlfriend in junior high school with the most beautiful red hair. The most beautiful skin. We took showers together a few times."

"That's good. How did that make you feel?"

"It was great! Then she moved away."

"Was that your only intimate experience with a woman?"

"Mm-hmm."

"Well, hell, that's not much to go on."

She pondered that, looking down at my handkerchief in her hand. "This is a really nice handkerchief," she said. "Is it linen?"

"Thank you, yes. My aunt Rosalie gave them to me last Christmas. She sent away to Ireland for them." The hankies were square and plain, except for a thin tan border, and my monogram embroidered in small tan block letters: LB. Aunt Rosalie had gone whole-hog and bought me two dozen.

"They are *très, très sophistiqués.*"

They did help my self-esteem, actually. My jeans and shoes were wearing out, but with a couple of elegant squares of linen in my pockets, I felt prepared for most any occasion.

Truby asked, "How did *you* feel about women when you were young?"

"Oh, I was intensely attracted to all of them. I thought my second-grade teacher was incredibly sexy. I fell in love with girls in junior high, high school, teachers—everybody. It freaked me out and made me ashamed, but at least I knew I was different early on. It's not the same for everybody, of course."

"Do you think you have to be born that way?"

"No. In fact, I really hate it when people argue for gay rights by saying we can't help being the way we are. Because the implication is that we'd be different if only we could. Bullshit. I want people to be free to love whomever they *choose* to love. *Feelings* of love aren't exactly a choice, but acting on them is. And it's a gorgeous, wonderful choice that everybody ought to be free to make."

Truby stared for a while into the blackness beyond the windows. "Well," she said, "I have to find out. Didn't you sleep with a couple of guys, just to make sure? What was that one's name, the one with the fur hat who wore his keys on his belt and—"

"I don't remember."

"I bet you don't. Well, I'm not going to be happy until I find out what it's like to be with a woman. And you have to help me."

"I hope you're not expecting—"

"No! Christ almighty! Here's what I want." She fixed me with her anxious, wide-set eyes. "I want to learn everything you know. How you date, how you get a woman to go out with you and understand where you're coming from. What's gaydar? What is it? How do I know if a woman might be interested in me? What are the mating dances? How the hell do you get a woman to love you?"

"You think I'm some big expert on all this?"

"Honey, you're the only expert I've got."

4

I have to tell you, I was relieved. Relieved not to have to figure out how to prevent the syndicate from disemboweling Truby to find the gems, relieved not to have to shield her from an FBI assassination attempt, relieved not to have to help dispose of Theo's body. How hard could it be to coach her through her first lesbian experience?

We talked late into the night, polishing off the bottle of Bordeaux and starting another. Finally, Truby revealed her plan.

"You know the Dinah Shore championship, the golf tournament?"

"LPGA hot spot. Isn't it always in Palm Springs?"

"Actually, Rancho Mirage. It's always in March. It's next week, and we're going."

A brilliant idea.

"Wouldn't it be booked up by now?"

"Sort of," Truby explained, "but one of the admins at work was going to go, but—"

"One of the whats?"

"Admins." Emphasis on the first syllable. "Administrative assistants."

"Oh."

"This admin," Truby continued, "was going to go, but her mother in South Dakota broke her hip, and now she has to go home instead. She gave me her pass."

"All right!"

"And most important, she gave me her reservation at the Howard Johnson's in Palm Springs."

"Very good."

"And before the last putt is sunk, I'm gonna get laid."

I laughed. "How many times?"

"Minimum four."

"We'll need two rooms, then."

"Well, we've only got one. We'll make do."

"I guess we will."

The Dinah. Lustiest of the annual tournaments held by the Ladies' Professional Golf Association—the LPGA. A gay women's fun fair on the magnitude of the Michigan Womyn's Music Festival. Thousands of dykes come from all over the country—from all over the world—to party down and root for their favorite golf stars, in the biggest of the tour's championships. I'd heard stories about the parties. Of course, lots of women on the pro tour are gay. Pretty deeply closeted, most of them. If you're fighting for equality in prize money, if you're competing to convince sponsors to sign you, you're reluctant to risk blowing it by coming out.

Why is the Dinah such a magnet? I supposed because it stays in one spot, allowing the massive lesbian population of nearby Los Angeles to build, over time, an impressive social infrastructure. Because it was founded by a beautiful woman with one of the smoothest voices in the world: the Tennessee Thrush, Dinah Shore.

I was old enough to remember her singing sentimental songs on television and radio. She was the embodiment of active, healthy womanhood: those sparkling eyes, that uncomplicated blond hairstyle, the good body, and always that sure, liquid voice. Chevrolet sponsored her TV variety show, and no one could have sung, "See the U.-S.A. in your *Chev*-rolet" with more verve. She was patriotic. She entertained troops during World War II and Vietnam. Bob Hope respected her. Bing Crosby respected her. Frank Sinatra respected her. Patti Page probably hated her guts, but respected her.

Yep, Dinah Shore was a classic. Then she got divorced and founded a charity golf tournament that grew into a major professional event. She'd passed on, and the championship was now officially "The Kraft Nabisco," but people still called it the Dinah. Among lady golfers, that trophy is the Grail. Why? For one thing, it's an invitational. You can't play your way in; there's no qualifying tournament. So it's like the men's Masters, exclusive and tough and historic, always on the same course. The first major of the year—and the most significant. You win the Dinah, you're The Woman, all year long. You're the broad who can get the job done.

And if you watched the tournament on TV, you'd have no way of knowing what a grand time everybody was having off the course.

Being a golfer, I'd always thought it'd be fun to go to the Dinah, but who had the dough for a vacation like that? Plane ticket, rental car, motel, tournament passes, party tickets—I could live for months on what a vacation like that would cost.

"Trube, it occurs to me that you don't even golf."

"Golf has nothing to do with it." She looked at me with sudden sternness. "And how are *you* fixed for love? Ready for some action, or have you met some little sexpot down the canned goods aisle at Farmer Jack's?"

I shuddered. "Whhf. Love? Real love? Hell. It's not that I don't try. God knows I try. But—I don't know, maybe I was born to suffer. I've sent away for membership information on various cloistered orders. That might be the answer."

She laughed. "If we lived in the Middle Ages, we'd both be in the cloisters."

"No other choice."

"And all the other nuns would be falling in love with your earnest face and your way with the lute. Hey, play me a song."

I got out the old mandolin and tuned her up. Choosing a flexible plectrum, I played a few tunes: "O'Donnell's Hornpipe," "Drowsy Maggie," and a sort of swing version of "Nine-Pound Hammer." It felt good to loosen up my hands. The familiar thin tones of my instrument made me feel grounded after a long day.

Between songs Truby remarked, "That little thing's more beat up than ever. Still sounds sweet, though."

I rubbed at a scratch on the mandolin's flat spruce face. "Yeah."

Truby really liked the hornpipe.

"Hornpipes are cheerful by definition," I said. "And on that note, I'm going to bed."

Donning her yoga leotard and bright-pink headband, Truby cooked a stack of marvelous pancakes in the morning, and we more or less got ready for school. She had a French press pot, from which the most wonderful coffee flowed, making me rethink my trusty stove-top percolator.

The sun was creeping over the edges of the West Coast, turning the ocean from slate to thunderous ultramarine. A fresh breeze blew in through the casement windows in the kitchen. White waves stroked the beach, where I could make out a few joggers and their dogs.

"We're going to Carla and Meredith's tonight," said my friend, spooning hot buttered banana slices over the thin cakes.

"Boy, do those smell good. Who are Carla and Meredith?"

"Women I sort of know. Carla's in makeup. Meredith manages Genie Maychild. They're having some people over, and I slightly begged Carla to let us come."

"This Meredith manages Genie Maychild?"

"Plus, I think, a few other golfers. Lona Chatwin, for one."

"What day is this, anyway?" I asked her. "Friday?"

"Yes, dear heart."

The tournament would start with practice rounds and charity benefits on Monday, then the real championship would run Thursday through Sunday. Truby told me she'd arranged to take next week off from work and had called in sick early this morning.

"That'll be believable," I said.

"You forget what a wreck I've been. They'll believe it. I don't care, anyway. Christ, my life is at stake here."

"Your sex life, anyway."

"One and the same."

She was looking better. A certain grim sorrow, or tension, had evaporated overnight. We'd both risen early to watch the dawn come up. She showed me a few yoga stretches.

I'd brought Todd out to the living room. He seemed to like the place. At one point he sidled naughtily over to a stereo speaker cord. A firm, "No, Todd," was enough to remind him of his manners, instilled by me through careful training. He was five years old now, almost middle-aged, but he still had the same patient, inquisitive personality that had made him such a good friend from the beginning.

While the last of the pancakes cooked, I feasted my eyes on the Technicolor vista past Truby's Sub-Zero and her Viking and her Waring and her Dualit. She owned all the good brands. Out in the water, black fins cut this way and that, catching the sun. "Are those sharks or dolphins out there, past the surf line?"

Without looking, Truby said, "Dolphins. How long can you stay?"

"I guess a week." I thought of the dismal late-winter cloud cover in Detroit. "Week and a half. Do you suppose we could go to a museum today?"

"I'll drop you off at LACMA this afternoon, but then I'm going shopping. I want something new for tonight." She looked at me and I could tell she was thinking, *You could use some new clothes yourself*. But I didn't want any, and she could tell that, too.

"Now," she said, "I'm ready for lesson one." We moved to the living room, where we sprawled and began to metabolize our breakfasts, with fresh coffee as a digestive. "What's gay-dar, and how do I get it, because I'm going to need it, right?"

"Forget gaydar" I told her. "It's simply a matter of paying attention. And it's not infallible, anyway. You begin by ignoring guys. When I say guys, I mean the kind of guys who feel they're the center of the universe. That's the first big step for you. They hate that, by the way. I think one reason men can't handle lesbians is that lesbians ignore them, and they're unnerved by that. It's so bizarre to them to be ignored by women that they perceive it as hostility. They get deeply uncomfortable. Then they get pissy."

"My God, you're right."

"At the Dinah, and I'm sure at this party tonight, whichever direction you walk in, you're going to bump into gay women. If you want to work fast, you're going to need a system to separate the—well, the Bordeaux from the Mad Dog. I've developed CUPCAKE. It's very effective."

"I should be taking notes."

"No, just listen."

"Cupcake."

"You see a woman; something about her appeals to you. Maybe it's just looks, for the moment. Before approaching her, use this simple quiz. Does she look chipper? C for chipper: By that I mean does she look as if she likes to have fun? Is there a spark in her eyes, something there in her face besides just beautiful curves? Then, does she appear to be unattached? Any partner lurking around, on the way back with a cup of punch? U for unattached. P is for piercings."

"Piercings. As in—"

"Does she look as if she just escaped the Spanish Inquisition? Call me a dinosaur, but having an up-close conversation with someone with eyebrow piercings makes my stomach feel funny."

"What about a pierced tongue?"

"I went on one date with a woman who had a tongue stud. All through the movie she clacked it around her teeth."

"I have to ask, what was the movie?"

"Oh, God, some Japanese epic she wanted to see. With all the colored uniforms. Then—well, those things are supposed to be great in bed, you know, but I guess she wasn't very practiced. Either that, or I was too afraid something unfortunate would happen. God probably wanted to punish me for going to bed with her on the first date. So I make it a point to check for piercings. You can't see certain ones, of course, but my research suggests that a lot of visible facial piercings indicates a high occurrence elsewhere."

"P for piercings."

"Yes. C and A are for cognitive abilities. This is beyond chipper. Is she just standing there waiting for something to happen, or is she engaged with what's going on? Could she sell you a set of encyclopedias? Does she look like the type who sends in her Publishers Clearing House entry?"

My friend's laughter swirled around the room.

"Cognitive abilities," I repeated. "Now, a very important letter, K. Can you picture yourself kissing her? Yes or no? If the answer is yes, and if you're still E for enchanted, then go for it. Make eye contact and talk to her."

"CUPCAKE."

"CUPCAKE. Chipper, unattached, piercings, cognitive abilities, kiss, enchanted. Now, there are sometimes exceptional cases where your knees suddenly go weak, and you don't need this CUPCAKE stuff."

"Tell me about your ideal woman," Truby said. "What kind of woman would you like to meet this week?"

I thought for a minute. "I guess I'm at a point where I'm looking for someone extraordinary. I mean, I'm past 'Oh, God, it's great to be in bed with a woman,' or 'Wow, it's great to be working on a relationship.' "

"What would she be, ideally? Come on."

"She'd be chipper—well, she'd be a CUPCAKE, plus she'd be doing something exceptional with her life: She'd be inspiring. She wouldn't just be working as a drone, beneath her capacities. She'd be challenging herself to do better, always striving for something important—whether it's inventing some new vitamin, or being a great kindergarten teacher, or competing in a tough business, or competing against herself. Someone who presents herself honestly and who isn't afraid of hard work, or being wrong, or being human. Someone who can take a hammering from life and come back up smarter and tougher and just as loving. Someone who would let me love her."

5

The party was in Bel Air. As Truby gunned her Jetta around blind curves, I looked at the street names and tried to remember where the Manson murders occurred. The evening was fine. A golden dusk was settling over Los Angeles, making the city look friendlier. Windows flashed in the low sun. The air was gloriously warm, pouring in through the sunroof.

"Meredith is supposed to be good friends with Billie Jean King," Truby said. "I hope she's there. Of all the women in sports, I'd like to meet her the most. She's done so much."

I agreed. "But the one I'd really like to meet is Tonya Harding."

"Tonya Harding?" Truby honked out a laugh at that. "Why, for God's sake?"

"I'm serious. I think she's fascinating. There she was, a champion athlete, and she decided that winning was worth the price of her soul."

"And she succeeded in destroying herself."

"I wonder what she's like these days. Whether she's more, you know, introspective."

Carla and Meredith's house, looming over a crescent drive, looked as if it'd been built to the specifications of a film producer with a very small penis. Everywhere you looked, there were things sticking up: columns and obelisks and turrets and spires. Very '30s, very grand.

A kid in a red jacket took the car keys, and we walked into a marble foyer where another rent-a-kid stood ready to take our wraps, had we any, which we hadn't.

Then on into an enormous room furnished with antiques and hulking postmodern pieces, all mixed together. On and around the furniture were women of all different shapes and sizes and ages, all beautiful, all wearing extremely stylish clothes. They stood or sat, holding drinks and one another, talking above the music, which was coming in from somewhere outside. I'd never seen so many attractive women at one time in my life, except for when I climbed a tree above the crowd at the Michigan festival.

Beyond the windows I could see the dusky sky, a swimming pool, more women gathered there. Other rooms opened off the main one, all spilling low-key party sounds.

"Do you know any of these people?" I murmured to Truby.

"No, I don't think so. There's Carla."

A short woman with smiling eyes came over to greet us. Truby introduced us, and as we shook hands I delivered my usual warm "How do you do?"

"Welcome," she said, then quickly scanned my clothes down to my shoes. I'd thought I'd looked fine in the mirror in my room at Truby's, but now I knew otherwise. This was not an unusual experience for me. There were other women in the room wearing—as I was—blue jeans and plain linen blouses and brown shoes, but their whole look was different. Very expensive, was what it was. Their clothes fit as if they'd been custom made, even the jeans. I hadn't asked Truby how much she paid for her new outfit, a brilliant Chinese-red sleeveless tunic. In silk, over a pair of gorgeous translucent white slacks. Manolo Blahnik shoes, I saw the label.

Carla said, "That is charming."

"Um?" I said.

"How do you do? That's what I meant. Nobody says that anymore. You're not from L.A., are you?"

"I'm from Eagle, Michigan, next to Detroit."

"That's in the Midwest, isn't it?"

"Pretty near, yes."

All women love shoes, especially dykes. Is this a widely known fact? I guessed that my twice-resoled Weejuns made me look like a runaway from a Brownie day camp. There were some gorgeous shoes in that room, I tell you.

Sweeping us by the arms, Carla introduced us to her partner, Meredith, who had the determinedly game expression of a not-natural-born hostess—and also couldn't seem to help checking out my shoes. Maybe I'd been misinformed about this bunch, and they were actually a coven of foot fetishists. I didn't see anyone famous.

Carla introduced us to a few people standing nearby. I truculently waited for any of them to look at my shoes, but none did.

Truby and I separated, and I made a casual beeline for a table near the center of the room, to look at something that had caught my eye when we came in. It was a food table, and the main feature was an amazing ice sculpture of a bag of golf clubs. The life-size bag was sculpted in the round, and the club heads sticking up were clustered together in a realistic bunch. I tried to make out a brand name, they looked that good. It looked as if a caddie had stood the bag there among the prawns and portabellos and gone off to sneak a smoke.

As I stood there admiring it, a young server in a hot black bodysuit swung by and said, "Champagne?"

"*Mais oui*," I said, relieving her tray of a shimmering flute. She gave me a little glint. Her eyebrows were minky, her figure graceful. I smiled back, enthusiastically, and she moved on, glancing over her shoulder.

There was, in the air, a sense of anticipation. A sense of possibilities, the feeling that we're here to celebrate an important event, we're going to have a good time, we're beginning to have a very good time, and we're being just a bit cautious to get this thing started off right. Something especially good might be ready to happen.

I noticed a few pale left hands in the room: the tell-tale sign of an avid golfer.

The appetizers looked good. There was a slew of vegetables crafted to appear architectural, like a sort of Carrot-henge. A little zone of cool air hung over them. Then there were some miniature, incredibly elaborate sandwiches that you'd be too embarrassed to eat anywhere except in a house like this. I enjoyed it all for a minute, drinking my champagne, then I moved over to look at a small bronze sculpture of a leaping woman.

My plan was to sort of edge around the pedestal,

inspecting all sides of her, then from her cover, scan the room for famous people, and perhaps pick out a friendly face to approach.

As I admired the statue—and I thought it was good, lively and free—I listened to the voices in the room, catching a few fragments.

"On top of that, we won the drawing for the free cruise, so we're going to Alaska at the end of—"

"Don't know when I could fit it in. I've got soup kitchen on Tuesday, literacy on Wednesday, crisis line on—"

"So I said to her, they *do not* owe it to us to stay together. Puh-leeze!"

I thought about women's voices. It always brought me up short when I met a woman who consciously modulated her voice. You know, that—well, is it an East Coast thing? A straight thing? An I'm-a-good-girl-therefore-I-speak-mellifluously thing? I knew a lot of gay women with unmodulated voices. And I heard a lot of unmodulated voices in the room. It was a healthy sound, it seemed to me.

Someone grabbed my shoulder and I jumped.

It was Truby. "Okay, Starmate, what do you say?"

"What are you talking about?"

"I mean what do you say first, once you've found a CUPCAKE?"

"Christ! You make eye contact. And then you just *say something*. You talk to her. Get her to talk to you. Listen to her. Offer to get her something."

"But she's a complete stranger."

"Didn't you ever approach a guy?"

I looked at her, in her brand-new little crimson number, her clear face shining, her quick knowing eyes. "Don't answer," I said. I was glad I'd never had any bawdy feelings

35

for her. We were so close it would've seemed incestuous. "All right, you say something un-wisecrackerish like, 'I like your earrings,' or 'That's an interesting scarf—did you design it yourself?' With a friendly tone and a smile, for God's sake, you can say anything, even if it's really lame. You can talk about the weather. Then listen. If you like what you hear, keep up the conversation. When she asks how you're doing, be ready with something upbeat like, 'Fine, I got out for a little sun today, and it was great,' leaving her the opening of 'Oh? Where did you go?' Look, Truby, you're not going to blow it. You don't go boringly on and on about yourself."

"That's all most men do. Theo said he wanted a woman with a good sense of humor. What he really wants is someone who'll sit there and laugh at all of his witty comments."

"Quit thinking about Theo. Where is she?"

"Out by the pool, where the music is. Do you realize it's a live band?"

"Oh! No, I hadn't."

"They're called Hannah and her Sisters."

"Oh."

"They're exceptionally famous, I was just told. Genie Maychild's out there, too."

"Go on, now."

I went back to studying the sculpture, slowly shifting to a casual survey of the room, when again someone took my shoulder from behind. I turned sharply, in annoyance, elbow out, ready to bark something at Truby, and felt my elbow hit a firm stomach at the wrong height. I looked up to see a tray of full champagne flutes tilting toward my head.

It wasn't Truby, it was the champagne server, and I saw the sexy grin disappear from her youthful face as she struggled briefly to reposition the tray beneath the shifting glasses, then I saw her give up as gravity asserted itself. There were perhaps a dozen servings on the tray.

I ducked, but the full load of champagne cascaded onto my head and back, more or less followed by the flutes, which bounced off me en route to the nice hard floor, where they, of course, shattered. Into a million pieces. With a sound like a rocket falling on Notre Dame cathedral.

In the silence that followed, I straightened up and met the horrified eyes of the server.

"I thought you were someone else," I said.

"Your glass was empty," she whispered.

Then I turned to the room at large. "I'm sorry."

After an incredibly awkward sixty seconds, a broom, dustpan, and mop appeared in the hands of two other servers, and the mess was cleaned up.

My server girlfriend disappeared. Truby was nowhere to be seen, fortunately. Perhaps it wasn't too late for her to pretend she didn't know me.

Carla and Meredith came over, kindly not having run up shrieking immediately, and I apologized to them. "I'd like to pay for the broken glasses and the champagne."

They wouldn't hear of it. "It's the caterer's glassware," said Meredith, "and to hell with the champagne. We've got eight more cases, I believe. I'm just glad it wasn't me this time. Thank you."

"Oh, not at all," I responded generously.

"Are you all right?" Carla felt my wet sleeve.

"I'm fine. Just don't set me out in the sun next to an anthill. Is there someplace where I can clean up?"

She directed me to a bathroom down a cul-de-sac off the foyer. It was done in a Moorish style, with complicated medallions on the wallpaper and a snake-charmer's basket next to the john. I lifted the lid and found a cache of tampons and minipads. Handy.

As I went out, washed and combed to a degree, I noticed someone waiting in the hallway. I stepped to the side, smiling at the floor, then to the other side, suddenly blocked in by this person. She put an arm up on the wall; I lifted my eyes.

It is a difficult thing to describe a moment of such impact that, like a violent car accident, you have no clear memory of it. All you remember is what came next: You're in the ambulance, you can't move, your shoes are gone, and someone is yelling at you to name the days of the week.

"Hello," she said.

I blinked. "Hello."

6

Have you ever met a goddess, a real goddess? I haven't either, but this woman was the closest thing I'd seen to one.

Mind you, she would not have won the Cutest Baby contest in her hometown, had someone even thought to enter her, nor would she have nailed prom queen. Second-string cheerleader? Nah. Her looks were neither golden nor rosy.

But she had *it*. Yes. *It* being a vivid aura of self-possession, of confidence. Of intelligence. Of fun. She had, also, strength: This was clear to me from the firmness of her body, easily visible through her clothes, even in the dim light of the hallway. I saw the quiet way her body rested there on her feet, the balance of it, the stillness of it. The readiness of it.

She extended her hand. "I'm Genie Maychild." Her grip was firm, all right.

"Lillian Byrd. How do you do?"

"Very well, thank you.

"That's one of us, then."

"I saw your mishap. That was spectacular."

"Uh, thank you."

I'd seen her a hundred times on television, of course: Genie Maychild, dominatrix of the LPGA tour. She'd been on top for years now, maybe eight years? Ten years? She'd won as many majors as Kathy Whitworth, and, last year, had broken the record of consecutive wins, five, held by Nancy Lopez and Annika Sorenstam. And she broke it by three. She was at her peak, but she wasn't a kid anymore.

"It was a disaster," she said, "that went almost in slow motion. I've never seen anything like it."

"You've never attended a stadium implosion?"

She laughed. "Look, how about some more wine?"

"Guess I could use another glass."

My next clear memory has me spending a relaxed and, yes, happy hour or so talking with this wondrous creature. We were back in the big room, seated on a fat tufted love seat.

"So," she said, "what's your connection at this party?"

I told her, blurting out Truby's story by way of explaining why I was in Los Angeles in the first place. I threw in preliminary details of the power failure, the storm, my plot against Monty, which made her laugh again, and the kindly Mrs. McVittie.

"God, I don't miss that weather," said Genie Maychild. "I'm from Chicago." She pronounced it like a native: "Chicaugo."

"Oh, God," I said. "That's even worse than Detroit. Christ, I remember the first time I was in Chicago, I had to walk fifteen blocks downtown, and it was eight below and it was blowing like a bitch, and they hadn't invented wind chill yet, and *I had no gloves*. I've never been colder in my life."

"Boy, do I hate that freezing rain."

"Me too, boy."

The details of her were ordinary: hair that was probably light brown to begin with, but bleached considerably on top by the sun, cut in a perfect bob and blown fluffy; eyes that were a color I really couldn't determine yet—green, perhaps, or possibly hazel, set close together—but this made for a look of concentration rather than denseness; a good classical nose with nostrils that could perhaps, I thought, flare nicely if properly provoked; a full mouth sporting an upside-down smile, you know, where the corners turn down instead of up; breasts a bit low-riding; the arms nicely shaped and evenly tanned, except for the left hand. The dead-white left hand announced where it spent most of its time outdoors: inside a leather glove, wrapped around the grip of a golf club.

I became aware of the scrutiny of other women. They sort of hovered; yes, hovering was occurring. Genie Maychild was like a magnet, and the women in the room were oriented toward her like needles. I saw Meredith looking at me. Then she came over.

"Genie," she said in a completely different tone than when she'd talked to other people, "I forgot to tell you I have a surprise for you!" Her voice was a full-blown simper.

"What's that?"

"Mary Lee Hume is here! And she wants to meet you!"

Genie's eyes cut to me. I'm sure I reacted. Mary Lee Hume had just won something like four Oscars for her movie *Skyhook and Breadfruit,* the story of a Malaysian princess who disfigures herself after learning that 10,000 of her people were massacred by the CIA, which unsuccessfully tried to pin it on the Chinese Mafia. It was a hell of a picture.

And the whole world was talking about Mary Lee Hume. And Mary Lee Hume wanted to meet Genie Maychild.

"I don't have time," said Genie.

I watched Meredith swallow that one whole.

"All right," she said, crouching low, "I'll tell her you've been *detained.*" She smiled a horrible submissive smile that somehow also conveyed firm dislike of me.

"Mer," said Genie, "I need a glass of guava juice, fresh. Do you have a guava in the house?"

"Anything, darling. If I don't, I'll send out for one."

"Do that, would you? Oh, and would you take this?" Genie extended her empty champagne flute.

"Wow," I said, after Meredith had gone, "is it because you make her lots of money?"

"Money's the only thing she cares about. I, personally, am nothing to her."

One thirtyish lovely wearing an odd fringed jacket circled very slowly, and as she passed Genie, she allowed her trailing fringe to skim Genie's arm, resting on the back of the love seat. Genie looked up in cold irritation, and we were alone again briefly, in a tenuous envelope of privacy.

It was quite clear that Genie had cut me from the herd. Why? Did she merely want quick sex later? I certainly hoped so. Her eyes searched my face thoroughly. I felt self-conscious, thinking about all my ungorgeous attributes.

My complexion tends toward sallow, my jaw is too long, and I'm thin-lipped. On the plus side, my cheekbones are halfway decent, both my eyes match (light-gray), and my eyebrows don't need plucking.

Then Genie's eyes quite deliberately moved downward and checked out my body, such as it was. I shifted in my seat.

I didn't know how sports idols operated. Were they all jaded from the adulation, or did they continually thirst for it? It seemed I was being given an opportunity of some kind.

All those times I'd seen her on TV, I'd never felt the pang of cupid's arrow. Never thought about her sexually. Never thought about any of them that way.

Why? Because they were *athletes*. Different brand of human. Athletic women always intimidated me, with their easy competence and equally easy aggressiveness. Their bodies were stronger than mine, bigger than mine—bigger around, anyway. They liked to wear equipment. They liked to move with precision.

Looking at Genie closely, I perceived a—a *something*, an aspect or an aura that wasn't previously visible to me, not visible at all on television. Was it a solemnity? A depth not revealed during the cold course of competition? Somehow, I didn't feel intimidated. Not very, anyway.

She said, "You don't look as if you belong here."

I smiled into my champagne. I was feeling good; I didn't take it as an insult and was quite sure it wasn't meant as one. I suppose this is a cliché, but I felt her power, felt it as a positive force all around her. If this was what she was like just hanging out at a party, what must she be like in competition? *Whoa*, was my thought.

"I suppose most women here are pretty significant people," I said. "It's all a bit rich for me."

Ever so casually, Genie touched one of my fingertips. The resultant spark could've powered Las Vegas for five minutes. "That's not what I meant," she said. "It's just that you're—I noticed you as a little island of calm, there, looking at the statue. You weren't frantic to talk to everyone, to, to—ingratiate yourself somewhere. To not be alone. Then, even when the champagne fell on you, you were calm."

"Where were you?"

"I'd come in from the pool a minute before, trying to get away from a group of groupies. I'm playing next week—"

"Of course."

"And well, the night is young, but I'm burned out on the flattery."

"I'd imagine almost any party you go to, you'd run into that."

"I was told this party would be different. But everybody's so...hectic."

Truby cruised by, looking at me in astonishment. She cruised back again, holding two full glasses and balancing a plate of food. I gave her a subtle wink.

"So," I said, "you don't know this crowd?"

"I know some of them."

"Meredith manages you?"

"She does now. Actually, she doesn't so much manage me as represent me."

"For endorsements and stuff?"

"Yes. I left the Blevin Group last year."

"Oh."

"I was with them for four years, but they went and lost their focus."

"What happened?"

"They signed Coco Nash."

"Ah."

"You dig?"

I had to laugh. "Yeah."

Coco Nash, a.k.a. Cornelia Rosa Parks Nash, was the upstart, the baby phenom, foe of every woman in the LPGA, but most especially of Genie Maychild. It was the natural thing. Genie was at the top, and Coco was rookie of the year last year and had given notice that the top was her rightful spot, and it was just a matter of time until she got there. She'd won four tournaments and finished in the top ten in all but one of the rest. People said she was just warming up.

Coco Nash talked very tough, and she was black, and she wasn't liked by a great many women on tour (so I'd read in a small item in *Golf Today*), and she didn't give a shit. She didn't give a shit about endorsements. What she gave a shit about was winning.

Genie's "You dig?" was a jab at Coco's lingo, which was half hep-cat, half Catholic school. I liked Coco Nash and rooted for her, and I could see how Genie might feel nervous about her.

"It mustn't be easy to keep up your confidence, when you've got the world snapping at your heels," I said.

"I don't have much trouble that way," she said.

"It doesn't bother you that Meredith manages Lona Chatwin, too?"

"Oh, no. Lona and I are friends."

"And she's not nearly as good as you, and everybody knows it. No threat. Right?"

She paused, and I thought I'd angered her. But she said, "Everybody's a threat when you get to this level. But—well. I guess you called it. It's not that I'm afraid of Coco. I just don't like her. I don't like the feeling I get when she's around me."

"How do you feel when she's around?"

"Hey," she looked at me closely, "I don't talk about this stuff."

"Sorry," I smiled.

"I hate her."

I laughed. But there was a deadly look in her eye. "Yeah? As in really actually hate?"

"Yes."

"How come?"

After a moment she said, "Because she hates me."

"How do you know that?"

"I just know it."

"But how? Have you guys had words?"

"What are you, a lawyer or something?"

"Something."

"Don't you read the papers, don't you read the magazines? She keeps telling everybody that I'm old and can't win anymore. She says she'll kick my ass. She says she's God's gift."

"But that's just talk. What have you said about her?"

"Nothing. I've been polite."

"Oh?"

"I have." She touched my finger again. "Look. I'd like to spend more time with you. I want peace before this tournament. I want to relax."

"You decided not to play in Phoenix."

"Right, I wanted to take the week off, relax, prepare myself."

"And you didn't go home? Where's home, anyway?"

"No. Heck, I live in Orlando now. I don't like timezone changes. I wanted to acclimate to Pacific time. And I wanted to work with Dewey for a couple of days."

"Dewey O'Connor?" Swing guru to the champs.

She nodded. "I'm staying at his house. One of his houses, actually. It's nice and..." Pause. "Private."

"Oh, is it?"

"Yes." She looked at me.

"I bet it's ever so nice."

"It is. It's ever so nice."

7

It was time to have a word with Truby, who'd been making some progress, it appeared, with a comely lass who sported no visible facial piercings. They were taking their ease in a little cabana by the pool. The musicians must've been on break.

"Go for it, Starmate," she said.

"Focus and execute," I said. "Please check Todd's water."

"Okay."

"Thanks."

And so, with Meredith pointedly looking utterly dismayed, Genie and I exited.

"Is Meredith freaking out?"

"She's keeping a lid on it. This'll give her more excuse to fuss over Lona. She knows I don't need a baby-sitter."

"Doesn't anyone travel with you?"

"Not really. What's this?" Genie asked the kid who brought her car up. It was a Jaguar, rented. She plucked an envelope from beneath the windshield wiper.

"I don't know," he said, pocketing his tip, "It was there." I noticed she gave him a fiver. *That was nice,* I thought.

When we stopped at a light at the foot of the hills, she opened the envelope, drawing out a small folded sheet.

"Fan mail from some flounder?" I said.

Her face went white as she read it. It was a short message. After a second she crumpled it in her fist.

"What is it?"

She didn't answer or look over at me. The car behind us honked; automatically, she let up on the brake and the Jaguar moved into traffic.

"Are you all right?"

"Yes."

She wasn't, though; a sudden heaviness had come over her, as if an iron bar had dropped down onto her shoulders. I watched her sideways and saw her mouth working. She touched her forehead, then rubbed the back of her neck. I looked out the window at the nightscape of Sunset Boulevard and breathed in the smell of the leather seats.

By and by, I heard her laugh.

Again I asked, "What is it?"

"It's just me." She'd shaken it off. "I'm an idiot some-times."

"Me too, lots of times. Where's the house?"

"Hollywood."

"Think we ought to pick up a six-pack along the way? Some Doritos?"

She laughed. "You. Are. Funny. Calm and funny. And you have a…a…"

"An earnest face?"

"That's not what I was going to say, but come to think of it, you do. *Goodness,* I need to relax."

"Maybe I should drive."

"Naw, we're almost there." We were climbing again, through narrow streets.

It was too dark to see much of the house, which was perched close to the road, but it seemed to sort of spill down the canyon in a multitude of rooms. A Hollywood house.

Inside, the style was sleek, minimalist. As Genie ushered me through I caught a glimpse of the kitchen, which looked as if you could walk right in and start doing brain surgery on any surface.

We went directly to the hot tub, an *in-ground* hot tub, I add, nestled in a bower of flowers out back. A few ground-level lamps in the shrubbery gave out a soft glow. The night had turned cool, and a skim of warm vapor hovered over the surface of the water.

I stood looking up at the stars as Genie pressed a few buttons, and the jets began their jet-thing. I saw one light in the house go off and another go on in a different room. I guessed they had sophisticated timers in Tinseltown.

"Now, my new friend," said my new friend, "I'd like to get to know you better."

I really wanted a drink of water, but Genie hadn't offered me anything yet. This minor lapse in hospitality disappointed me, for I assumed her to be perfect in every way. That is, I was operating under the perfect-until-proved-flawed system, which has its perils, but is more generous than prove-to-me-you're-wonderful.

We helped each other out of our suddenly cumbersome clothing and descended the tiled steps into the roiling water. Very nice. The water felt perfectly clean, but didn't have that chlorine reek I remembered from the one other hot tub I'd been in, in somebody's backyard in Melvindale. That one you had to clamber up a ladder to get into. This was Hollywood. The seats were nicely positioned. There was room for half a dozen people comfortably, plus a flotilla of rubber ducks.

Genie's body was more exciting than even my fevered imagination had pictured. She was *smooth*. A firm waist, a real waist with muscles I could feel. Breasts that looked like Sno-Kones of the angels, and a wowzer pair of legs I could hardly begin to appreciate when they disappeared into the churning depths. Even seated, she moved with poise.

This was one serious whirlpool. I allowed the small of my back to be battered by one jet, while my feet found pleasant abuse before another.

We enjoyed the water quietly, each of us heaving sighs as the tensions of the party dissolved. Yes, it was very quiet. Thus I was able to hear sudden footsteps close by and coming closer.

My heart jumped into my throat as a tall figure loomed over us, blotting out the stars.

"Oh, hi, Hesper," said Genie, looking up. "Thank you. Lillian, this is Hesper."

A large, large woman set down a silver platter laden with a water pitcher, glasses, a plate of sliced fruit, and delicate cookies. She swung an ice bucket down from one elbow, containing—what else?—more champagne. She was a burly one.

"How do you do?"

"Good evening, Ms..."

"Lillian Byrd."

"Ms. Byrd."

Hesper's eyes glowed like a cat's in the dim light. Crouching easily, she poured the champagne and arranged the tray so we could reach everything, then disappeared.

"I thought you said it was private here," I whispered.

Genie looked at me. "It is. Oh! You mean—oh! That's good!"

Hesper reappeared with an armful of towels, and set them on a low stool nearby.

"We won't need anything more tonight," said Genie.

"Good night, then, Ms. Maychild," said Hesper.

We laid back in the tub, hooking our necks over the edge and letting our stomachs and toes bob up to the surface. We drank a little more champagne, each of us knowing better than to get drunk. I read the label on the bottle. "Dom Pérignon. I've heard of that."

After a while Genie reached over to the tray and made as if to feed me a slice of mango. "Aren't you hungry?"

Ignoring the mango, I looked into her eyes and said, "Yes. I'm very hungry." And she had the sense to know what I meant. It'd been a long time—oh, I hate to tell you the length of the drought I'd been through. Her eyelashes fluttered, and I hoped they were an indicator of her heartbeat.

She took my hand. "Look, I don't know how to say this, so I'll just say it. I like your company. I like you. I wish..."

"What do you wish?"

Her finger drew circles on my palm.

The bedroom was exactly five paces away.

I'd never made love with an athlete. Genie Maychild had the strength of three gym teachers, combined with the finesse of a Renaissance glassblower.

She understood skin the way I understood it: our best organ, one we humans, tragically, tend to underrate.

"Do you feel that?" she murmured. "How about now? Can you almost not feel it? That's it. Yes, that's it, love. I want you to barely feel it." She had a marvelous talent for the phantom touch, the touch that flies and settles like a breath of air, then flies and settles again.

By way of compliment I said, "My backside never had it so good."

It seemed everything I said made her laugh.

Genie did with my body exactly what she wanted to do with it. Which was fine with me, except I eventually worried that I wouldn't be permitted certain liberties of my own. A silly worry, as it turned out.

At one point I remember being supported for a moment, acrobat-style, on her solid feet, looking down at her composed face. As she lowered me she began to describe my skin in terms Keats would've envied. I listened carefully, mercenarily, thinking to what good use might I put those words myself someday.

After a while I took the opportunity to explore the world of her, which, as I've said, filled me with awe and longing. It wasn't merely that she was in great shape, and it wasn't merely that she was exquisitely sensitive.

She seemed to have a sixth sense, an extra something, that made her deliciously—how can I put it?—anticipatory. It was as if she could guess what I was going to do next, even though I was mixing up my pitches pretty well, so to speak. She guessed, then she allowed herself the luxury of anticipating the sensations, then actually feeling them. As if she felt everything twice. I sensed more than saw this happening. In making love to her, I came to learn more about making love, and to love it still more than I already did.

Love through the perceptions of a self-possessed body, a body singing with life—well, we should all be so lucky, every one of us.

Genie sang, and I sang, and then we slept, and the house was very quiet.

8

I awakened to Genie climbing over me on her way to the bathroom. "It's morning," she announced, planting a big smack on the back of my neck. "It's morning and it's a fantastic day—let's go, let's go."

I closed my eyes again, listening to the running water in the bathroom, and opened them when the bed jounced slightly.

Hesper had silently entered and placed a breakfast tray at the foot of the crisp white coverlet. Reflexively, I clutched the sheet to my bosom, but she glanced only into my eyes.

She had one of those haircuts where it's buzzed short in the back, then kind of floppy on the sides and front. Her neck was heavy, swelling into her shoulders like poured concrete. Yet she moved lightly, and I saw that her feet were quite small.

"Will you want a hot breakfast, Ms. Byrd?" She bent her broad back over the tray to adjust a tiny silver vase holding a pink tea rose.

"Uh, no, thanks. This looks great. Jeez." There was plenty of food—fruit and buns and such.

When Genie came out, she said, "Good. Hesper makes popovers to die for."

"Did she come with this house or is she—you know—yours?"

"Came with. Hey, let's go. I'll drive you to get your stuff. Because I love you and you're going to stick with me all weekend, right?"

"I had a wonderful night."

"Me too. *Goodness,* I needed that."

I stood up and stretched. She watched me. "You are built like a blade of grass, you know that?"

"I know it."

"I think I got bruises from your hipbones."

"You did not."

"Where'd you get that mark? I didn't notice it before."

She was looking at my right thigh, where a maniac had shot me a few years ago.

"Oh, it's an old dueling scar, I'll tell you about it sometime."

She was the kind of person who accepted a response like that with a look that said, *I look forward to it.* I've known women who would've said, "No, no, tell me now, what happened?" and insisted on hearing the whole damn story, who couldn't *rest* until they'd heard the whole damn story, then would've gone drama queen over it, deciding I was either a marvelous hero or a complete dimwit (I'm half of each, actually), and would either insist on a commitment ceremony on the spot, or run off to change her phone number.

But not old Genie. She understood privacy, and timing. She valued her own privacy, I'd noticed. There were things she didn't want to tell me, stuff about before she was famous. As a journalist, I'd occasionally met famous people and had gotten particularly interested in that gap between nonfamous and famous—you know, that magical time that comes when hard work, or luck, breaks through that barrier that separates the stars from the asteroids. What was it like to go from being a washroom attendant to having somebody ask you for your autograph? That's what I ask about, and I'd tried to get there with Genie last night, but she deflected me. It was fun to be deflected, given the other things we had to do.

I thought about the offer I'd just been made. It seemed like an offer, anyway. I'd imagined a morning of lazy talking, and more hanky-panky, followed by a fond adieu. Now I figured Genie and I would have a voluptuous weekend, then on Monday we'd go our separate ways. She gearing up for the tournament, I melting into the crowd.

I showered, my body feeling brand new.

Genie's morning-after energy propelled us to Truby's, where we found her doing yoga, with only Todd for company.

Everything was okay. I introduced Genie, and we sat and shot the breeze for a few minutes. I was afraid my friend would be downhearted from not having scored last night, but no.

"I'm making progress, Starmate," she said. "You know the woman I was talking with when you left?"

"Yes," I said.

"Well, we kissed."

"Right on. How was it?"

"Scrumptious...absolutely...divine."

"Will you see her again?"

"Tonight."

"She coming over here?"

"Eventually, I hope. We're meeting for dinner at Cobalt. She lives in Burbank."

"Good," cheered Genie, smiling her upside-down smile. "You won't have any trouble." She was holding her palm out to Todd, who was sniffing and inching closer.

"Right," I said. I could tell Truby felt fine about me taking off for the weekend. We'd reconnect on Monday. "Come on, Toddy, we're going for a ride."

The crack made by the collision of the face of Genie's driver with the backside of a golf ball was a sound of authority, the likes of which I'd never heard.

"That's it," said Dewey O'Connor.

"I felt like I hardly hit it," said Genie, looking after the ball, which was racing a jet through the crystalline sky.

"That's what I'm talking about," said O'Connor. "When you hammer at it you lose power." He was a jockey-size Irishman and sounded like it. *When ye hommer at it, ye lose power.* "Your hands were gettin' too quick."

We were standing beneath a high flat L.A. sun at O'Connor's golf academy in the San Fernando valley— "the Valley," people in L.A. call it. The Valley may be suburban and dreary, but O'Connor's spread was super-luxe, catering to professionals and high-rolling amateurs. He'd built a special lesson tee for his most precious clients; we were shielded by a thicket of cedars from all prying eyes and spy cameras. I'd brought Todd because I felt he'd missed me overnight and needed to hear my voice. I kept him in his travel case on the ground nearby.

I was feeling extremely sparkly. Tagging along with Genie I felt as if a big hand were following over my head, throwing glitter down. Every time she glanced my way, my heart wiggled in my chest. I yearned to wrap my arms around her again.

When we arrived, O'Connor scanned me all the way down to my shoes, as my party hosts had done. I was wearing shorts and my faded pink polo shirt, plus my black high-top Chuck Taylor basketball sneakers. I understood perfectly well they weren't appropriate golf wear, but they were the only shoes I'd brought besides my loafers. Back home I did have a pair of golf shoes, but I played in my sneakers sometimes, liking the feel of the ground beneath the worn soft soles. I expected O'Connor to curl his lip, but he gave me a kind smile and said, "Do you golf, then?" His face appeared unnaturally healthy, no spider veins, no rheum in his eyes—as if he never touched a drop.

"Gimme the six," said Genie, looking downrange and holding out her hand. Needless to say, she looked perfect in an outfit of fine knits and impeccable leather.

O'Connor looked at me. Realizing my role, I pulled Genie's six-iron from her absurdly large golf bag and handed it to her, grip first, as I'd watched caddies do, and received her driver. I propped it against the bag, thinking she might want it again.

She raked a ball over to a clean piece of turf, set herself, and hit it.

It was as if her body had no bones, only resilient muscles. She was as supple as an otter. She made the *club* look supple. With a pure click, the ball left the clubface, rose into the sky, and fell to earth at the distance most of my drives go. Its flight path was perfectly straight; the ball bounced and stopped to the left of a fluttering yellow target flag.

"I was trying to fade it in a little bit." A crease of disappointment appeared in her brow. I wanted to leap forward and kiss it away. "Just a second," Genie said. She handed me the club, then bent down and rummaged in her bag. She came up with something I recognized from my childhood: an asthma inhaler. She flicked it open and took two long puffs, exhaling through her nose.

"There's something in the air out here my tubes don't like," she said.

"Asthma?" I asked sympathetically.

"I don't call it that. I just need a shot of this stuff once in a while."

"How's your breathing been?" O'Connor asked.

"Not bad. My tubes just don't like California. Now, Dewey, listen." She took her stance again. "I'm thinking I'm coming over a little bit and pulling it. What's wrong?"

"Nothing," said O'Connor.

She hit another shot. This one started out straight, then curved a bit and stopped closer to the flag.

"I still feel like I'm fighting a pull, like I'm changing my plane at the top."

"Quit thinking, Genie. Now's no time to be thinking. Forget the fade, you don't need a fade. You hit a naturally straight ball. It's a gift. Just because everybody else thinks they've got to work the ball doesn't mean you have to. Merely see the shot and hit it. See it and hit it. Feel it and hit it. Easy, now."

She hit a few more, in silence. I could've watched her

forever. She switched back to the driver, and hit four balls that disappeared over the horizon—I suppose they landed in Nevada or Texas, maybe.

"Oh," she said at last. "I get it."

"That's it," said O'Connor.

And the lesson was over.

"What would you like to do now?" Genie asked as we zoomed onto the Ventura Freeway. "Tomorrow we'll play golf. I want to go over to Woodley."

"You don't want to play golf with me."

"Yes, I do. But how about now?"

"Well," I said, "you think there's any way we could, you know, test the old mattress again? In the Biblical sense?" I touched her arm, stopping short of grabbing it and stroking it madly, stopping short of diving into her lap as we rolled gaily along.

"I want to look at you again," I went on. "I want to look at you all over. You're so—Christ, alive!"

"Lillian."

I stopped.

"Later," she said. "Later we'll ride the hurricane. All right? Let's talk about it all day."

I liked that. "Well," I said, "first we should drop off Todd at the house and give him a little safe space. Then...well, what would you like to do?"

"Do you like to shop?"

"I guess it depends where. I like"—and I knew this was dorky, I knew it—"I like hardware stores. If I have a few bucks, that is. They have so much cool stuff."

She cut me a look and slung the Jaguar around a tour bus and settled neatly into the blind spot of a guy in a sparkling Lexus. The Lexus was white, trimmed in gold.

"That car looks like a Fabergé egg," I said. "And I like Army-Navy stores. Because, well, for the same reason, plus everything's so cheap. For instance, I got this Vietnam hat last year? It's the neatest thing for the rain, and it only cost—"

"I was thinking," she said, "Rodeo, but now I'm thinking Melrose."

So we checked out the latest boutiques, the latest L.A. funk and junk, on Melrose Avenue. We went into a place called Golf Punk, where they sold little tiny teenager clothes that I couldn't imagine any professional golfer wearing, even the cute diminutive ones.

"You actually golf?" I heard a clerk ask Genie. The clerks had no idea, but they were very nice, and even though we didn't buy anything, they insisted on giving us a handful of stickers with the store logo on them.

Then Genie spotted a sign across the street, for a particular brand of boots, those ones from Australia. We waited at a stoplight, and when it turned, Genie started across, her eyes already searching the shop window.

I happened to be watching the traffic. And I happened to realize that a minivan with a Jack-in-the-Box head on its antenna wasn't going to stop, was in fact still trying to beat the light, and was accelerating fast.

With a quickness I can only describe as supernatural, I lunged for her arm and screamed.

She perceived in an instant, and leaped backward powerfully, knocking me over. The minivan honked and barreled on, practically grazing us.

"Wow!" I said, getting up.

The few other people near the corner were looking after the minivan and shaking their heads.

Genie said nothing. She'd gone white. Sinking sideways against a light pole, she was on the verge of fainting.

I took her arm. "It's all right."

"My God."

"It's all right."

"You saved my life."

"No, I didn't. You jumped away."

"I almost died," she said wonderingly, "I almost died right there on that street—right there." She pointed to the spot as if pointing at a ghost: arm straight from the shoulder, finger out. "I could be dead right now."

"Hey, let's get you a cold drink. Let's sit down somewhere. Over here, come on."

I escorted her to a little table at a sidewalk joint. "Do you like raspberry? Two raspberries, please."

For a few minutes we just sat there and breathed.

By now I guess you've figured out that this was that year. The year the Dinah ended unlike any championship ever. If you were there, or if you saw it on television, or if you read the papers afterward, you know a little bit about it.

Well, you're going to find out what really happened, what it was to be inside the ropes when it appeared that the world was ending, and when, for a few people, it did.

9

That evening was a quiet one. A breeze swirled around the canyon, bringing smells of gnarled vegetation, spicy smells, green smells. We took Todd out for a romp on the terrace before dinner. I'd brought a harness and lead for him, and used them now. Thick shrubs surrounded the terrace; were there fences beyond? Impossible to know. Of course, you can no more walk a rabbit than a frog—it walks you. But Todd responded well to my voice. And I'd learned what to do if danger came around and I wanted him to freeze so I could pick him up: stomp very hard, as rabbits themselves do to signal danger. It's not that they stomp so much as launch their hindquarters skyward, which then fall to earth with a bang.

I'd known of this habit of Todd's and thought it was random, until I'd inadvertently made him freeze when I opened my post-Christmas credit card bill.

Some people rely on Valium to relax, but I relied on Todd. Whenever I was near him, I felt a warm, special kind of serenity. It's hard to explain.

I hoped a little of Todd would rub off on Genie, who still appeared shook up from our brush with the minivan. Now and then she'd close her eyes and take a deep breath.

Todd was still pretty frisky when it was time to go in, so Hesper and I fixed up a run for him up and down the hallway that led to the bedroom Genie and I were using. Hesper shut the other doors that opened onto it, and I pushed some furniture and plants that I hoped were nontoxic into the other end. He liked it.

"But won't he just jump over this stuff?" Hesper asked. Her face had gotten sweaty as we worked; she lifted the hem of her T-shirt and ducked her face into it. I got a shot of her belly, which was a stack of perfectly curved, perfectly white rolls.

"You'd think he would," I said, "and he would if he wanted to, but that's not the way rabbits think. He sees this wall of plants, and he has no idea whether jumping over them would be worthwhile. Maybe he doesn't know he's being confined. Anyway, if he thinks he's safe where he is, he's happy to stay there."

For dinner, Hesper turned out a platter of the most darling little lamp chops you've ever seen, plus baby vegetables and an odd delicious pilaf made from oats. There was a lovely wine, all for me; Genie was not drinking from now until after the tournament.

We talked through the meal, which we took outside.

Part of the terrace extended into a deck that stuck out over the canyon. You could see the lights of L.A.

That evening I learned many things about Genie, and didn't learn others. She considered winning the Dinah her first year on the tour to be a fluke. She hadn't won it since and was anxious to repeat her victory. I learned she didn't have much in the way of folks.

"Your parents are dead, then?" I asked.

"More or less."

"I see. Brothers, sisters?"

"One of each, but they've both disappeared."

"What do you mean?"

"Just that."

"I see."

I learned that the camaraderie on the LPGA tour wasn't what it used to be. In the old days the gals on the fledgling tour shared rides to tournaments, shared motel rooms, and, one could safely suppose, beds every so often. Prize money was paltry. Today it's only paltry compared to what the men get.

"Oh, everybody's friendly," said Genie. "You know, you're polite enough—you say hi and everything, but there's, like, an edge to everybody. That look in the eyes, you know?"

"What's it like?"

"Your mouth is smiling, but your eyes are saying, *I'd just as soon kill you.* The money's bigger, the girls are better trained—not just as golfers, but as athletes—heck, nobody even eats doughnuts anymore." She looked wistful. "There's more at stake. The media attention's bigger, not that it's big enough."

"I know. They cover the whole last round of the men's

majors on TV, and I'm lucky to get the last six holes of the women's. That is so sucking."

"It's very sucking." She liked that construction.

I like to watch golf on television. Even if you're not really interested in golf, televised golf is a valuable tool for wellness. The next time you're home sick on a summer weekend, or have really bad cramps, or whatever, close the blinds, find some golf on TV and curl up on the couch with a nice cold glass of ginger ale. You can sort of drift in and out to the subdued tones of the announcers, the murmur of the crowd, the cool green glow of the screen. You'll feel better after an hour or two.

Genie said, "You know, the LPGA and the sponsors work like crazy to minimize the appearance of lesbianism on the tour. They're always playing up publicity for women with husbands and kids."

"The stigma thing. Dykes hurt the tour, right?"

"That's what they think. But the truth is, it's prejudice *against* gay players that hurts the tour."

Every so often as we dined, Hesper would come out on her little cat feet and remove a dish or refill something.

I told her, "Hesper, this is all just wonderful." She smiled, then cocked her large head toward the shrubbery, listening. I'd heard nothing but the birds and the bees; I guess after a second Hesper decided that was all she'd heard, too. She withdrew to the kitchen.

Genie said, "I'm glad I'm not a rookie anymore."

"Tough times?" I knew she'd come up from a pretty humble beginning; that much I'd retained from reading magazines.

"Oh, those days. I was on my own. All those black golf gloves."

I was baffled. "What about black golf gloves?"

"Well, they wear longer than any other color. The black dye makes the leather stronger. Plus they don't look dirty after one week. Serious golfers on the cheap wear nothing but black gloves."

I made a mental note to look for black gloves the next time I went through the sale bin.

"Did you stay with families at the tournaments?" I asked.

"Yes, my whole first year."

At most tournaments, people living near the course, some of them, offer their homes to the golfers. At the high end a golfer can rent a luxury home right next to the course for a fat fee. At the low end, some families simply make a spare room available for nothing to a young pro on a tight budget.

"They're all nice, the families," Genie said. "Only once in a while you sort of have to sing for your supper."

"Yeah?"

"Like, they make these nice meals for you, and then they sit with you and ask you your life story, and they tell you theirs, and they try to get you to gossip about the other golfers. But you know, even that's not so bad compared to guys who want to help you with your swing."

"You're kidding."

"No, I'm not."

"You mean, like you're sitting there at dinner after your round, and the dad says something like, 'You know, I noticed that your right elbow is flying a little bit on your backswing'?"

"Exactly," she said. "Once I had a host—this was at the

Tour Championship—this guy takes me out in the yard after dinner. It was Saturday night, and I'd gotten into the lead by two shots. At first I thought he wanted me to correct *his* swing, but suddenly I'm realizing that he's trying to coach *me*. He kept talking about my hips, my hip turn. 'Do you know you're tilting slightly, he says?' "

"Oh, God."

"The next day during my round, I just kept hearing this idiot's voice in my head, talking about my hips. I tried not to think about my hips, but it's like the blue horse in that movie, you know?"

"Yeah," I said. "What's-her-name tells the jury to think about anything but a blue horse."

"All I could think about was my hips. So essentially, I blew the round and tied for fourteenth. That wouldn't happen today."

I nodded. "You've learned greater mental discipline?"

"I've learned that sometimes you gotta belt people in the mouth!"

I laughed.

"I'm kidding, yeah," said Genie.

Hesper came in with some coconut sorbet for dessert.

Genie's knowledge of golf history was awesome. I'd thought mine was pretty good, but I didn't live and breathe the game. I did know who Glenna Collett Vare was, after whom the Vare Trophy was named, and I owned instruction books by Vivien Saunders, Judy Rankin, and the great Mickey Wright.

"Have you ever met Mickey Wright?" I asked. Most people have never heard of her, although she won almost as many titles as Kathy Whitworth and received the highest compliment in the history of golf: Ben Hogan was on record saying that of all the golfers he'd ever seen, the one with the best swing, man or woman, was Mickey Wright.

"Oh, she's my total idol," Genie said. "I've met her a few times. She's getting old. I wish she'd been born later, so I could study her at her peak, in person. She's the chairman of the board. That swing, she could do anything with it. Of course, it wasn't just that she could put anything she wanted on the ball."

"It was her confidence."

"That's right." Genie leaned in to me, her sandy brows scrunched. "Knowing how to do it and doing it when you have to—do you have any idea what a difference there is between those two things?"

"I've never hit a golf shot under pressure. Say, you said you didn't want to dwell on golf this weekend."

"This isn't dwelling. You don't know what dwelling is. If I was dwelling on golf, we'd have the Golf Channel on all the time, then I'd be going over every hole at Mission Hills shot by shot. I'd be talking about all my past rounds there. I'd be speculating how thick they're growing the rough this year—plenty thick, that's always a safe bet. I'd be obsessing over whether I'm going to go for the green in two on eighteen or lay up—"

"Ah, the water hole, right?"

"Yeah. There's a few of us who can do it—Laura Davies can, when her head's straight, which is most of the time. I can. It's a risk for anybody. You've got to have two perfect shots. Should I go for it in the early rounds? Or just if I need a miracle?"

Suddenly she leaned forward and drilled her eyes into mine. "How old are you, anyway?" Her eyes, I'd determined, were hazel, tending very slightly to green. Beautiful flecks of color that changed all the time.

I drilled her back. "I lie about my age."

"You're too young to lie about your age."

"You're never too young."

"You're older than me."

"You have a beautiful smile."

That made her laugh, and she looked out at the lights of Babylon. "Peaches and I've been working on course management," she told me. "We'll get together tomorrow and go over our plan."

"Who's Peaches?"

"Peaches Oshinsky, my caddie."

"Are you happy with her?"

"Peaches is a he, you goof. Oh, my gosh, I'd die without him. You will not find a better caddie on the tour. He knows every blade of grass on every course we play."

"Peaches—that's so funny." It made me smile.

"His real name is Herman or something. People call him Peaches because of his beautiful face. He makes movie stars look ugly. He's a doll, completely, and he's a good guy. I'd put my life in his hands any day. You'll meet him. He's been with his wife in Tallahassee. She just had a baby, so he was glad to get a week off. But we're gonna buckle down tomorrow."

"How're you going to have time to shoot a round of golf with me *and* meet with Peaches?" I asked.

"We'll start early."

"In that case."

"Yes. To bed."

I liked Genie's directness, her up-frontness. She was a specialist at golf and a specialist in the sack. Oh, yes.

Before we dropped off to sleep, I asked, "Where do you get your drive from?"

"A lot of who I am, I invented."

It didn't occur to me until later that she had answered a different question.

10

Sunday's highlights most certainly did not include the round of golf Genie and I played at an out-of-the-way public course called Woodley Lakes, starting at daybreak. I mean to say, my play wouldn't have made any highlight tapes, except the accidentally wonderful shot I hit by viciously topping my ball off the tee on one of the par threes, which ricocheted off a bunker rake and came to rest a foot from the cup. I missed the putt. It was a typical outing for me. Using rented clubs and Genie's advice on strategy, I shot a 97.

"You're really not that bad," Genie said as she slammed the trunk on the Jag. "You hit some good shots." She'd slaughtered the course.

It's interesting to realize that pros don't hit every shot

great. When you watch them on TV, you mostly see the leaders, who are all over their game, or they wouldn't be out front. You don't see the pro who can't hit the broad side of a brewery that day. Genie had a fine morning, but even she hit a few lousy shots.

"The main difference between you and me," I observed, is that your bad shots come only one in a row. Then you make the putt for your par or your birdie anyway."

"You gotta make putts." She felt good.

A guy in a primer-painted Buick, about a '79, zoomed up from behind and cut in front of us as Genie was trying to merge onto the expressway.

"Goddamn it!" I yelled, as Genie braked and swerved. "What an asshole!"

Genie just kept driving. "You can say that again."

"You never swear, do you?"

"It's not my style."

"That's nice," I told her. "That is very nice. I've been swearing like a sailor since I could talk."

"What, did you grow up in a bar or something?"

"Yeah."

"You grew up in a bar?"

"Yeah! Even people who run bars have kids."

"Well," she said, "I take pride in not having to use gutter talk."

I played with the power window control, fighting feeling ashamed. "Good for you, Goldilocks, but every time I try not to swear I feel flaky." I sat there wishing I hadn't brought it up.

When we got back to the house, Peaches was already there, drinking iced tea at the kitchen table and flipping through his yardage book. I didn't spend more than a minute meeting him before leaving Genie alone with him, but I liked him at once. Unlike many strikingly handsome people, he didn't appear conceited: You could sense his warmth right away. Beneath his impeccable skin and dimples, he had that scoutmaster look, as if he'd wade through a lava pit to rescue a stranded fawn. Plus he was big enough to haul Genie's heavy leather golf bag all over a championship course, hustling back and forth with divots and towels, without needing supplemental oxygen.

They talked strategy while I looked after Todd, taking him out for a stroll on the terrace, then brushing him and talking to him. I felt him all over, feeling for his bones, to make sure he was eating enough.

I wondered whether he and Hesper had made friends. She was like a hologram—there, then not there, then somewhere in the distance. I felt like shooting the breeze with her, but she went out on errands.

I got out my mandolin and played a few tunes into the canyon, testing the acoustics. They were pretty good. I'd played for Genie the night before, and she liked it. She got up and danced to the music, moving so sexily that my fingers trembled.

Peaches would stay to dinner, I thought, but he left after a couple of hours, driving down the canyon in his rented Altima. He and Genie would meet in Rancho Mirage the next afternoon to play a practice round.

That night something jolted me awake. Something had happened—a vibration, an earthquake? Only a noise? Whatever it was, it brought me fully awake, nerves tingling.

I listened.

Genie was breathing slowly and regularly, curled next to me. I realized that what had awakened me was one of Todd's thumps. It's amazing how loud they were.

Then I heard another one. A second later, I heard a sound like static, like something brushing against the wall just outside the bedroom door. I grunted in surprise. There was a sharp rustle, then footsteps.

I sprang naked out of bed and rushed into the hallway. There was a night-light out there; Todd hunkered in its greenish glow. At the far end of the hallway, I saw a plant teeter and fall over—one of the plants I'd moved to block in Todd. I ran down to the foyer, hearing the front door bang open. I reached it and paused there, flailing my hand on the nearby switch plate, searching for an exterior light and not finding one.

The door was in the deep shadow of a patch of cedar trees. There were no streetlights in this neighborhood anyway. I stepped into the night toward the street, looking everywhere, seeing only blackness. I thought I heard a rustle to my left, where a dense hedge blocked the next house.

"Hey!" I called. I stood there uncertainly, the concrete of the walkway gritty beneath my bare feet, the cool night breeze slipping around my body. I listened for a car door, an engine, anything. The night was still.

I went back inside and found my way to the other end of the house. I opened doors and flipped light switches until I found Hesper's bedroom.

She was snoring, spread-eagled on her back, no covers on. For pajamas she was wearing a yellow T-shirt that said WEST COVINA DEMOLITION VOLLEYBALL. Between her legs a huge bush of hair rose up like a mountain.

She sat, blinked at the light, saw me standing there with no clothes on, and said, "Is there something you need, Ms. Byrd?" I saw that she had one of those nose strips on, like football players wear.

"I'll explain later," I said, backing out.

I woke up Genie, told her what happened, and reached for the telephone. She was taking little whooshing breaths and rubbing her forehead. "Ohh, ohh. Rats, rats, rats. Wait. What are you doing?"

"Calling the police."

"Don't."

"Why not? You're not awake yet. Listen. There's somebody out there, maybe not far. Somebody was in this house, Genie."

Very quickly she grabbed the receiver out of my hand. She was awake all right. "No police," she said.

We got dressed and went into the kitchen. The clock on the microwave said 2:54. Hesper appeared and began preparing cappuccinos. Nothing appeared to be missing. I scouted around and found that a small sliding window in the laundry room had been jimmied open and the screen removed. I closed and latched it.

Hesper, who had added a pair of black bicycle shorts to her ensemble, produced a flashlight; I took it and went outside. I could see faint marks in the dirt beneath the window, like the edge of a smooth shoe, and there was a smudge on the stucco wall where a shoe or dirty hand had rubbed going in.

"Here's why no cops," said Genie when I reported back, "First of all, whoever it was is long gone. What would the cops do anyway?"

Hesper and I made automatic "Yeah, cops" faces.

"Second, I'm out of here tomorrow for tournament week. Third, I just want to forget all about this. I don't want to dwell on it. I have to prepare for the tournament. I don't need this. I don't want to think about this anymore."

"Hesper," I said, "this is your main home, right? How do you feel about not reporting it?"

She shrugged.

Genie said, "And I don't want Dewey worried with this."

"I understand," said Hesper.

So the prowler in the night would be our little secret.

I picked up Todd and held him in my lap while we drank our cappuccinos. Genie motioned for Hesper to sit with us.

"Well, Todd," said Genie, bending to look him in the eye, "you're the hero of the night, aren't you?" She was trying to be casual, but I noticed her hands trembling.

When we went back to bed, she said, "Play me some music, will you? Know any lullabies?"

I got out my mandolin and slowly played "Green Grow the Rushes-O," and "Lord of the Dance," and a few other tunes, while she snuggled down beside me in bed. Her eyes flicked around anxiously, then, it seemed with great deliberateness, she willed her body and mind to relax, and she drifted into sleep. Her face in repose was beautiful and somber, I thought, like a medieval princess's.

I sat up a while, playing soft two-note chords.

11

I didn't know what to think. This weird thing had gone down, and Genie wanted to pretend nothing had happened, but she was scared, very scared.

I'd been feeling a growing protectiveness toward my lover, along the lines of "Wouldn't it be fun to look after you." But now it was more like "Goddamn it, I don't want anybody bothering you." It was real.

When I saw dawn pinkening up the sky, I slipped out of bed, showered, and started to pull my stuff together, so Genie could quickly drop me off at Truby's, then swing over to the highway to Palm Springs.

She woke up looking glad of the day, then, remembering, she clouded over. While she was in the bathroom the phone rang. I didn't answer it, and neither, I guess, did

Hesper, as it rang ten times then stopped. Genie came out of the bathroom, toweling her hair and trailing a wake of warm Neutrogena smell. The phone rang again. She glanced at me, then casually went over and, turning away from me, picked it up.

"Hello?"

After a moment she made a half-sound, a truncated exhalation that caught in her throat. Her shoulders jumped up around her ears. She put the receiver back.

I waited, trying to gauge her thoughts by her sleek naked back. With effort, she was breathing regularly. As I watched, she began to regain her usual easy control of her body: Her breaths moved from tight in her chest down to her belly, her shoulders slowly dropped.

"What is it?" I said.

She heaved a huge sigh, then turned to me. "Wrong number."

"You expect me to believe that?"

"I don't care whether you believe it."

"Genie."

All of a sudden her eyes welled up, and her lips got tight. I went and sat down next to her, putting her robe, a blue silk kimono, around her shoulders, which started to tremble. She choked out something I couldn't catch. I reached her a tissue and said gently, "Why don't you tell me about it?"

She looked at me miserably. "I can't."

"How come?"

"I just can't."

"Who's bothering you?"

"I—I don't know." She looked down at the crumpled tissue. "I honestly don't."

"Well, then—"

"Look," she said, sounding suddenly tough, then she stopped. She sat there thinking.

I was outraged, absolutely livid, that someone was harassing her, right at the beginning of the most important tournament of the year. My heart was bursting with the desire to protect her. I didn't let it show, though.

"Are you afraid?" I asked.

"No."

"I'm not convinced."

She leaned close. "I love you."

"I love you, too." You know how you just automatically say that?

The fact was, I *liked* Genie a hell of a lot, I was in awe of her, and we sure clicked in the sack, but it was too early to know whether I really loved her. It was certainly too early to *let* myself start loving her deeply. She was this big superstar, and I was this little Larry Fortensky over here, and everybody knows how those things work out. On the other hand, maybe we could beat the odds.

I pictured Genie Maychild and myself aboard an ocean liner, en route home from winning the women's British Open, feeding each other oysters and throwing the shells out the porthole while "It Had to Be You" drifted in from an orchestra somewhere. I pictured Genie ramming laser-straight drives down the throats of the fairways at the Dinah while I walked outside the ropes, nodding, frowning, providing discreet encouragement. I pictured myself sitting at a camp table beneath a palm tree on a tropic isle, working on my important new book about clean energy or Baroque troubadour songs or the secret life of Eleanor Roosevelt, while Genie massaged my shoulders with her strong good hands and hummed softly.

"Look," she began again, "you've saved my life once, and your rabbit saved maybe all our lives. That's twice, and so it's very clear to me that you are powerful magic."

I smiled, hiding the fact that I thought so, too.

She explained that she'd rented a house near the tournament course, and that Todd and I were to stay there with her through the week.

"Us and who else?"

She looked at me curiously. "Most golfers on the tour travel light. I hadn't counted on meeting somebody like you. I hadn't counted on any of this."

So I beat it out of L.A. with star athlete Genie Maychild, pausing only to phone Truby and arrange to meet her for lunch at the Howard Johnson's in Palm Springs, where we were supposed to stay. I caught her as she was packing and wondering where the hell Todd and I were.

It's 130 miles from Los Angeles to Palm Springs, but it travels fast because you're leaving Los Angeles. Roads out of L.A. always travel faster than roads in. After a while the lanes open up and you can get out from behind the semis and roll down the windows and breathe clean desert air. Cleaner, anyway.

We drove through to Rancho Mirage and stopped at the house Genie had rented for the week, inside the Mission Hills complex. It was a low stucco place—the kind people these days call a villa—that on the outside didn't look like much. But inside it was rich with wrought iron, mosaic tiles, and a host of peculiar statuary nooks. Comfort-wise, it was tricked out with everything you'd need to entertain a sultan, or whoever's left of the Onassis clan.

There was a very nice den-type room that I quickly rabbit-proofed. I set up Todd with some provisions and his newspapers and hung out with him for about an hour while Genie changed clothes and fussed over her equipment. The house was right on the tournament course. It was the sixteenth fairway lying there just beyond the patio, Genie told me. I looked out at the velvety golf course dotted with contestants and their caddies.

I thought she'd run me over to the HoJo's, but she drove straight to the clubhouse. Golf pros, caddies, and security guys bustled around, everybody looking fresh and eager. It was the beginning of tournament week and you could smell the optimism.

"There's Peaches," said Genie. "You take the car after he gets my clubs out. I'll get a courtesy car to take me home later. Or why don't you and Truby come out to the course after lunch?"

"Will do. You'll be all right without me for a couple of hours?"

She laughed a genuine, relaxed laugh. She felt safe and happy here, you could tell. She was about to greet the majestic Dinah Shore course again.

The Howard Johnson's was right on Palm Canyon Drive, the main thoroughfare of Palm Springs. When Genie and I passed through, I'd expected the main drag to be swankier, you know, like Beverly Hills, but the few fancy boutiques were squeezed in between T-shirt stores, travel agencies, and sandwich places. I think I saw a wig shop. Nothing against any of this, it's just that I was thinking about all the movie stars that supposedly hung here. Later somebody told me the movie stars had gotten bored with Palm Springs and moved over to Palm Desert. It was strictly retirees for a while, and now gay guys who couldn't afford San Francisco were buying up the vintage mid-century houses and redoing them.

The Jaguar, an XJ sedan, drove beautifully. I'd heard that model of car has an unbelievably powerful engine, supercharged up to about 300 horsepower, but after about four minutes behind the wheel I believed it. Not lightning off the blocks, but smoothly responsive to the gas. A very rich, heavy car. This one was finished in a deep burgundy lacquer that was flawless. As big and comfortable as the car was, though, I could still feel every pebble in the road through the steering wheel. Genie and I had driven in with the windows down, letting the desert breeze cool us.

A young lass on a Harley-Davidson pulled up next to me at a red light. The growling Harley was one of the big ones, and the woman was one of the small ones, but she was enough for that bike, all right. Every inch of her was drawn up straight in the saddle. Mirrored sunglasses, studded leather with lots of fringe, and great big black leather boots. Her arms were tanned to perfection. She gunned her motor and gave me a tough look. I smiled and showed my tongue, and she responded with the sweetest, hugest grin.

Only after getting blasted by the air conditioning in the HoJo's, which actually turned out to be a Denny's attached to a HoJo's motel, which was disappointing, did I realize how hot it was outside. I bet it was above ninety. The fabled dry heat of the desert. The climate inside the restaurant was a dry cold. I walked past a bus stand and smelled the bleach water for the wipe rags. Then I smelled a good hamburger and my mouth watered.

The place was doing a fantastic business this lunchtime; dykes from all over the world were fortifying themselves for a week of golf-watching and parties.

"Becky! I can't believe you made it!"

"Wouldn't have missed it. Been coming since '81."

"How're you keeping your sweet self?"

I don't guess the place saw this much hugging in all the other fifty-one weeks of the year. An elderly couple watched knowingly. They wore normal retiree clothing—no Palm Springs logos—so they were locals. I nodded pleasantly to them as I looked for my friend.

She was drinking a Coke at a table in the corner, away from the glare bouncing in from the windows.

"Starmate," I said.

"Starmate. Sit."

It was good to see her intelligent, quick face again. "You go first," I said.

"What's a dental dam?"

"Oh, Lord. Where the rubber meets the road." I explained about the little latex sheets and their varied uses.

"I don't get it," she said, "I mean, why?"

"To ward off disease, basically. I mean, lesbians can get AIDS and pass STDs back and forth."

"Have you ever used one?"

"No. I'll have a Coke, too," I added to the waitress who'd stopped by. She was young and buff, with spiky hair and sleek black glasses, and she was getting rather special attention from her customers this day. I think she was having a pretty good shift.

"Just a second," Truby said to her. "Have you ever used a dental dam during sex?"

"I would if you wanted me to."

Truby shook her head pensively. "I can't imagine it."

I stopped laughing long enough to tell the waitress, whose name tag said OH MISS, "Give us a few minutes, please. Trube, why don't you back up a little bit? Did dental dams come up in a discussion with your *amour*? What's her name, anyway?"

"Yes. Lucy. She's a little strange, but she really likes me."

"Do you really like her?"

"Well, we've had these tremendously long talks, mostly wonderful. About all sorts of things. And she's beautiful."

"She is, I do remember."

"I find myself staring at her breasts and going all dreamy."

"Have you masturbated while thinking of her?"

"Yes."

"Good."

"We've had dinner twice now, but—"

"Did you tell her you're experimenting?"

"Oh, yes. I decided I had to be totally honest about this, even if it slows me down."

"I'm impressed. I expected you to lie."

"Lillian!"

"Well, gosh, hon, you seemed so desperate. All's fair in love and Roller Derby, anyway."

"She told me it didn't matter to her that I'm inexperienced with women. I think if I were a kid, you know, really young, she might've gotten spooked."

"But you haven't hit the sack yet?"

"No!"

"Well, what the hell did you talk about?"

"It was so much fun to talk about what buttheads men are. It was like being with you. Turns out she's had a boss who shoved his tongue down her throat, too. When we started talking about pop culture, though, I sort of lost my way. She talked about all these singers and comics I've never heard of, except for, like, Ellen. And movies. I never knew there were so many lesbo movies out there, and here I'm working in the film industry!" She took a pull of her Coke. "Then the subject of books came up, and she said she was a big mystery fan, so I started mentioning P.D. James and Minette Walters, and, oh, Patricia Highsmith, but she started talking about these totally different writers—"

"Like who?"

"I can't remember."

"Katherine Forrest? Mary Wings?"

"Yeah. Both of those, I think. Plus she's wild about some Calico something. A series about a detective, that sounds like complete shit."

Ouch. "Ah, yes." I said. "When cultures collide."

"I don't feel they collided so much as just sort of blew right by each other."

"Yeah."

"I've got some homework to do."

"Yeah. Did politics come up?"

"No, thank God."

"Thank God."

Truby was the only person I knew, besides Mrs. McVittie and my own self, who never could stand Bill Clinton. All the rest of my friends went on worshiping him through every bad decision, every betrayal, every self-pitying whine.

Our waitress came back, and I ordered a hamburger, Truby a grilled cheese. She licked her lips and seemed about to say something more to OH MISS, but changed her mind.

"She's kind of cute," I prompted, after she left.

"Not my kind of CUPCAKE."

"Oh, well." I waited.

"Okay, here's the thing," Truby said, "We *talked* about sex and even made out on the couch both nights, and I was really ready, you know—Jesus Christ, the feel of a woman's arms, a woman's body..." She stopped, searching for words, finally giving up, saying simply, "Wow."

"I know."

"But every time it seemed like the next step should happen, like when we were at my place and I said, 'It would be the most wonderful thing if you could stay all night,' she sat up and started talking about her ex. Somebody named Beryl, who liked to have the TV on during sex but who could make her come like Vesuvius. Plus she talked a lot about a special cleansing diet she was about to go on, and a retreat she did last year that had a fire walk. She did a fire walk, and she did a survival course the year before, and she went on and on about it, and she, like, made a parallel between all that crap and sex. Dental dams and dildos, which I'm not terribly interested in. 'The challenge of sex,' she said."

" 'The challenge of sex.' "

"She got very philosophical, and I'm sitting there trying to relate, you know, go with the flow and hope we get somewhere, but it just didn't happen."

"Trube, is this a challenge you want to pursue?"

"I'm not sure. What do you think?"

"Dump this one and go to a party tonight. That chick from work did give you party tickets, didn't she?"

"The whole package."

A couple of the big hotels hosted enormous parties—dance parties, comedy parties, pool parties. Everybody went.

"Go then and renew your search." Our food came, and we dug in.

"Are you coming?"

"Well," I said, then told her the story so far. "So, Starmate, you'll have the room here to yourself for at least tonight."

"Just tonight?"

"I'm only thinking about eighteen hours ahead right now," I said.

Truby smiled. "Probably a good idea. Do you love her?"

"Too early to say. Yes, to tell you the truth and goddamn it. She says she needs me. And I want to protect her. I don't know what's going on in the outback of her life, but something is, and if I want to keep on being her lucky charm, and I do, then I might have to find out what it is."

12

When we caught up with Genie she was on the thirteenth fairway waiting to hit her approach shot. Her practice round partners were Lona Chatwin and one other pro I didn't recognize. They and their caddies were all standing with their hands on their hips, watching the group on the green.

The course was gorgeous; the grounds crew, I judged, must have put in piles of overtime. The trees and shrubs were perfectly shaped, and the fairways stretched green and lush away toward the mountains to the west, that ridge of peaks that prevents the ocean from sending any nasty old storm clouds over. A dusting of snow clung to the rocks way up high. The sky was so clear blue, it would've shattered if you threw something at it. Yet hovering just beyond those peaks, pressing against them, was a swirl of gray clouds, just aching to get over here and throw down some rain. They wouldn't, though.

Palm Springs, Rancho Mirage, Indian Wells—these desert towns lie on a finger of a flat arid basin that stretches north into the Mojave Desert, America's most serious hot place. In Death Valley, on the other side of the Mojave, the faucet taps in peoples' houses are reversed: The water coming out of the pipes in the ground is so hot you can almost cook with it, and you make cool water indoors by storing it in your hot water heater tank with no heat on. I was amazed when I learned this. To the east lie the Little San Bernardino Mountains and Joshua Tree National Park, an otherworldly place of tortured rock and gnarled trees and throat-tightening vistas.

The desert stopped wherever the ground was watered, and began again past the reach of the sprinklers. You could smell the difference as well as see it: Green grass smells like bread next to the mineral smell of hot dirt. When I was little I had a book, *The Living Desert,* with pictures of a fearsome fight to the death between a tarantula and a wasp. I read that book over and over, building a permanent belief in the desert's uncaring treachery. Anything can prick you to death in the desert: cacti, tarantulas, wasps.

The soft turf of the golf course cushioned my feet benevolently. A raft of coots and mallards clucked from the pond between the thirteenth and fourteenth holes. I caught Genie's eye; she gave me a tight smile, then, catching herself being tense, blew out a long breath and rolled her shoulders. I gave her a wink.

The group on the thirteenth green was taking its time

putting out. This being a practice round, things always go slowly as players hit two or three balls, sometimes, and chip and putt to different places around the greens, testing the contours and speed.

But somebody was taking a real hell of a long time up there, and as I walked closer I saw that it was Coco Nash. Her chocolate-brown skin shone in the clear sun. She was calmly putting a handful of balls from the back of the green to the far right side, where the pin might be on Saturday or Sunday, trying to gauge a break exactly, oblivious to the fact that her playing partners had finished and headed for the fourteenth tee.

A silver-headed female fan wearing a Dove Soap visor à la Nancy Lopez said with quiet excitement, "This has been going on all day. I wonder when Genie Maychild's gonna blow."

I looked back at Genie, who was talking and gesticulating to a course marshal. The marshal shook his head and shrugged lamely. She stalked away from him, cupped her hands to her mouth, and yelled, "Hey, Your Holiness! Move it already!"

Coco Nash looked up in surprise. Then she deliberately lined up another putt, stroked it, lined up one more, stroked *it*, then walked off, as her caddie scurried around picking up her balls.

The Dove lady spoke again. "She's gotten inside Genie's head now. Better watch out."

The instant the caddie's hind sneaker left the surface of the green, Genie fired a shot in. The ball climbed to an impossible height, then dropped softly onto the center of the green.

"Genie's no head case," I said proudly.

After the round, Truby and I watched Genie walk past Coco, who had stopped to sign autographs and chat with a gaggle of fans. I couldn't see Genie's face, but Coco gave her a look that would've stripped varnish. Genie stopped and stood still for a second, then went on into the clubhouse.

That night, Genie and I had Chinese dinners delivered and ate on the patio. I kind of missed Hesper. The evening was coming on cool, as it always does in the desert. The mountains flattened out black against the gleaming Western sky. I looked for Venus but didn't find it. A sparrow paused on a bush, cheeped once, then vanished. It was some species of desert sparrow I didn't know.

"How do you feel about the course setup?" I asked.

"Good. It's good. The greens are like linoleum. Just the way I like it."

"I almost needed a machete to find my way to the lemonade stand."

She laughed and leaned over to give me a garlicky kiss. "Oh," she said, "the rough's not that bad. You know, we get a better setup than the men. The current fashion for the men is to grow the rough so high they can only hack their way back to the fairway with a wedge. No chance to make a good recovery shot. Here, the rough's thick but not so long, so we can use a longer club. It's better golf. It rewards guts."

"You playing in the pro-am tomorrow?" I asked her.

"Uh-huh."

"You want me to find out when Coco's teeing off so you can get ahead of her?"

"Princess Coco," Genie said. "I just wish she'd grow up."

"Looks like she just wishes you'd drop dead."

"Nothing would give her greater pleasure, I'm sure."

After a minute I said, "You think she deliberately tried to annoy you out there?"

"No doubt. What's up her butt? When she was a rookie, she used to act respectful to me. Now she thinks she's queen of the world. I'm not afraid of her."

I knew then that she was. Suddenly, I began to hate Coco Nash. How dare she? Genie was the number 1 player in the world, having paid her dues all over the place. Coco hadn't proved she was anything but a one-season wonder.

We talked of other things. While washing my hands in the clubhouse women's room, I'd picked up a juicy bit of gossip about one of the older European stars, who was here this year. I overheard a woman with a bayou drawl say this star's name, then go on to her friend, "She was, too! I was there last night and saw it. She was higher than a Georgia pine, sister—she kept trying to get the waiter to take his pants off! Her caddie finally came and practically carried her out!"

I repeated this to Genie, but she seemed uninterested. I asked her about a story I'd heard—well, a story every-body's heard—you know, the one about that same golfer who supposedly went semi-nuts five or six years ago in the off-season and tried to hold up a gas station in Mexico for drug money. "Do you know if that's true?" I said, "Because, jeez—"

Genie gave me a sharp look. "I don't care what people did a long time ago."

For a few minutes I was ashamed of my prurient streak. But much earlier in my life I'd made peace with it, along with my morbid streak. They were there in me, and I had to pay them some attention sometimes—feed them, you know, or I'd get depressed. Once in a while I'd have to run over to the newsstand and pick up an armful of tabloids—*The National Enquirer, Weekly World News, Star*—plus that sluttiest of the slicks, *Vanity Fair*. After an hour or so leafing through them I'd feel all right again.

After dinner we spent some time playing with Todd and listening to a Shirley Bassey retrospective on National Public Radio. We danced together in the Mediterranean living room, our steps light on the cool tile floor. The room smelled pleasantly of leather furniture and green plants. The radio station shifted over to a set of the Chieftains, and I couldn't resist getting out my mandolin and playing along with a few songs. One was "Hardiman the Fiddler," a slip jig Genie liked a lot. I was glad she liked music. I can't live without it.

Some athletes, I know, eschew sex before competition on the theory of conservation of energy. Others need sex to ease the tension and worry. Lucky for me, Genie was one of the latter. I settled Todd down with "Wildwood Flower," his favorite song, and Genie and I retired.

We enjoyed each other in a quiet way—almost, I'm tempted to say, in a meditative way. We'd already learned some things about each other, and now we took the time to explore those things in greater depth.

For instance, there was a small glade of fine golden hair in the hollow of Genie's back. This glade cried out for exploration; it invited me to enjoy it, to breathe it in and memorize it. I wanted to write a guidebook to it. I wanted to build a shrine around it. That glade of silky hair, the perfection of it, made me very happy.

Moving along, caressing her, I noticed some whitish lines on her belly and thighs and wondered how they'd gotten there. They seemed like scars, yet they weren't raised, as scars usually are. She guided me away from those areas and into the tulgy wood between her legs, where I chortled in my joy. Did she burble as she came, you ask? Don't get so smart.

I was joyful afterward, too, but restless. I didn't know why. I felt so relaxed, but I got up quietly, put on Genie's kimono, and went out to the patio. The air tasted good. A half moon was coming up, and by its pale shine I saw sprinklers shooting water in big glittering arcs over a distant fairway. The yellow gallery ropes sliced back and forth against the dark green grass. Faintly but distinctly the sprinkler sounds came to my ears: *chik-chik-chik-chik-fwoosssh*. I listened for owls and nighthawks.

I thought about how much I like golf: the challenge of it, the beauty of it. The feeling of striking the ball cleanly and seeing it fly. The look of an open fairway stretching out from the tee, so green and inviting.

I play at the cheapest municipal courses at the cheapest times of day, and I've endured being paired with drunk guys in undershirts, so being this close to a championship course felt magnificent. This was a place where drunk guys in undershirts weren't welcome, and I felt grateful.

I like golfers who don't talk much. I like old people with crummy clubs who walk fast. I like teenagers who take it seriously and who bet each other Cokes and tacos on making tough shots. I like off-duty cops and firemen because five-foot birdie putts don't faze them; they face death every day. I like golfers who know how to tend a pin. Who replace divots. Who at least have read the USGA rules.

I heard something nearer. A ground squirrel? Falling

palm fronds? I listened, my eyes open wide, as if that would help. Nothing except the sprinklers.

I moved silently to the edge of the patio and saw something moving on the fairway quite near to where I was.

It was a person moving stealthily along the border of a shadow cast by a large tree. I stood perfectly still.

My pulse quickening, I watched him walk slowly along, now veering into the rough, closer still. He wore a cap pulled low; his figure was dark and slouched.

Onward he walked, nearer and nearer. I heard his breathing. Sweat squirted from my palms. Abruptly he dropped to his knees and bent low, hands brushing the ground. Then he stood up and stepped quickly toward me.

I heard myself say "Hey!" in a low, sharp voice.

Instantly the figure sprang back, stumbling.

"Hey!" I repeated, "What are you doing?"

Before I'd finished the sentence, he took off running. I found myself striding after him, jumping the potted plants at the patio's edge and running, too.

He led me on a straight vector across two fairways, the both of us hurdling the gallery ropes, then he cut to the right and swerved toward some houses. My toes got good traction on the grass. My quarry was gaining distance on me, but not much: He was a fast runner, but I realized my legs were longer than his.

He disappeared into the mist of the sprinklers. I charged on, slipping only a little on the wet grass, hoping to pick him up again on the other side. As I emerged from the spray I saw no one, then I heard a clunk and a grunt that sounded like someone tripping on something. Out of the corner of my eye I saw him, picking himself up and darting into the deep shadows between two houses.

More slowly, I followed, feeling suddenly vulnerable. I made for the street, the wet kimono slapping my legs, and saw a light go on outside of a garage: one of those motion-sensor lights. My prowler sped through the pool of yellow light and kept going down the street. My lungs burned. *Are you a quitter?* I mustered another burst of speed. Houses flashed by; not another soul was out.

It wasn't enough. I lost sight of him and at last in the distance I heard a car door bang, an engine catch, and a brief *scree* of tires. I was alone on the dark street.

13

I decided not to tell Genie about this one. When I came out of the shower that morning, she wasn't in the bedroom, and I had a feeling. I padded out to the living room and heard her voice, low and hard, coming from the den. The door was shut. I crept up and sealed my ear to it. It smelled of a very good grade of wood polish.

"Yes, I can," she was saying. "You don't know what I can do to you." Pause. "Listen to me. You're not going to ruin this tournament for me, and you're not going to ruin my life." Pause. "You don't understand. You are nobody. You think you're the most important person in the world, but you're completely insignificant." Pause. "To me, to everybody." Pause. "Leave me alone. I'm telling you."

I scurried back to the bedroom.

After breakfast I drove Genie to the clubhouse for the first day of the pro-am, intending to follow along. She'd come back to the bedroom, pretending very well not to be upset.

The day was as clear as yesterday. You could still smell a little of the morning dew that hadn't burned all the way off. The birds were chirping away, a whole host of passerines up in the trees, the males displaying their plumage and singing their springtime song: *I need sex, I need sex, I need sex right now.*

Genie made her way over to the practice range where Peaches and Dewey O'Connor were waiting, and I wandered around. I watched Laurie Bradmoor chipping balls with surgical precision, and I watched Ying Lam Pan tee off on number 1 with her wide, powerful swing. It was amazing to me how few spectators there were. I'd volunteered at the Men's Open one year at Oakland Hills, and it was so mobbed, even on the practice days, that you really had to scheme and strategize to get a good view anywhere. But here the players were fairly accessible: Nobody was getting mobbed; fans were able to speak to their favorite players, albeit briefly.

You have to be respectful of the players while they're working. You wouldn't barge into an operating room and say, "Hiya, Doc. ¿Qué pasa? When's lunch? How do you make those seams so even, anyhow?" No, you wouldn't. But people do just that to golfers sometimes. I guess that's showbiz, which of course is the essence of professional sports.

I thought about Genie's troubles. She was going to have to tell me something sooner or later, but I had a feeling it was going to be later. I was no detective, but I knew that the top ones on TV and in books always start at the most obvious and take it from there.

Somebody, or somebodies, were harassing Genie, and she either wanted to deny it, or hide it, or both.

Who could gain by threatening her before a big tournament? Who would gain by Genie's being off her game, or out of the way altogether? Well, the other players. They could all gain a little bit, but who could gain the most? Who was Genie most afraid of?

Coco Nash blew past me, walking fast.

All right, who else? Who were Genie's friends—her real friends, her close friends? Who were her exes? Who was back there, you know, in the tear-bedimmed mists of the past? Who, for that matter, might be hiding somewhere out in the future? I didn't know.

Was someone trying merely to terrorize her, or kill her? Why send messages in advance? If you're going to kill somebody, why not just kill her? Why creep around at night unless you intend to do physical harm? Does she possess something somebody wants? Some object?

She wore little jewelry—gold earrings, a gold neck chain, a small ruby ring on her right hand. Her luggage was minimal, and she didn't appear overly concerned about its safety. Her golf bag was the exception, but not because the clubs were particularly valuable; she was paid to play the brand she used, so she received sets of clubs adjusted to her specifications for free. If they were to be stolen, however, it would be a hassle to replace them in a hurry. But the clubs were hardly ever out of her sight—and never, when he was in charge of them, out of Peaches's sight.

Maybe none of this had anything to do with golf. Who hated Genie? Who, perhaps, loved her too much? Was there a psycho fan out there stalking her? I hadn't noticed anyone watching Genie yesterday who appeared odd. Not that that meant anything.

My thoughts returned to Coco Nash. As she'd sped by, something about her had registered in my brain, but I was thinking so hard I couldn't tell myself what it was. I went off in the direction she'd gone and saw her talking to her caddie at the putting green. As I approached, she turned toward Janet Anson, who was approaching her from the opposite direction. Janet Anson was a middle-of-the-pack player who'd gone to the same Alabama college Coco had attended on a golf scholarship. They'd known each other as teammates. Eavesdropping, I pretended to watch Vi Spaniel practice four-foot putts.

"Hey, girlfriend," Janet said.

"Hey." Coco looked up from adjusting her belt.

"What happened?" Janet was noticing what I had half-noticed before: a big Band-Aid on the point of Coco's chin.

"Cut myself shaving," said Coco.

"No, really," said Janet.

"When're you teeing off?"

"It looks like you got stitches under there."

"Shut up," Coco said irritably. "I heard you choked over a two-footer in Phoenix."

"You shut up."

"No, you shut up."

I sidled away.

When Genie and I finished dinner that evening, I said, "You've got to stop acting dumb, or coy, or whatever the hell way you're acting. Somebody means you harm, and you've got only two choices."

She sipped the tonic-and-lime I'd fixed for her and

looked at me mildly. "I was wondering what you were getting yourself worked up about."

"One," I went on, "is to do nothing. You allow this harassment to go on, you allow whoever it is to escalate this, and you allow yourself to be harmed. Do you have a death wish? Is there something I don't know about you?" I was straddling the chaise, while she rocked back in her chair at the patio table.

A shadow crossed her face, and for a moment she was a million miles away.

"Your second option," I pressed, "is to do something, which breaks down into two sub options, which are one, involve professionals, either the police or some private security firm; or two, and I do not recommend this option, have me look into what the fuck's going on. You've got to do something."

Something in what I said made a little light go on behind Genie's eyes, and I thought she almost smiled.

"You're right," she said.

"Finally. Thank you. Okay, do you want to know what I think's going on? I think Coco Nash is the next Tonya Harding, and you're the next Nancy Kerrigan. Only I don't think you're just going to get whacked on the knee."

My lover sat silent for some time. I started to say something more, but she held up her hand and said she was thinking. So I waited.

At length she said, "It could be Coco."

"Behind it all," I said.

She sucked the left quadrant of her lower lip, her beautiful lip.

"I wish you'd tell me more," I said. "You've been talking to her, haven't you? You were trying to warn her away this morning, weren't you? You don't even know what happened last night."

"What happened last night?"

I told her, and watched her swallow.

"Ohboyohboyohboy," she said in a breath.

"I figure your troubles would stop if you hired some bad-ass P.I., you know, to pay her a visit and let her know you're onto her."

"Oh, my dear," she said. "No, no."

"Yes. That's exactly what you should do."

"Oh, no, no." She slipped her hand under my shirt. "No, you can understand why I wouldn't want to put my trust in somebody I don't even know."

"Well, I know some cops back home who could maybe rustle up a real solid local recommendation out here." Her fingers were exploring my midsection with utmost delicacy. "Stop that right this minute."

"I want you to handle this. You've been my magic all along."

"You know, maybe—"

"Say you'll handle it."

"I don't know what I'm doing."

"You know more than you think you do."

"But—"

My last protest was sucked out of my lungs as Genie eased me back in the chaise and took it downtown, right there on the dark, dark patio.

Late that same night I sauntered down a street in Indian Wells, then darted behind a parked car and crouched there. Catching my breath, I watched a scorpion skitter across a patch of gravel near my foot. "Hello, happy little sweetie," I whispered fearfully, on the theory that a soothing tone might make it feel friendly and not so misunderstood, as scorpions must generally feel.

I held still, and it stopped at the edge of my sneaker, thought a minute, then skittered around and came to the next sneaker. I could've peed on it. After another minute it shuffled sideways and disappeared under the car.

A breeze kicked up, and I smelled dust and something musky. Maybe there was a dog around.

I was looking over the house that Coco Nash had rented for the week. It happened to be trash night; someone had wheeled a large bin from the garage to the curb shortly after I took up my watch. The someone wasn't Coco; it was an older white woman in a head rag. I could see her faintly, by the light of the moon and a porch light. She looked as if she'd just blown in from a women's shelter in Oslo or someplace. She had a thin sad face and big shoes.

I waited a while after she went back in, gathering my nerve. Now I stood up, strode over to the bin, and wheeled it away down the street.

I'd learned the address of Coco's temporary home base by approaching her caddie before they teed off.

"Hi, I'm Nancy Rogers from the Blevin Group. Coco doesn't know me from a bale of hay—I'm just a drudge." I talked in a rush, consulting a piece of paper in my hand. Coco was talking to the starter across the tee box. "I'm supposed to run a goodie basket over to where she's staying. Is she renting from that couple, the ones Sheila Kahn used to rent from before she got that tumor—what the hell's their name, over in—"

"No, she never rented from—"

"Oh, right, those other people in—"

"Indian Wells. Um, hey, Coco, who're those people you're renting from?"

Quickly, I turned away and sneezed.

"Hancock. Otis and Julie Hancock. Who wants to know?"

"Blevin."

"Oh."

When he turned back to me, I said, "Yeah, I know the house. It's right on a—what do they call those things?"

"Cul-de-sac."

"Yeah."

"Thanks a bunch. Go get 'em, hey?"

So now I was trundling this trash bin down the street. I'd remembered that Tonya Harding had gotten busted for her role in the Nancy Kerrigan hit because she'd dumped her trash containing incriminating notes in the alley behind a bar she liked. Pissed that somebody was filling up her Dumpster, the bar owner fished out the stuff and went through it.

What could I gain by snooping into Coco Nash's trash? All I can say is, you gotta start somewhere. What could I lose?

I wheeled the container into a clump of bushes at the end of the street. Out came my Mag-lite Solitaire, which I'd clipped to my key chain last year after getting stranded with a flat tire at night miles from nowhere.

The bin was large but not much was in it. Holding the light in my teeth I found a handful of Power Bar wrappers, empty golf ball sleeves, a copy of *Time* magazine with a graphic showing something about the stock market on the cover, an egg carton, a recipe for blueberry waffles written in a jagged hand, welcome literature from the tournament, and many used Kleenexes. Grossed out, I put the stuff back in the bin and trundled it back.

Just as I got to the house, the door opened, spilling out yellow light. I dropped to the ground, where I was more or less hidden by the bin and a spiky bush.

Someone came out, walking heavily. I didn't dare peek. The steps came closer, then stopped right next to my head. There was a huge *thunk,* then the footsteps retreated to the house.

Someone had dropped a cardboard box next to the bin. I scuttled back to my hiding place behind the parked car to reconnoiter. The box was obviously heavy. Should I try to carry it away, or risk picking through it right on the street? In the hour since I'd arrived, only two cars had come by, both while I was hidden.

Before I could decide, the door opened again and I saw the silhouette of a woman standing there uncertainly. She seemed to be peering out. After a minute she came out and walked slowly toward the street. It was Coco, strolling carefully, as if approaching something danger-ous. She stopped before the box and gazed down at it, hands on her hips.

Suddenly, she stooped and with a grunt hoisted the box onto her shoulder. She headed into the driveway, and a minute later I heard the slam of a trunk.

I stood up and started walking toward the Jaguar, which I'd parked about a quarter-mile up the road. Over my shoulder I saw a car backing out of the driveway. After it passed me I ran the rest of the way and jumped in.

I caught up with Coco's silver BMW, then dropped back and followed close enough to keep her in sight. She stopped at a Circle K in what must pass for downtown Indio. I watched from a parking lot across the street as she came out lugging a bag of charcoal briquettes. She put the bag in the trunk, looking neither left nor right in the glare of the parking lot lights, her face focused inward.

She got on the I-10 going east, then got off a few exits later and headed into the desert on the secondary road. She drove a few miles, then slowed down, then pulled off. I whizzed by, pulling off farther along, past a swell in the land that cut off the sight line back to where Coco was. I cut the lights, got out, and began to creep along the roadside. The ground was sandy, and from it grew skeletal bushes that gave me a little cover.

The moonlight helped me. I saw Coco haul out the heavy box and dump it on the ground. She picked up the briquettes and upended the bag on top of the stuff from the box. Then she moved around busily in the dark.

I saw the flare of a match and decided to get a closer look. I stepped onto the asphalt and kept walking. My Chuck Taylors were noiseless on the smooth surface. Another match flared, then a flame took hold of something in Coco's hand and grew. She dropped it, and a fire began on the ground.

A feeling of tragedy came over me. She was destroying something, destroying something important enough to have to do it in secret. I quickened my steps as the fire burned brighter, flashing on Coco's face.

The breeze had stiffened into a real wind. Coco was speaking in a strong voice, but I couldn't catch any words. It occurred to me that she was gaining something in this fire. I saw her body begin to rock rhythmically, comfortably, as if she were getting in tune with something.

Before I knew it, I was running. Hearing the slap of my

sneakers she looked up. I kept coming, running into the circle of light to see what was on fire.

"I want to talk to you," I blurted.

She stared at me with gigantic eyes, and she screamed a scream that split the night like an axe. In two bounds she was in the BMW, cranking the starter.

"Wait! Wait!" I yelled, torn between saving whatever was burning and throwing myself on the hood of the car. Some instinct made me not jump on the car; I'm sure she wouldn't have hesitated to run me over or drag me all the way back to Indian Wells.

A shower of stones peppered me as the car fishtailed onto the road. In a second it was gone.

I kicked dirt over the fire and stomped on the briquettes, which hadn't really caught. Panting, I pulled what was left away from the ashes. There was a pile of stuff that hadn't burned yet—scrapbooks, it looked like, and bundles of pages from magazines. I looked around for body parts and weapons and decoder rings, but found none.

I carried what I could back to the Jaguar, then drove it over and loaded in the rest.

14

Wednesday was the second day of the pro-am. That's where the pros play with a few non-superstar celebrities, and anybody else who coughs up the five grand charity fee. I could only imagine the bullshit the pros have to deal with during a pro-am. There's one before every tournament, I think, except the men's majors. Most of the amateurs are these big executive types who may stand in awe of people who make more money than they do, but they really revere professional golfers. For even though an executive can get by—even succeed spectacularly—by faking it half the time, there's no faking it on the golf course. There's no loyal staff to make you look good, no scapegoat flunky to soak up blame, no rival department head to connive against and score on. There's only you, and you either can hit the goddamn ball or you can't.

Every executive wishes to behave well and honorably on the golf course, and it can be done, even lacking solid golf skills. You can laugh off a bad shot or a bad hole and settle yourself to calmly do better on the next, or you can stomp around and get tense and embarrassed and ruin the day for yourself and your party.

That's why executives respect professional golfers so much. The pros have conquered their inner assholes enough to play the game at the highest level; they're athletic enough to have that body awareness that makes it possible to execute good shot after good shot, and their mental discipline is the ideal blend of focus and relaxation.

Unnerved by the competence and cool of the pros, most amateurs try too hard and end up stinking up the course. Imagine the excuses, the painful rationalizations, the nervous laughter. As if the pros really care how the amateurs play.

"Is it really as much of an ordeal as it looked from the sidelines yesterday?" I asked Genie.

"Absolutely, but *none* of us ever says so in public. You get used to it. Most of them are really nice people; they just go brain-dead when they golf."

After I dropped Genie off, I went back to the house and dragged the charred stuff out from behind some plants on the patio, where I'd hidden it. I spread it out in the shade of the awning. It was a hot morning.

There were three fat scrapbooks and an assortment of loose clippings. The books were your ordinary dime-store scrapbooks, in dark-red leatherette. Do teenagers keep scrapbooks these days? What about autograph albums?

In less than five minutes I determined that everything in them was about Genie Maychild.

There were stories from what appeared to be her home-town newspaper, the Pearl Center, Illinois *Bugle;* the *Chicago Tribune; USA Today; Golf Digest; Golf for Women; Sports Illustrated;* and more besides. It was a compilation of the history of Genie's public life, beginning when she was a junior in high school.

There were the usual small notices about the winners of local and state amateur titles, then bigger, well-written stories in the prestige publications. The early stories from the *Bugle* were smudgy and printed on copy paper—gleaned from microfilm, maybe, or just copied on a crummy machine. The headlines for those stories were heavy on the "Magic Genie" theme. Everything had been pasted in carefully, though, nice and straight.

Going through the unmounted items, I saw something that made the hairs on my arms stand up. It was the most recent big piece on Genie, a pullout from the February *Golf Digest* showing her swing in stop-motion.

Using a black marker, someone had drawn an unmistakable noose around her neck, tied to a tree in the background, along with arrows shooting at her kneecaps. The marks were rough and angry.

I went through the books carefully, looking for other marks like those on the photos, but didn't find any.

Now what was I supposed to say to Genie? "Welcome home, sweetheart. I've cooked pasta and shrimps, and by the way, Coco Nash has been nurturing an obsession with you that has turned murderous"? I looked up at the blue blue sky and the hot, hot sun and thought.

I hid all the stuff again and went into the air-conditioned house. Todd was dozing in a corner of the den. I changed his newspapers and washed his food and water dishes, and filled them again. He woke up and bumped over to me, first rubbing his chin on my shoes, then sniffing the charred smell that still clung to my hands.

"Toddy boy." We played one of his favorite games: Mad Scramble. You take a balled-up sock and push it along the floor very slowly. Todd turns his back as if uninterested. Then you make a little low sound like *juuu, juuu,* and in an instant Todd explodes into a frenzy and runs in figure eights around the sock and you. Then he stops and the game begins again. We did this for some time.

It didn't help me, though. I got in the car and drove over to the clubhouse, deep in conversation with myself.

Me: I'm so freaked out and pissed at Coco Nash I could spit.

Me: Easy now.

Me: I have to confront her.

Me: Why? When?

Me: Now, goddamn it, today! What can I gain by waiting? I've got evidence, solid empirical evidence that she means harm to the greatest creature ever to tread ground. That's *why,* for Christ's sake. I almost caught her twice. Three times.

Me: Wait. I really think Genie should know. Let her decide what to do.

Me: What, are you crazy? She's already *said* she doesn't want to make a big thing out of this, she doesn't want to stir up this kind of publicity, and for sure she doesn't need the emotional turmoil that'd go with it. The fucking tournament starts tomorrow! It's time!

Me: You're acting rashly.

Me: Am I? Or am I simply taking appropriate measures to ensure my beloved's welfare?

Me: Would you consider admitting that you're doing this for purely selfish reasons? To win points with Genie? To impress her so that she'll love you forever? To make up for the many inadequacies in your life?

Me: No, I would not.

Me: I thought not.

Me: Look, if she were in a burning building, would I stop and dither, or would I rush in?

Me: You'd rush in.

Me: I rest my case.

Me: And I rest mine.

This argument took so long I had to drive past the clubhouse and around again. Finally, I turned in.

The pro-am was wrapping up; there was to be a party and charity auction afterward. I stationed myself near the clubhouse and wondered how to get a private audience with Coco—just walk up to her and start talking? Slip her a note?

Player after player came in; Genie went by chatting with a couple of the British pros. After a while I asked a club official where Coco Nash was.

"I believe she's inside already."

"May I go in—just for a minute?"

"Are you a pro-am participant?"

"Yes, I am."

"May I see your pass, then, please?"

"Oh, never mind."

So once again I found myself lurking late at night outside the house in Indian Wells, but this time I didn't lurk long. After a brief reconnaissance, I strode up and rang the bell.

The Norwegian woman opened the door and stood there looking at me hostilely.

"Coco Nash, please."

"Who are you?" Her face was a narrow wedge.

"Lillian Byrd." I handed her my card. "She's expecting me."

"This is concerning?"

"She's expecting me."

She shut the door and I heard her throw the bolt. I waited.

Coco came to the door and stood with her hands braced behind her hips. She still had the bandage on her chin.

I said, "Do you recognize me?"

She looked me over, sizing me up. "It was dark," she said. "Was it not?"

"Yes." I sure didn't need to size her up. She projected the same graceful athleticism Genie did, but she had an edge, an anger in her eyes that I'd seen in the eyes of kids in the projects in Detroit. Those kids' eyes betrayed a baffled anger; Coco Nash's anger, though, was knowing.

She said, "I want to talk to you, bitch."

"Good, because I want to talk to you."

I followed her through a fancy foyer to a fancy living room. We stood in deep pile carpet facing each other. The carpet was Air Force blue; I saw a grand piano in a large room beyond. No one else was there.

"Who the fuck are you?"

"My name is Lillian Byrd, and I'm a friend of Genie Maychild."

"Why are you spying on me?"

"Why are you bothering Genie?"

"What are you talking about?"

"Somehow I knew you'd say that. You know what."

"Suck my dick! What do you want?"

"I want you to leave her alone. You'd have to kill her to stop her, do you know that?"

"Kill her!" She lunged for me, but I sidestepped fast. I could have tripped her, but I'd made up my mind not to hurt her, no matter what. She whirled and seized me in a hug and kicked my knees out. I went down backward, my head bouncing on the carpet. She sat on my stomach and pinned my arms over my head.

She was awesome to look up at, I'll tell you. The cords in her neck were like cathedral columns.

And she was so frenzied that spittle flew as she said, "Now what the fuck are you talking about?"

"All right. You've tried to frighten her with threats. You've prowled around at night trying to scare or hurt her." I tried to launch some spittle back. "Obviously, you're obsessed with her. She's your dream and your nightmare rolled into one. Anyone can understand that. And I've got evidence that you're planning to execute her. You hauled it out to the desert last night to destroy it. I've got it!"

"Why do you say I want to kill her?"

"That picture! With the noose around her neck! You drew a noose around her neck! You want to lynch this white girl who's in your way, you sick self-aggrandizing bitch! I'd call you something worse, but I'm too polite!"

My adversary arched her back, lifting her face to the ceiling. I didn't know whether she was going to slam her forehead into my face, or bite off my nose, or what. I probably would've bitten my nose off if I'd been her.

Her hands were like iron bands around my forearms.

To show I wasn't scared, I said, "Make it happen, bitch, whatever you're going to do. I'm getting bored with this."

She let out another shriek of the kind she'd let out the night before. Suddenly, her face was an inch from mine.

"I should kill your candy ass."

I waited.

"You're the biggest asshole I ever met," she said.

"Eat me."

"You eat me."

"I would, if it'd make you leave Genie alone."

She collapsed as if she'd been shot. All in an instant she released my arms and rolled off me, burying her face in her arms. I hoped maybe she was having a nervous breakdown. I sat up.

Pretty soon she sat up, too, and I saw she was laughing. "Oh," she gasped, "Oh." Her body shook.

No one had come in to check on us during this chaos.

"You are the stupidest bitch in the world," said Coco Nash. "I mean to say, you are *not bright.*"

"That may be," I acknowledged, not for the first time in my life. We looked at each other. "Something has changed here, hasn't it?"

She closed her eyes, then slowly opened them. Something certainly had changed: All the hard, sly anger in them was gone. I realized she'd been afraid of me. And now she wasn't.

Speaking for myself, I was shook up. I took a few deep breaths and rubbed my forearms, which were bruising already. A pack of cigarettes lay on a small table. They were Shermans, an expensive kind. I reached for them, found them temptingly fresh, and lit one with a butane table lighter fashioned in the shape of a penguin. Its mouth, or beak, flipped open to shoot the flame out.

"Butt me," said the number 2 lady golfer in the world.

"You smoke?"

"Kick me one, you jackass."

"If you're going to call me that, you'd better prove it."

"Gladly." Coco Nash smiled at me as if I'd dropped a bouquet of gardenias into her lap.

15

She made herself comfortable against a gold brocade couch, while I scooted to lean against a matching armchair. I practically wriggled with the pleasure of the relief I was feeling. She exhaled a stream of rich smoke and said, "Okay. Part of what you said is partly true. Obsessed with Genie Maychild? Not me. Not anymore. But I was."

"I knew it!"

"Where is my box of gold fucking stars? Shut up. Yes. I thought she was God. She was God to me. When I was a kid, I collected all that shit about her."

"It goes up to pretty recently."

"Shut up. I tried to be her. I memorized her every statistic, I watched every minute of her on television I could. When I met her, I was nineteen and playing in my first

Open. When she shook my hand I almost fainted. I won the Amateur that year."

"Like Tiger was with Jack."

"H'h," she spat, "that son of privilege. Do not compare me to him. Big daddy was there for him every step of the way—that boy had everything handed to him, even his dick when he needed to piss."

"Except the wins."

"H'h."

"You came up the hard way, I know it." To impress her I sent forth a series of small, very thick smoke rings. She watched carefully.

"Those are good," she said, then hollered, "CARLENE!"

My ears were still ringing as the wedge-faced Norwegian came in.

Coco said, "Ashtray."

Carlene opened a cabinet, took out a silver saucer, placed it on the coffee table between us, and left again.

"But you do not know about the way I came up," Coco said. "My mama killed herself when I was ten. She drank Drano one day until her windpipe was gone and she could scream no more. I consider that the beginning of my blessed life. My granddaddy, he raised me up. He was a Gabriel in toe joints all around the South Coast."

"I'm sorry about your mother. The Gulf Coast?"

"Yes."

"Did you ever pick up the horn yourself?"

"I did not. I see now that you are hep."

"No, but I'm not so off the cob as you thought. I grew up in a gin mill in Motown."

She laughed, a delighted squeal that was startlingly high-pitched. "Off the cob! I have not heard that one in years!"

"How come you talk jazz cat from forever ago?"

Again she laughed.

I said, "How come you like to intimidate people? Part of your image?"

"Damn straight. You can believe it or not, but I grew up whacking rocks in a pasture with a stick."

"Sure I believe it. There are plenty of things a little black girl can do."

"I made my own way, just like Genie Maychild made her way. See? She was it. All the way up to last night, she was it for me. I dragged all that shit around to every tournament with me. I collected that shit for years."

"Did you also collect the articles where you insulted her?"

"I insulted her?"

"Well, she says you did, in interviews all over the place. That she was old and couldn't win anymore, and you were going to show the world who's boss."

"Oh."

"Something like that."

Coco's mouth curved into a half smile. "She is speaking of the *Sports Illustrated* profile on me in which I said— and I am quoting myself verbatim—quote, Older players have experience on their side, but younger ones like myself have a passion for winning. We got the brio. That is an advantage, no matter what anybody else says. I intend to win often. I will be swinging those trophies around my head while everybody else is checking their tickets home. Unquote."

"Oh."

"I did not even mention Genie Maychild."

"Oh."

"She took it a little personal, did she not?"

"Yeah, I guess so."

"Look, I would not dis somebody like Genie Maychild. I would not dis anybody. People look for dis in what I say and do, and they find it. But not because it is there, dig?"

I certainly did.

"She was my ideal."

"Her caddie's not bad, either."

"Yes, Peaches Oshinsky."

"She told me she's never lost a stroke, never taken a penalty, due to a mistake made by Peaches."

"I'd love to take him away from her," she said.

"All right, Coco. Why burn all that shit?"

"Because it was time, man! Because it stopped working. It started to work against me, even. Because I cannot shoot for something I have already surpassed. I have been playing on the level of the heppest bitch in the game! I had to cut her out of me. Had to cut her out of my mind. I said, 'Cornelia Nash, you got to find a new way.'"

"Well, there are other role models for you out there. Not necessarily golfers."

She looked at me searchingly. I could see her wondering whom I might suggest, but she wasn't going to ask. All she said was, "Right you are. I put that shit out for trash, but I kept seeing it going to Alcatraz, or whatever dump they use, and all of it lying there in the dump getting covered deeper and deeper, and I could see it there in the dark just like it was still in my hands. So I decided to burn it, right that night and—" She broke off and glared at me. "Where did you come from, bitch? Where did you come from?"

"I'll tell you after you tell me about the noose in the picture."

"Lord. Lord. I was studying her swing all the way

122

through last week. It is not a noose. I drew a cord, a wire if you will, around her neck connecting it to the tree to inform myself how steady she keeps her head through the swing, like as if it is wired in place."

"And—"

"I put the arrows in to show myself how her swing originates there, at the knees. At the feet, really, but you can see her activate her knees before any other part of her, if you look just right."

"Oh."

"Do you know I wanted to fuck her? I wanted to fuck her until she cried and said Cornelia Nash, you are the greatest in the world, you are greater than I myself. I wanted that, oh, man."

"Did you get it?"

"No. Did you?"

"Of course I got it," I told her. "That bank opened up wide for me. D'you think I'd go to all the trouble of crossing you if I hadn't got it?"

"What's she like?"

"Like going over Niagara Falls in a Dixie cup."

"She strong?"

"Very."

"Stronger than me?"

I paused. "Yes."

"You are lying."

"Well, all I know is you're a good thug, but I have no idea if you're a good lay."

There was a silence.

"Well, if you no longer want to go to bed with her, what were you doing sneaking around her place?" I asked her.

She stared at me, her mind working. "You mean—"

I stared back.

"That was you?" she said, touching her chin. "Who chased me through the sprinklers?"

"Yes it was me! Christ almighty!"

"That was her place?"

"Yes!"

"For this week? Right there on sixteen?"

"Yes!"

"Lord."

I waited.

In a heavy tone that said she wouldn't blame me if I didn't believe her, she said, "I was checking on something on the course."

"Well, what?"

"I wanted to know where the nearest sprinkler head is to where I intend to land my drives on that hole this week."

"How come?"

"Because the ground is always a little bit softer near a sprinkler head, here in the desert. You get a little bit different bounce."

"Wow."

"So."

"Why sneak at night, though?"

"The notion had just occurred to me, and I wanted to go see right then to fix it in my mind. I have not played this course so many times."

"Well, why did you run, then?"

What a smile she gave me. Oh, my. It was a smile of superiority mixed with thirst for my approval. Her teeth were big and beautiful. "For the hell of it. You startled the living Jesus out of me, first. Then I wanted to see if I could get away for the hell of it. And I did."

"Not without shedding some blood."

"You run like a jackrabbit. I almost died beating you."

For an instant I wished I had a wall of fire to walk through for Coco Nash. I breathed a long, happy sigh. "Now all that's left are the odds and ends," I said, "which I can guess about. But tell me, if you would, why did you climb through that window in Hollywood? And what about that note on the car? And the phone calls?"

She looked at me for a minute. "Do not cast a kitten," said Cornelia Nash, "but what window in Hollywood, what note, what phone calls?"

16

It was some time before I left the house in Indian Wells. I slipped into bed beside Genie. She didn't wake up. For a long while I watched her face in the dimness, her composed fourteenth-century face, there so close to mine on the pillow.

The next day, Thursday, was go-time for the Dinah. The course looked as though God had pulled an all-nighter on it: spectacular—not a petal or a stalk was out of place. But beauty can be treacherous, as we know. From every player the course would demand the accuracy of William Tell, the courage of Saint Catherine, the patience of Siddhartha, and the stamina of Ma Joad.

The jets were still coming in, disgorging the last big wave

of spectators; the hotels were straining their corsets, and rental cars were careening all over the place.

Genie had time to breakfast with me. She'd lined up a courtesy car for herself for the duration of the tournament, meaning that a volunteer would drive her to and from the course; she didn't want the distraction of driving herself even the short distance around the course to the clubhouse, and she didn't want me chauffeuring either.

"You use the Jag," she said. We were having toast and my special veggie eggs with the secret ingredient of tiny bits of chopped pickle. She chewed and swallowed. I loved the shape of her mouth: a perfect bow with those curled corners. "These eggs are good," she said. "It's all business for me from here on in."

"I know." I watched her getting herself into a zone, her zone, a bubble of concentration she would strive to stay in for the next four days. There was a look taking hold in her eyes, a look of intensity, a look of gathering strength.

The phone rang, as I hoped it would, and I jumped for it as Genie said, "No!"

"Hello."

A liquidy male voice said, "He'd be almost fourteen now."

"Who are you calling for?"

I heard the sound of a mouth opening, or shifting, in surprise. A quick silence, then a click.

"Ah," I said into the receiver, "there's no Alejandro here. I think you misdialed. Unh-unh. Bye."

"Who was that?"

"Wrong number, sweetheart."

There was a long pause before she said, "Oh."

"Would you like more coffee?"

"Oh, no, just the two cups. Thank you so much, Lillian. Darling. How did it go last night?"

I squinted out the window at the postcard colors of the golf course, carved out by the desert light that exposes everything. I said, "I'm not going to burden you with a lot of trivia. All I'll say is, Coco has no clue I'm keeping an eye on her."

She looked at me.

"I've do have some covert operations experience," I told her. I didn't tell her how half-assed my experience was, but of course it didn't matter. "And I know how to take care of myself," I added. If I kept saying that, somehow I felt it would come true.

Genie said, "Well, I'm not going to think about it anymore."

"You don't have to think about it. There's your car. Let me kiss you. That one's for good luck. And that one's for good measure."

"Oh, I do love you."

"And I love you."

As I slid into the Jaguar, a little bolt of *Hey!* shot into my head, and I scrounged around the driver's seat. After a few minutes I came up with a crumpled piece of paper. It was a receipt from Randy's Donuts, that place on the surface road by the L.A. airport with the giant doughnut. I kept digging and found the scrap I was looking for. Uncrumpling it, I read: "You can afford it." It was written in blue pen in very even characters—very even and small. A careful, perhaps obsessive person. A neat person. I put the note, the one Genie had found on the windshield after the party in Bel Air, in my pocket.

I rendezvoused with Truby at the practice range. Genie

had teed off nicely and was gone, with Dewey O'Connor following her group.

Truby sneaked up behind me while I was observing a rookie I'd never seen before work magic with wedge shots, and goosed me. My heart rammed into my throat, then I heard her laugh.

Turning, I said, "God-*damn,* Starmate. You shouldn't do that. Sober up now."

We found a patch of grass in some shade.

"Man," she said, chicken-winging her arms, "it's hot enough to melt the tits off a brass monkey." She looked good, as always. Cute outfit, just right: tailored shorts, sleeveless blue chambray blouse, bright white sneakers and anklets. Chunky silver bracelet, smooth black shades.

"Did you highlight your hair?" I asked.

"Uh-huh. What do you think?"

"It looks really good."

"Thanks, I thought it'd make me look more outdoorsy."

"It does, it does."

She still hadn't scored yet, I could tell. But she looked upbeat in an unforced way. I didn't doubt she'd succeed. She was waiting.

"All right," I said, "the plot thickens. Somebody's giving Genie a hard time, and it's not who I thought it was. She knows who it is, but she won't tell me. She thinks I think it's a rival golfer."

"What's the matter with her?"

"I guess she just doesn't want me to know, doesn't trust me enough. It's something she really wants to keep quiet." I felt a kink in my back and stretched it. "My philosophy this week is, whatever Genie Maychild wants, Genie Maychild gets. She wants me to think the enemy is this golfer—fine, that's what I act like. She also wants the problem to go away, that's very clear. Well, I'm going to make that happen for her. I got a little bit of information this morning, sort of a—an opening. It's given me an idea."

"What are you really up to here, Lillian?"

"It's just ridiculous, hon. Really. I mean, if I told you I was going to spend this afternoon looking at somebody's charred old scrapbooks that I pulled out of a fire in the middle of the desert the other night, then fly to Chicago tonight to tie up a loose end of Genie's life for her, thus preventing an ugly situation from unfolding, would you—"

"You're really going to fly to Chicago tonight?"

"I might."

"When would you come back?"

"I don't know. Maybe one day'll be enough. I don't know. Hon, I really don't know. I don't even have my own thoughts sorted out yet. I could be totally wrong. All I can say is, Genie is a good woman who needs help, and I love her. That's it."

An oven-like breeze stirred the trees. I watched a plastic drink cup roll in a wide arc on the paved path near where we sat.

Truby said, "Let me come with you."

"No, you've got your own show to run here. Besides, the stuff I'll be doing isn't dangerous, let me assure you. It's scut work, you know? Like most investigative work is."

She looked at me steadily. I shifted on the grass.

I said, "Come on, Truby, you know me."

"Yeah."

Now we were both watching the cup as it skittered back and forth, making an annoying sound. I got up and picked it up and put it in a trash basket. The trash baskets were decorated with Nabisco's logo, a modified woman symbol—ever noticed that?

"You might as well tell me how you've been doing," I said, "I'm dying to know."

Running her fingers through her goldeny hair she said, "Well, I've been learning about this femme-butch thing."

"Ah."

"I've been to two parties now. There's as much posing at those as there is at straight-people parties. More!"

"This surprises you?"

"It disappoints me."

"I see."

"Okay, so I know that you don't have to be either a butch or a femme, you know, but my question is this: Can two femmes make it together?"

"Certainly. Certainly they can. But you look confused."

"I thought I knew what a butch was and what a femme was, but I guess the real question is what the hell—I mean, everybody seems to know what butchy qualities are and what femmy qualities are. Everybody but me."

"Oh, no. Dear God, no. The opinions are endless, the arguments are endless, the permutations are endless. That I cannot sort out for you, because it's un-sort-out-able. Maybe you haven't heard the old, 'Butch in the streets, femme in the sheets.' Even within the same person things aren't what they seem."

A dyke couple walked by looking as if they were on vacation from their jobs as bookkeepers in Grand Rapids, wearing identical new Tilley hats, along with their Nabisco Championship logo golf shirts. Truby dismissed them with a pitying *tsch*.

Another couple stolled by, smoking cigarettes and wearing tight shorts.

"What *is* it with that hairstyle?" Truby said. "I used to only see guys wear their hair like that back home. Like hockey players."

"Yeah, the mullet, that's what it's called. God knows why it's called that, and God knows why anybody would wear their hair that way."

"Well, I guess it's convenient to have it short in front so it doesn't get in your eyes, then long in back to show you're still a babe. Or if you're a guy, to show you're a rebel."

"Yeah."

"I find," Truby said, "a certain swagger some butches have to be very appealing."

"Yeah? Tell me."

"Well, I was at this party over at the Wyndham, and this ultra-butchy type comes on to me very cutely! She had on this white linen suit and these *shoes,* so at first I was like, oh, right, *Fantasy Island,* but then, I don't know. She looked like she'd just walked out of a barbershop. No mullet, needless to say. We started talking. There was really something about her. I was thinking hey, maybe this is it! But it turns out—" She dropped her eyes.

"Yeah?"

"I don't want to tell you."

I waited.

She muttered, "She didn't know who Colette was."

"Hon—"

"Don't say it, Lillian, all right? I know. But it'd be like you trying to make it with somebody who'd never heard of Chaucer."

"Oh, I've managed to do that."

"You give me so much grief."

"You give yourself so much more than I ever could."

"Look," Truby said, "okay, so we didn't work out, but like I say, there was something about her, and something about some of the other ones."

"That irresistible combination of female beauty and that sort of assertiveness."

She peered at me attentively over her sunglasses. "Yeah!"

"I stop short of saying 'aggressiveness.' Because I find that whole stone-butch thing slightly repulsive. Well, it's like the whole machismo thing. I understand it, I accept it, I even respect it, but—" I stopped.

"Yeah," Truby agreed. "But it's like, who doesn't want a partner that takes the lead during sex?"

"Boy, have you nailed something. You know, lesbians who've been together for a while, some of them don't have sex very often, and I think a lot of that's about both of them wishing the other would initiate sex. Both are reluctant to do it."

A light dawned in her eyes. "That must be why gay guys have so much sex—you've got two guys initiating sex."

"Plus the hormones."

"Yeah."

"Then again, Trube, there's the attractiveness of that femme-role thing. Everybody wants a wife. Who doesn't want a wife? Straight women want a wife. That part's about support. Receptiveness."

"Right. Because I met another woman I really like who is totally different. She's beautiful and soft but not simpering."

"Good! A CUPCAKE?"

"I don't need that crutch anymore."

"Good!"

"She owns a gallery in Fort Worth. We didn't leave together, but we're getting together tonight."

"All right," I said. "I'll keep my fingers crossed."

We watched the people go by, lots of gay women chattering and laughing, happy to be on a holiday in the sun.

"Lillian?" said Truby.

"Mm?"

"Don't get into trouble?"

I took her arm. "Truby. I swear to you."

"It's going to happen. Don't tell me, because I know."

"No. Look at me."

"You turn into an idiot when you're in love. I know it, goddamn it."

"I know how to take care of myself."

17

After finding Genie on the fifth hole and blowing her a discreet kiss, I slipped away and went back to the house.

Again I dragged out the charred memorabilia, and this time examined it more thoroughly, making notes as I went along.

Aside from the ominous-looking marks Coco Nash had drawn, only two things stood out to me:

One was the fact that in none of the articles was there any information about Genie before she picked up a golf club at age fifteen and a half, other than the flat statement given by Genie in several interviews, "I had no home to speak of. Golf became my home."

The other was a spread from the Pearl Center *Bugle*

about the retirement of Marian Handistock, a local gym teacher:

What befits a legend most?

When it comes to Marian Handistock, whose very name calls to mind gym and winning sports teams at Pearl Center Consolidated High School, it's a city-wide day of recognition. Last Tuesday, under sunny skies that matched the mood of the crowd, Mayor Dick Coggins declared Marian Handistock Day in Pearl Center. The widely beloved Ms. Handistock, or "Handy," as her students affection-ately called her, retired from PCCHS after 25 years of service...

The article noted her popularity, the records of the teams she coached, and featured a quote from Genie Maychild, who had flown back to her hometown to speak at the ceremony. The article went on:

"Marian Handistock was the best thing that ever happened to me," said the sprightly linkswoman, noting that it was Ms. Handistock who not only introduced her to golf, but coached her to her first junior championship trophy.

Currently ranked the top female golfer in the world, Ms. Maychild stood before a crowd estimat-ed by the PCPD at more than 300. She spoke at length about the kindness and wisdom of Ms. Handistock.

"The Pearl Center Con girls' golf team consisted of me alone," said Ms. Maychild. "She drove me to the matches and back to Pearl Center at all hours. She was there for me. I remember her lending me her own golf shoes to play in before I could afford a pair. You couldn't say the word 'can't' in her hearing. There was always a way to make the shot you needed, always a way to learn. Always a way to win. I see some of the girls from softball and volleyball here. I'm sure they have their own special memories of Handy."

The old expression "A good time was had by all" certainly applies to last Tuesday's festivities.

The day was marred only by a brief incident during which a spectator, wearing a mask and a bedsheet spattered with a red substance, appeared in front of the platform as Ms. Maychild was speaking. Ms Maychild appeared shaken by the sight and stopped speaking for a few moments before regaining her composure. The shrouded figure left the area a short time later.

When asked to comment on the strange incident, Ms. Maychild said, "No comment."

Indeed. I returned to the country club. Before heading out on the course, I made a few calls from a public phone. I got hold of two people who were eager to see me, and was unsuccessful at getting hold of a few others, but I didn't consider that a bad score. I bought a plane ticket for a hideous amount of money and reserved a car.

I caught up with Genie on the fourteenth hole, where she was lining up a lengthy putt. Peaches was tending the pin, his handsome face a study in concentration. It was as if his will could guide the ball into the hole. Man, it was a beautiful stroke she made, just as solid and smooth as Foucault's pendulum. The ball dived in, for her second birdie of the day.

I'd been gone for almost three hours; after she holed the putt, she saw me and gave me a "What gives?" kind of look. I gave her back a warm, knowing, reassuring smile, and a thumbs-up. I'd picked up a pairings sheet and found that Coco's tee time had been well ahead of hers.

Genie had a good round that day, shooting two under. This is a tournament where plain old even par wins it some years.

When we met up after the round I let her think I'd been looking after Coco, doing some scouting work, secret work—whatever.

"I'm just not sure about her," I said.

"Let's talk later," said Genie, looking over her shoulder. She went into the clubhouse to shower and change.

While cooking up a stir-fry for dinner, I repeated what I'd said. "But the main thing," I added, "is for you not to worry."

"What do you think is going on?"

"I'm working on it. I know you were wondering what the hell I was doing out there today, but you know—" I stopped.

"What?"

"Well, this is going to sound drama queenish, but if you don't know what I'm up to, you'll be safer."

She looked at me uncertainly.

"What I'm trying to say is, if I fuck up—I mean, really fuck something up really bad—well, if you have no knowledge, then you'll be in the clear. No problem."

The quick gears of her mind went into hyper-drive and she went quiet. Sucking her cheek, she slowly asked, "Do you think you might have to—you know—do something to her?"

I hadn't expected her to latch right onto that. The way she said it made me go over a bump. I looked at her.

"You mean, like, kill her?"

"You said it, I didn't."

The very thought made me laugh. She laughed, too, and after a minute I felt fine again.

She leaned over and kissed me and said, "I'm a lucky girl."

"You sure are. The loyalty of Lillian Byrd is not to be taken lightly."

She smiled like the break of day.

"Now," I said, "I'm going to ask you for something."

"What is it?"

"Just some understanding. Truby's having a hard time. I mean, not in getting laid, which she seems to be heading inexorably for, but—well, see, she gets—see, she has a little trouble with panic attacks."

"Oh."

"And she's asked me to spend the night with her. Not *necessarily* spend the night, but be there if she needs me to. You know? I'm good at getting her settled down from these—states she gets in. I've promised her I'd meet her for a drink, anyway."

"You know, I feel I could use a night alone," Genie said. "Don't be so apologetic. Hey. I need you. You're my charm, my touchstone. But you've got a life, and if another friend needs you, I guess I can lend you out."

"Oh God, Genie, honey, thank you. Thank you for being understanding. All right. I'll plan to see you on the course tomorrow. But you might not see me."

"Uh?"

"Remember what I said: The less you know, the better."

"Would you—would you leave Todd with me?"

"Oh, certainly! You know what to do; he's easy. He'd love to play with you. He likes you." He did, too.

When I left the house that night, I stopped first at the Nash hacienda, where she and I had a quick little conference.

"I need to go out of town tonight and tomorrow, and probably tomorrow night. I'm worried about her. Not terribly, but I am. And I was wondering—"

"Listen. She has got Peaches to look after her on the course, and I have got some security I can direct her way."

"You do?" I thought about my barging in and our rasslin' match in the living room.

She laughed quietly. "Yes. They are discreet. She will be all right. She will not know a thing about it."

"You're fantastic, Coco."

"I am beginning to think you are, too."

"Thank you, but what I am is an earnest-faced fool in love."

I left her laughing and hit the road.

The Palm Springs airport is small and convenient, and I could've caught something to LAX there, but I distrust those little short-hop airplanes. Anyway, in the Jaguar I made as good or better time, given the waiting and the boarding and the taxiing and all that.

Fortunately, I had a row to myself on United's 11:38 red-eye to O'Hare. Before going to sleep, I looked over my notes and composed my thoughts, focusing on the facts, trying not to go too far with my inferences.

It was obvious that something from the past was trying to take a bite out of my athletic lover.

She'd left behind a childhood that had dissatisfied her, let her down, damaged her.

Someone was trying to blackmail her.

And terrorize or hurt her.

And had been at it for a while; it'd been almost a year since Marian Handistock Day.

A person doesn't exist who would have been "almost fourteen now."

Life today, for Genie, was her golf career.

The past for her was everything that happened before she met golf. Therefore, that was the past I needed to look into, that was the place where I could do her—I suspected and hoped—some concrete good.

I felt in the pocket of my coat for my pint of Ballantine's. Never do I travel without some whisky. I asked for a cup of water, drank most of it, then poured in a shot and sipped it. I slipped off my loafers, pulled out *Valparaiso Farewell,* and read a little. It won't be ruining it for you to tell you that Calico Jones suavely manages to escape from the ambassador's residence, but not before enjoying a zestful romp with the ambassador's soon-to-be ex-wife. Then Calico hunts down the guy who counterfeited the government bonds, but learns the shocking fact that his *real* racket is running Cambodian orphans into Quebec via Panama, for use in French-language snuff videos.

After a while I rolled myself in two blankets and relaxed into the roar of the engines and the clink of the beverage carts, grateful to feel drowsy.

18

Pearl Center, Illinois, pop. 2,560, is 63.8 miles north-northwest of the Alamo rental car lot at O'Hare airport. At that distance, it's stayed out of reach of the suburban creep that has made places like Northbrook, Lombard, and Downer's Grove into extensions of places like Evanston, Villa Park, and Oak Park.

The utter flatness of the terrain heading out from the airport gives you a clue as to what lies beyond, as you segue from the Pizza Huts to the places that used to be Pizza Huts but are now used sewing-machine shops. It's farm country; it's Farm Aid country, where people eventually stop fixing the motor on the RV and just let the weeds grow. Little welfare office on the prairie. A gray place, an uneasy place, it felt to me.

Pearl Center's motto, I read on the sign at the town limit, is, "Honoring the Past, Envisioning the Future." *Anything to avoid looking hard at the present,* I thought.

It was nine in the morning and, despite the dreariness and the wet March thaw, I was feeling fairly wholesome. I'd eaten a good solid breakfast of bacon and eggs at the terminal and was ready to implement Operation Save Genie Maychild.

In Pearl Center, which hugs the banks of an apparently nameless small river, there were five taverns, four stoplights, three churches, two police cars, and one newspaper.

Every small newspaper office is different in every detail from every other one, yet they are all exactly alike. That is, you will find different people working there, different stories on the layout boards, different advertisements, different contact names in the stacks of press releases, a different brand of sugar cubes at the coffee shrine—yet the smell and sound and feel of the place is like that of any other you've been in: You're aware of the stale coffee, carpet lint, copier toner, hand soap; you're aware of the low clamor of plastic keyboards, voices on the telephone, the odd crinkle of a candy wrapper, the jingle of coins dumped onto the front counter by a carrier.

If you've worked in the business, you can also walk in and tell what day of the week it is, whether the issue's just gone out to the printer, or just about to go out, or somewhere in between. You can feel it in people's voices, in the tension of their movements.

I'd noticed that the Pearl Center *Bugle* published on Thursdays. That was good for me; Friday, then, was a day of nothing pressing.

Skip Doots, staff correspondent, heard me ask for him in the front office and came bounding out to meet me.

"Hi there, Theresa. Good to meetcha!" His grip was sweaty but firm.

"Skip, how do you do? Good to meet you, too." I liked him instantly, knowing that ninety-nine percent of reporters would've waited in their office for the receptionist to get up, come in, and announce me. Then seventy percent of them would've stayed seated behind their desks while she showed me in. I also liked his title, staff correspondent: just a trifle over the top for Pearl Center, Illinois. His name, Doots, was one of those funny Northern European names common in the Midwest. I'd gone to school with a DeVroot, a Waards, and even a Doody.

He offered me a chair and coffee. "Jenny just made a fresh pot, so hopefully it won't strip the skin from your throat," he said, as he handed me the cup.

"Thanks. You drink yours black, too? Then I guess we're both gluttons for punishment."

"You said it." He was a beanpole with acne scars and crooked teeth, but his eyes and smile made him look like a best friend waiting to happen.

"Nice setup you've got here," I observed.

"Thanks!"

"I really appreciate your taking the time to talk to me."

"Well, it isn't every day somebody from *Sports Illustrated* comes to Pearl Center."

"Heh, yeah. Um, you've been with the paper for quite a few years now, right?"

"Yeah, how'd you know that?"

"Oh, I've seen your work in an archive, a sports thing— you know."

We heard a growl just outside the door, which Skip had left ajar. Another growl coalesced into words. "Jenny, I will not take the call!" It was a haggard male voice. "Would that all *my* accounts paid me net thirty! I told him he'll get the money in his grubby little hands as soon as *I* get it! And he says, my hands are not grubby! That bastard's hands are grubby, all right."

The boss. Skip laughed silently. I smiled.

A low, soothing voice said, "I know, but I can't lie to him."

"Then tell him I'm in conference with Skip!"

Skip's door flew open and a fellow shaped like a fireplug jumped inside. "Skip," he yelled, "have you called Ellen Schmidt yet about that goddamn flood insurance program?"

"Yes, we're meeting Monday to go over it."

"I'll never understand it!" He twisted his ear as if he wanted to throw it away.

"It's very complex."

"Who are you?"

"My name's Theresa Sanchez."

"She's with *Sports Illustrated,* doing a piece on Genie Maychild."

"What's she doing here, then?"

"Skip was kind enough to agree to talk with me about what it's like to—"

"I gotta go." The door slammed.

"He's a trip," said Skip. "Where were we? Oh. Yeah! I guess you guys have all kinds of resources."

"Yeah, pretty much. So—"

"Are you on staff at *Sports Illustrated,* or, like, doing a freelance thing for them?" He wore a small wooden cross on a cord around his neck, and a school ring on his hand.

"Well, quite honestly, Skip, my angle here is, when a sports figure makes it big and leaves town, how do the home folks feel about them? Like, how do you, as a local reporter, cover Genie Maychild? The people here know her, remember her. Her roots are here, and yet she's moved on. That coach she had in high school—"

"Marian Handistock."

"Yeah, her: How does she feel about Genie now? I'll be talking with her today, too. Her friends, you know—"

"She wasn't terribly popular around here."

"Oh, yeah?" That surprised me.

"I didn't know her myself. I mean, I knew who she was, but she was like three years ahead of me in school, so, you know. But it just seems like nobody around here cares very much about her. I tried to interview her parents one time, and they wouldn't even answer the door. Kids from school—I mean, kids who were kids with her—it's funny, but they don't know her very well. They're not comfortable talking about her."

"Yeah?"

"I think Genie Maychild was one of those little nobody-type people, mousy people—maybe one who got picked on, you know. Then something happens to them. For her, it was discovering golf. And they bloom, and like overnight nothing's ever the same for them. It's like they become a different person nobody knows anymore."

"Uh-huh." I couldn't imagine Genie being mousy.

"You can only milk 'Local Girl Makes Good' so far."

"Yeah."

"Are you doing any other celebrities, or just Genie?"

"Oh, you know. Yeah. I'm not sure, though. The editors

are dithering. You know. I decided to go ahead and get a little legwork done anyway."

"Oh. They do dither, don't they?"

"You gotta love 'em. Say, have you heard the one about the writer and the editor who get lost in the desert? They're walking and walking, trying to find water. Then they're crawling. Finally, they come to an oasis, and the writer plunges his head in and drinks. He looks up to see the editor peeing into the water. 'Hey, what are you doing?' he says. The editor says, 'Improving it.'"

Skip really liked that one. "You got that right! Boy, have you got that right! Sometimes I—"

"So," I said, "did you ever know any, like, boyfriends or girlfriends of Genie?"

He was too eager to help me to get insulted because I kept interrupting him. "No," he said, "like I say, I never really—"

"Ever look her up in the old yearbooks?"

"No, I never thought of that." He looked crestfallen.

"Maybe I'll swing by the library later. There is one here, isn't there?"

"Yeah, not that they have any kind of *collection*." He raised an eyebrow, a college man through and through.

"I hear ya." We sipped our coffee. "Skip, tell me, do you want to keep on in journalism? I'm just curious. Do you—do you see it as a long-term career for you?"

He smiled into the distance. "Once," he said, "I left here and moved to Chicago, to take a job at the *Tribune*. I offered to work for free, just do anything, you know, so they'd see I was a hard worker, and maybe then one day I could work into a foreign correspondent position. I was studying Arabic and Russian."

"Wow."

"And I worked like a dog there," he went on. "I did everything they asked. Gosh, I did everything up to and including mopping the men's room. They wouldn't give me any real assignments, but I wrote features, ones that I'd think up myself at night. I did some investigative stuff on the road commission and public health. But they didn't like my work."

"Really?"

"It's kind of hard for me to say this, but I feel you'll understand." His eyes were clear and noble. "They said I didn't have the killer instinct."

"Oh, Skip."

"Yeah. What could I do? So I came home. And now my goal is to buy the *Bugle* someday and run it myself."

"Well, Pearl Center's a nice town."

"It is. I was born here."

For some reason I had to keep from crying. After a minute I said, "Well, heck, journalism's a crazy life."

"You said it."

"Hey, you know that rally last year for that teacher of Genie's that retired, Coach Handistock?"

"Yeah?"

"Somebody came up in some kind of costume? What was that about?"

"Oh, yeah, that was really bizarre. This person just sort of appears, right in front of the podium, you know, and Genie freaked."

"What exactly did this person look like?"

"Well, like I think I said in the article, he or she was wearing a mask—"

"What kind of mask?"

"A rubber mask, like for Halloween. It looked like a pig."

"A pig?"

"You know, a fat pink pig face. And then this sheet that was supposed to look bloody, I guess."

"Did you get any pictures of this person?"

"I don't think so." He rubbed the point of his chin with his thumb. "I can look back over the proof sheets just in case. We didn't have the digital camera then. I'm the whole news bureau around here, you know."

"I do know. Would you do that?"

"Yeah, sure."

"And how did Genie react when this Halloween person showed up?"

"She just—it's like she just froze for a minute. I was standing practically next to her and she looked—well, like she'd seen a ghost. Her face went totally white, and she just stared for about—I don't know, half a minute."

"Did the person say anything?"

"No."

"Did Genie say anything?"

"I almost caught something under her breath."

"What was it?" I pressed. "Did you hear a word?"

"I don't know. No. Then she, like, shook it off, like I could *see* her getting ahold of herself, and then it was like the person didn't exist. She just went right back to talking. I went back to writing notes, and then when I looked up, whoever it was was gone."

"Did people say, 'Who was that masked man?' or anything?"

"Not that I heard." He looked sheepish. "I guess people around here aren't too curious."

We both sat and thought on that for a moment.

"No," he suddenly said, "it's not that."

I smiled.

"You know what I think?" he said, "It's that people here could feel that Genie wanted that—whatever it was— goblin to be invisible, so just naturally it became invisible to them, too."

"Out of politeness, then."

"In a way, I guess."

We looked at each other and laughed. That's the Midwest for you: land of the pathologically polite. It was good for Genie that Skip Doots was just as polite as his brethren.

Just to see how polite he could be, however, I said, "Seems Genie and Coach Handy were pretty close."

"Yeah, I guess so."

I waited. Then, to push him to his utmost limit of politeness, I said, "Well, did people talk about that?"

"Oh! Uh. Gosh, I don't know. You know, Theresa, it isn't that people don't gossip around here. I mean, it's a small town."

"Yes, that speaks for itself."

"I try to stay out of it," Skip said. "I hear things. But my philosophy is, this town needs somebody to look after it. Somebody to help people feel happy and proud. Somebody who doesn't just criticize and find fault, but somebody who can tell the truth and who cares. Somebody who *cares* that a lady with no vocal cords comes once a week to the senior center and helps them make baskets, somebody who *cares* if the garbage truck guy has to keep rigging the clutch in the dead of winter with a piece of wire because it never gets fixed right, somebody who *cares* that even though the clock on City

Hall doesn't keep the right time, the *finches* are going to come back any day now and nest in it!"

For a minute I wanted to move to Pearl Center and marry Skip Doots. But I just said, "You have a fine career ahead of you."

"You think?"

"Yes, my friend. Yes."

19

The Pearl Center Public Library could've fit into a cigar box, but it appeared that the staff tried hard to keep their chins up, given what must have been a zero-sum budget game with the city council. On the bulletin board, there were notices for two different fund-raisers, a bake sale and a karaoke festival. Tonight was to be Karaoke Night, with soft drinks provided. Suggested donation was two dollars per song. I wondered if I'd be able to stop in for it.

The librarian was up on a chair pinning gold crepe paper and inspirational pictures of singing stars to the ends of bookcases and walls. She'd gotten up Elvis Presley, Conway Twitty, Jim Nabors, and June Carter. In her on-deck pile I saw Garth Brooks and Dolly Parton. The librarian rubbed her neck as if it hurt.

The only patron, a great-grandpa in a Ford jacket, was reading a newspaper at a table. He made a continuous, deep throat-clearing sound.

The librarian climbed down and showed me the shelf of yearbooks from Pearl Center Consolidated High School and went doggedly back to her decorations.

I found Genie Maychild's senior picture and her junior picture. She looked about as I expected her to look: strong neck and jaw, shy smile, yet the suggestion of immaturity, especially physical immaturity. As most teenagers do, she looked as though she hadn't grown all the way into her face yet. Even so, I saw a quiet determination in her eyes. Almost a somberness.

And there she was also, among the sports photos, bundled in pants and a jacket, swinging a club against a dreary backdrop of muddy ground and bare trees. And there she was again, leaning on her driver, Coach Handy at her side.

Coach Handy appeared in most of the team photos, a solid presence with a challenging look, as if she might jump out of the photograph and recruit you on the spot for half-court basketball, or maybe cross-country.

I flipped through the pages of candid shots, too, looking for Genie with other students, looking for references to her. In her sophomore year her picture wasn't among those of her classmates, nor was it there in her freshman year. I looked for the golf team; there was none. Coach Handy was there in the sports pages, but no Genie Maychild.

Puzzled, I looked through the candids for those years. "God, I'm glad I'm not a kid anymore," I muttered, the pictures taking me back to those awkward days of yearning and frustration. One picture drew my attention, of two students caught necking in a stairwell. A high window caused the shot to be backlit, with a silhouette-like result. You couldn't see the faces of the couple; I suppose that was how it got past the censors. They were a couple of slobs, it appeared to me, lumpy and straggly, but the body angles of the girl made me look more closely. I'd seen that body. The boy, in profile, had an obvious hard-on. The caption said: "Sitting in a tree: G.W. and D.D?"

This was Genie's sophomore year. I searched through the head shots in the W's. Christ Almighty, was that her? Could that be right? "GENIE WICKERS," it said under the picture, of a surly, chubby, dull-eyed girl. Yes, it was her— there she was, my beloved beautiful athlete, my Tarzana, staring into the camera like a stupid pumpkin. *What the hell? What happened to Genie Maychild?*

I went to the D's, and found the only boy with "D" for a first initial: Dominic Dengel. He looked even more stupid than Genie, but somehow more optimistic. In spite of his incredibly mangy haircut, there was an eagerness about his face. I looked at the picture for a few minutes.

Well, no wonder I hadn't been able to find anyone in Genie's family by phone. She'd changed her last name and had somehow drastically changed her appearance, her self, between her sophomore year in high school and the rest of her life. The woman I knew was Genie Maychild. So the question became, what happened to this Genie Wickers?

I consulted the directory in the library and found two Wickerses, both on the same road, and one Dengel. I noted the addresses and left.

To hell and gone was where Gristmill Road was, a long lonesome rut west of town. I drove past the first of the two

Wickers addresses, number 11; half a mile down the road was the other one, number 15. Both homes were the kind of places you'd go and photograph for a bleeding-heart feature on the rural poor.

I turned around and went back to number 11, the bigger of the two lots, and pulled over. Someone had thrown down a single-wide prefab about forty years ago, it looked like, then attempted to bond a board-and-tarpaper shanty onto the side of it. A variety of adhesives had been used over the years, I noticed, to keep the pieces together and seal out the weather: expanding foam, red epoxy, duct tape. I expected to see Dorothea Lange and Walker Evans bump heads between the junked cars any second.

My Weejuns slipped on the mud, which still harbored ice crystals between the clumps. There was no name on the mailbox.

Standing at the front door wearing my pea coat and my hopeful-kid-at-Christmas expression, I listened. Inside somebody had a television blaring. I knocked on the kick panel of the storm door: *bam-bam-bam!* Glancing up, I saw a huge satellite dish pointed skyward, attached directly into the shingles of the shack with tenpenny nails.

After a few minutes I knocked again. The inner door creaked open to reveal the most repugnant hag I have ever seen, which, I feel, is saying a lot.

The woman wasn't terribly old, but she had that weathered, skaggy look that retired prostitutes have, whether they've tried to take care of themselves or not. And this one had really let herself go.

Before she opened her mouth to talk, I could tell she'd be minus all but about four teeth. Her vaguely beige hair was wispy and wild. Pouchy in the face, she stooped miserably, as if a large dead dog were strapped to her back. She pushed open the storm door a crack and looked at me with bee-stung eyes.

I smiled warmly. "Mrs. Wickers?"

She stared.

"How do you do?" I went on, "My name is Theresa Sanchez and I'm doing an article about Genie for *Sports Illustrated*. I wonder if—"

She let the storm door fall shut, but I quickly pulled the pint of Ballantine's from my coat pocket. She stopped, I kept smiling, and she let out half a cackle.

"Come in!" she said. "Hah!" I was right about the teeth.

The smell of the place triggered my gag reflex, but I controlled it. I forced myself to breathe through my nose, to filter the germs and cat dander, and wondered how I could get a dab of my mentholated lip balm into my nostrils without appearing rude.

Well, we're talking cats, we're talking cigarette butts in hubcap-sized ashtrays, we're talking mildew, we're talking dirty underwear. There. I'm sorry, but that's how it was.

The television was on absolutely full blast, tuned to a soap opera.

"*But didn't Asher tell you? He's going to marry ME!*"

"*That's what you think, Bethany. You know, if you weren't PREGNANT, I'd shut that poisonous little trap of yours for good!*"

"*Who told you that, Valda?!*"

"*Let's just say a little BIRDIE, dear.*"

Daytime TV. Whoever said television was a wasteland?

Mrs. Wickers dropped into the couch facing the TV and indicated that I should take a seat with her there, but

I stepped into the kitchen and brought out a straight chair. It was wooden and very greasy, but at least I didn't think it'd give me VD or crabs, as I was certain the couch would.

"Sorry to interrupt your story," I began.

"Oh! Hah! I know how they all come out!"

Sloshing the bottle, I coughed and murmured, "Maybe a glass or two."

"Oh! Hah!" She heaved herself up and all but scurried to a cabinet. "Of course!" A scrofulous yellow cat darted from behind the cabinet and made as if to climb up the back of my chair. I made a sudden movement and it changed direction to the kitchen. I saw at least five other cats around, all old-looking. I thought that was strange; in a houseful there's usually a few kittens in the bunch. I supposed kittens aged fast in that place.

I poured a couple of fingers into the cloudy glasses she set before me on a trash-encrusted coffee table, then said, "Mrs. Wickers, I'm wondering—"

"Hah! Cheers!"

"Cheers."

She smacked her lips. "Ah, that's the good stuff! Good stuff!" She had on a pink sweatshirt appliquéd with seahorses, and those stretch pants nobody over age twelve should ever wear. She kicked off a pair of filthy scuffs and eased back in the couch. Her feet looked like poached footballs.

I poured again, for her.

She said, "Genie was a—a disappointment, you know."

"Yeah?"

"She never gave a damn about me."

"Oh, I'm sorry."

"She's rich, you know."

"I guess she is. What I'm wondering about are Genie's formative years, you know, her school days—"

"Hah! That Bethany's gonna drink poison, y'know!"

The audio track of the soap opera pounded along—

"*Dempsey, I know you never meant to hurt me.*"

"*That's right, Bethany. Up until an hour ago, you're the only one I ever loved. But I guess you always knew that. Now that it's too late—*"

"*But Dempsey—*"

"*No, Bethany. Not now. Not here. Asher's waiting.*"

"*If only I hadn't—*"

I grabbed the remote from the coffee table, hitting the power button. "Goddamn it. Let Bethany drink poison, then. I want to talk to you."

Mrs. Wickers, her lips wet with Ballantine's, peered at me. "You a cop?"

"No. Listen. Did Genie have a boyfriend in high school?"

"Unh." She began cursing softly, slurringly, something like, "Godzhdamn. Damn. Godsham-damn."

"What was his name?"

Mrs. Wickers cursed again, and I realized she was saying the name I'd already seen. "Dom. Goddamn Dom."

"Dom? Yes? Dominic, uh"—I flipped open my notes—"Dengel? Dominic Dengel?"

"Dang. Goddamn. Sumbitch."

I felt like backhanding her into coherence, like in the movies, but it never works in real life.

Sharply I said, "Did she have any other boyfriends? Mrs. Wickers! Hey! Work with me here! How about her father? Did her father have sex with her?"

"Unh." She cleared up a little. "He was gone before she got periods."

"What about—"

"Why d'you care about tzhese shings? Who cares?"

"I'm trying to help your daughter."

"Trouble? She in trouble?"

"I don't know."

"She never gave a good goddamn about me."

She reached for the bottle and sloshed a lot more into her glass. I took the bottle back and took a slug out of it. After a minute I felt calmer. The bottle was almost empty.

"Why didn't she care about you?" I asked her.

"Dunno."

"Maybe because you were a drunk? Maybe because you never gave a damn about her?"

"Mm, ah, did. Did, too."

"Listen. Mrs. Wickers. Did Genie have an abortion back then?"

She gave me an answer I wasn't expecting.

"I hope she did. Yepsh, I sure hope she did. 'Smy daughter you're talking about."

"What do you mean, you hope she did?"

"You—all ya want—all ya people want—"she appeared to be gasping, struggling for air. I waited, poised to do something, I didn't know what. Suddenly, with an effort, she got it together and screamed, "Get out! Offa my house! Get out—getoutgetout!" Her face went shiny, and she began what I can only describe as projectile sobbing. A lifetime of grief spewed out of her, fearsomely. Terribly.

"You don't care!" she screamed. "You never gave a damn!" Her face swelled and turned yellowish, mottled with purple. "You never gave me a damn thing! Damn! You hear me? Gimme!" she slobbered, "Gimme it! Look what you made me do!"

Recoiling, I leaped up and headed for the door.

As the storm door fell shut she got the TV going again.

"Asher, if you walk out that door now, don't you EVER expect to come back!"

20

One Wickers was enough for me, but for the sake of thoroughness I stopped at number 15, a brick cottage overgrown with yews and junipers, which closed behind me as I pushed toward the front door.

I heard a phone ringing inside. No one answered my knocks.

Dominic Dengel lived in an apartment above the Wash-n-Fold back in town; I struck out there, too.

Still, I was doing all right. It was one-thirty. I picked up a microwaved burrito at the Stop & Snack and ate it in the car while I thought about the angles I had left.

The existence of Dominic Dengel signified a big break, I felt. If Genie had had an abortion as a teenager, or more than one, this guy might've decided to blackmail her about it now. But I couldn't imagine who'd really care whether Genie had had an abortion fourteen or fifteen years ago. The media? Come on. Sponsors? Well, maybe. Genie had a few big contracts for clubs and apparel; you saw her face looking out at you from *Golf Digest, Golf for Women,* the usual. Still, sponsors are so frightened of lesbianism you'd think they'd be *glad* for some proof that one of their stars had had heterosexual relations at least once in her life. Is this nasty? I don't know anymore. The thing was, Genie didn't want this information coming out. That had to be enough for me right now.

I remembered Genie saying sharply, when I was gossiping about that European star, "I don't care what someone did a long time ago."

My appointment with Coach Handy was at two o'clock.

Why had Genie changed her name? Why do people, other than giddy new brides, change their names? To reinvent themselves. To get away from the past. To gain something.

The summer I was eleven, I read *True Grit* twice through and immediately changed my name to Mattie Ross. I wanted to be everything Mattie was that Lillian Byrd was not: fearless, smart, driven. Driven from within to fight a good fight to the death if need be.

Carrying a sharp stick, I rode my bike through the crummy streets of Detroit's south side, into the weeds in vacant lots, along railroad beds, looking for criminals and rattlesnakes. In those days, criminals were not so easy to stumble across. There were no rattlesnakes in any event.

During the summer that I was Mattie, I felt brave, square, and true. Confidence braced up my posture as I patrolled the neighborhood, convincing my playmates to join my posse.

Then, I suppose, school started again, and I resumed my journey to actual adulthood, with its anxieties and consequences and exhilarations. I have never felt as capable, though, never again as fearless, as when I was Mattie Ross.

Marian Handistock lived in a house with a white picket fence around it and a basketball hoop in the driveway. I had to go past it and park on the next block down, because the street on the coach's block was torn up and men were digging a trench. I thought it would be presumptuous to park in the driveway.

She stood in the doorway watching as I came up the walk. The house and yard were tidy, notwithstanding the mounds of dirty snow still clinging to life here and there. In the summer the yard would be shady: Maples and shagbark hickory trees, their bare branches thinking about all that great sap down there starting to thrum, towered overhead. I caught sight of a goshawk perched on a high limb; it was silently watching a cluster of plump chickadees that were taking turns pulling seeds from a feeder. The chickadees kept in touch with each other with a constant chatter: *dee-dee! diddy-dee!* The goshawk was thinking about food, too.

"Welcome," said the coach, who filled the doorframe gracefully, I thought. She was stocky but not fat. Not tall. I recognized her aggressive chin from the pictures. She could've been a utility infielder, or possibly a goalie, apart from golf. She wore the prettiest blue blouse you've ever seen. Silk, maybe. Such a pure cerulean. Gorgeous. Around her neck was a clever ornament: a miniature coach's whistle made of silver, on a fine silver chain. *What a nice retirement gift,* I thought.

She sized me up; of course, she was accustomed to sizing up women: *How strong are you? How fast? The legs? The back?* Her eyes drilled deep into mine for an instant: *Fighting spirit? Team player?*

"Benchwarmer," I said, shaking her hand. It startled her, but then she gave a friendly laugh, embarrassed that she'd been caught. I smiled and thanked her for seeing me, then wiped my feet carefully on the mat.

"Oh, don't trouble yourself," she said pleasantly.

"Water-main break?" I asked.

"Yes. What a mess it's been! They say they're almost done, though." She directed me into the kitchen and took my coat. She had a pot of coffee going, and there was a plate of windmill cookies on the table. A clean kitchen, a civilized kitchen, it was. *And a civilized woman,* I thought with a measure of gratitude.

"It's great to be talking with someone from *Sports Illustrated* again," she said, pouring coffee.

"You've been interviewed before."

"Several times. Do you know Tommy Pursell?"

"Uh, no."

"Jane Metz, then?"

"Actually, I'm really new. I was working for the *Motor City Journal,* and I'd done a few freelance things before that, and one thing led to another. You know. Crazy business."

"Right, sure. So—"

"So what I'd really like to talk about today, Ms. Handistock—"

"Please, I'm Marian."

"Marian, thank you—and of course I go by Theresa— are Genie's early days; I mean, before the record starts. I feel there's a gap between obscurity and fame, a sort of magical time, and it seems important because Genie came from very humble beginnings. I think a lot of fans would be interested in how you worked with the raw material of Genie, so to speak, how you took this young person and helped her on the path to sporting greatness. Like, the Nick Bollettieri angle, the Jack Grout angle."

Coach Handy sipped her coffee, which she'd served in nice china cups with saucers. She'd set out a ceramic sugar and creamer in the shapes of bluebirds. I glanced around for evidence of a roommate but saw nothing conclusive. I did notice, through an archway to another room, a couple of antique golf clubs on a wall, and a pair of new space-age snowshoes, the kind you can jog in. Yep, old Handy was still a jock.

An extremely serene Golden Lab walked in, sniffing, circled the table, then settled beneath it. It was a nice dog, with a smooth coat and that sort of concerned expression those dogs have.

"Some people," I prompted, "would say you created Genie Maychild."

"That's not for me to say. But it is true that when she came to me she had no swing at all. We built it together."

"You won the Illinois Amateur, didn't you?"

"Yes, in college. I thought I'd turn pro—but that's another story."

"The point is, you knew the game as well as anybody in this state."

She smiled. "Genie was like a lot of young golfers: all power and no balance, no real finesse. She wanted—"

"Who first put a club in her hand?"

"I did."

"When was that, Marian? How old was she?"

"She was fifteen-and-a-half. It was toward the end of her sophomore year in school. You see, they'd made a mistake on the sports budget at Pearl Center Con, and we had more money than we thought, for once, going into June. It was the end of May. If we didn't use the money by the end of the school year, it'd go away—you know how that works. So I pushed through a request for some golf equipment. I'd seen Genie in my gym class. I could see she was a natural athlete, in spite of being out of shape. She had a gift."

"Yeah?" I took a cookie.

"She could move. She was coordinated. I invited anybody to come after school and try out the equipment, and she and oh, half a dozen other kids showed up. From the moment she took a grip, I knew I had something special on my hands."

I'd gotten my reporter's nod going as I made notes. The reporter's nod in the seated position isn't so much a head nod as an upper body rock, a rhythm you get going more or less in time to the speech patterns of the person you're listening to. The purpose is to create an atmosphere of receptivity and encouragement. Every now and then you vary things, do different head movements—a head cock, an upward chin tilt. Reporters do this naturally, unconsciously. The TV ones, however, have to force themselves to sit practically still, at least while they're taping the reaction shots, because the reporter's nod on TV looks idiotic.

"There was something about Genie then," Coach Handy went on, "It was like a world opened up to her. She took to the game. The other kids didn't have the patience for it, or if they did, they weren't interested in playing for the school. This is the heartland, Theresa, you know."

"Football country."

"Right. Golf is sissy to boys, and girls would rather play team sports."

"Or lead cheers," I put in.

"Ufh! Yeah. It's a short season here, too, of course. In the spring you get some pretty raw weather."

"But it didn't bother Genie."

Coach Handy said, "No, she had gumption."

"I like that word." She smiled in agreement. I asked, "What was Genie like before she picked up that club?"

The coach took a big long breath, then let it out. She leaned forward and cupped her chin in her hand. For a while she gazed at the tabletop. I waited.

She looked up. "May this be off the record?"

I hesitated, pretended to consider, then put down my pencil. "Of course."

"I felt there were problems at home. I have to tell you, the teachers at the school—you know, when a girl is as— as marginal as Genie was—I say marginal—I—I mean, it was as if she was invisible. She wasn't attractive; she wasn't bright. I don't mean she was actually stupid, I mean she didn't appear bright. Never spoke up. She was shy in gym, and she was fat. Big belly. Still, she could move." She paused. "I got away from what I was trying to say. When a girl is like that, it's usually the gym teacher who tries with her. The other teachers don't even know she's there."

"What kind of problems were there at home?"

"Theresa, I don't know for sure. She never talked about her home, her family, at all. To this day I've never met her parents. There were a couple of older kids, I heard, who lived someplace else—Minnesota? I wondered about—are we really off the record here?"

"Yes. More than you know."

She looked at me. I shouldn't have said that. Too cute.

But she went on. "I wondered about incest. But—but that's not the kind of thing you talk about. Is it?"

I shrugged sympathetically.

"Not the kind of thing you bring up," Coach Handy asserted. "You sit and you wonder at night, you know. You ask yourself questions. Finally, I decided that if something's buried, it ought probably to stay buried."

"Yes," I said. "Is Genie's dad dead?"

"I don't know. He's as good as dead to Genie."

"What about friends? Did Genie have any?"

"The way Genie's life went was, nobody paid her any attention when she was a nobody, except, I suppose, to tease her. You know how young people can be—my God, they can be cruel."

"Yes, they can."

"And then, when Genie's confidence went up, when she became fanatical about golf, she was practicing and working out four and five hours a day, then I think other girls and boys came around her, but by that point she didn't need them. Didn't want them."

"Sounds like she went from needy to entirely self-sufficient, all at once."

Coach Handy bit a cookie. "Well, she had me."

"You really took her under your wing."

"Yes." She put the cookie on her saucer and lifted her eyes to the kitchen window and the tree limbs beyond it. "Aside from teaching her the game, I taught her about diet and nutrition. I taught her the kind of physical regimen a golfer needs for strength, I taught her about clothes, even, and her hair." Coach Handy looked at me. "She was like a thirsty plant. She lost the extra weight, gained muscle, and became…beautiful."

She smiled a funny smile: one of those fake-modest smiles that indicate a deep, wide pride and the attempt to cover it up.

I said, "I know you devoted a lot of time to Genie. She's said you practically gave her the shirt off your back."

Marian Handistock said, with sudden tension, "I would have done anything for that girl."

Oddly, my heart began to pound. I was getting jealous. Pushing it down, I said, "It's that way sometimes between mentor and student."

"She gave me her Open trophy."

Whoa, I thought. "I didn't know that. So she was like a daughter to you. Do you have children of your own?"

She just watched me from across the table. Suddenly, the whole situation felt very uncomfortable. The look in her eyes was like, *I could take you any day, you fraudulent bitch.* Everything was wrong. The little ceramic bluebirds began to appear menacing. The dog stirred under the table.

I realized that Marian Handistock and I were both deeply in love with Genie Maychild. I pressed to the end. "Did Genie have a boyfriend that you knew of?"

"No." That was the shortest answer she'd given.

"Did you know a kid named Dominic Dengel?"

"No."

"Okay," I said. "Well, I'll be catching up with Genie this weekend. She's agreed to an interview on Sunday."

"I see."

When you ask somebody if they know a certain name, you can tell things. A person answering honestly will stop and think, say the name over, and at least run a brief scan of the old brain cells. But Coach Handy had that "No" ready for me.

"Do you see Genie these days?"

"Oh, yes. Not often, I mean, she doesn't come back to Pearl Center very often." She gave a frosty laugh. "But now that I'm retired I like to go to her tournaments."

"Do you give her advice?"

"She has another coach now."

Man, it was getting cold in that kitchen.

"How come you're not at Mission Hills this week?" I asked.

She stared at the tabletop for a minute. "I've learned that I have a heart condition. My doctor said I should avoid extremes of heat and cold. The desert, well."

"I'm sorry to hear that," I said, glancing at the snowshoes.

She didn't reply, and the interview was over.

21

Skip Doots was editing a pile of junk copy when I popped back in to talk to him. He looked at me with a little gleam; I didn't know why.

"Skip, my man, my time in Pearl Center runs late. I've got just one more question for you."

"I didn't find any shots that show that pig-mask person," he said.

"Thank you for checking anyway. Skip, if a girl gets pregnant in Pearl Center, where does she go for an abortion?"

"You know, they don't know you over at *Sports Illustrated*."

"And I don't know them, so we're even. Look, man, we're in the same business, you and me. I'm trying to help someone. You can take me at that or not. I wish I hadn't lied to you."

"It's all right." He sat there thinking. "That wasn't supposed to be a pig, right? That person?"

"No."

"Somebody was trying to mess with her."

"Yes."

"And they're still doing it?"

"Yes." I glanced at my watch.

"These days, if you want an abortion, you go to the women's clinic in East Horton. Next town over."

"How long's it been there?"

"Oh, yeah," he said. "Only about, um, five years. In that event...she wouldn't have gone to Dr. Carlsborg here. She would've gone to Dr. Fischell, the old G.P."

"Where's he?"

"East Horton, too."

"All right. You don't happen to know a guy named Dominic Dengel, do you?"

"Yeah, I know Dom Dengel. Why?"

I waited for it to click.

"Oh. Oh, man. Oh, man." He shook his head.

"What?"

"Sometimes I serve as an escort at that clinic I just mentioned."

"Yeah?"

"I know Dom from there."

"You mean he works there? I'm looking for him."

"No, he—well, I guess he feels he works there, in a way. He's a regular protester there."

"God! Really?"

"Yeah, he's—he's, you know..."

"Is he one of those quiet sincere ones," I wanted to know, "or one of those loud nasty ones?"

"He tends to the nasty. He's likely to be there now, in fact."

"Yeah? You mean right now?"

"Yeah, he likes the afternoon shift." Skip picked up a pencil and rolled it between his palms. "The place was bombed last year."

"Did he do it?"

"I'm certain he did. It was a screwed-up job. It didn't destroy the place, but somewhere he'd learned how to make a bomb. The investigation didn't really go anywhere, so he's free."

"I see. You know, Skip, I wouldn't have pegged you as a guy who'd run the gauntlet at an abortion clinic."

"How come?"

"Well, you seem like such a straight arrow. You wear a religious symbol."

He fingered the small cross that hung inside the V of his shirt. "Well," he said, "I've seen more than you might think. Things aren't so simple as people want them to be."

"You said it, friend." Skip Doots was about the swellest guy I'd ever met.

"Would you like some help?"

"Skip, you're an absolute dreamboat. But I have to say no. I want to get friendly with Dom."

"I understand."

"How do I get to this clinic?"

He told me. "So it's just maybe five miles. And the doctor's office, Dr. Fischell's, is out farther, maybe three miles more, out from town. It's all by itself next to the road. You can't miss it."

"Is there a Salvation Army store in Pearl Center?"

"Uh, Salvation Army? As a matter of fact there is. On Redbud Street, three blocks, I think, south of Center."

"That's great. Thanks. I think I'll be leaving town tonight."

"That's too bad."

"You kidding me?"

"No." Looking down, he pulled on his upper lip. "Theresa, I don't see any ring on your finger."

My heart began ripping itself into shreds. *Oh, hell. Hell, hell, hell.* "Skip, oh. I wish we could go steady."

"Me too."

"But I gotta go."

"One of those things, huh?"

"Yeah."

When Truby and I were at Wayne State, we bought our housewares and clothes—except for underwear—at thrift stores, mostly Salvation Army and St. Vincent De Paul. We called them "Sally Ann's" and "Paulette's." It was fun to shop at those places; you were always surprised. Truby became a connoisseur of bowling shirts and cocktail dresses; I once found a pure-wool bathrobe for a dollar. Someday I'll tell you about my flamingo mirror.

The Sally Ann's in Pearl Center was just the place for what I needed. It had that up-from-the-basement smell they all have. I zeroed in quickly and picked out a navy blue polyester twill skirt and a long-sleeved blouse in mauve polyester with a pattern of dark red and gold tulips on it. I added a thick acrylic cardigan in a sort of avocado shade, and found a pair of beige service oxfords that fit.

At the last second I ran back and grabbed a head scarf, a Vera design involving fish shapes in varying shades of turquoise. I cashed out for just under ten dollars.

Color me gorgeous, no?

I found the abortion clinic easily, and parked around the corner. Two sentinels, a man and a woman, were on duty, sitting in lawn chairs on the sidewalk across the street from the clinic. The man was talking; both of them had a glazed look, as if they'd been sitting there forever and had no plans for later. He droned on. Whatever he was saying, she'd probably heard it a thousand times.

I used my First Communion glide to approach the protesters. "Peace be with you," I said, interrupting.

"You too," said Dominic Dengel, whom I recognized from the yearbook. He looked exactly the same, as raw and young and uncomprehending, but with a certain rigidity. Yes, it was that frustrated-guy anger, that hardness you see in guys whose lives have turned out drearily different from what they had expected.

The woman said nothing. She was a farm-wife type with an impressive fluffy hairdo. It looked like a cluster of fine gold wire. She had on a white zip-up jacket with black and brown insets at the shoulders, which made her look like a linebacker. Her face was a linebacker's face, too.

Dom Dengel slowly got up from his chair. It was a cold day but he only wore a ratty sweatshirt and jeans. The gray sky above us was ratty as well.

The two of them looked at me with somnolent curiosity.

I peered across the street at the clinic: a grim little office with fake-rock siding and a caduceus decal on the glass door. PRAIRIE WOMEN'S HEALTH AND FAMILY PLANNING, said the sign. Little abortion center on the prairie.

"That's where they do it, is it?" I said.

"Yep, that's the place," said Dengel. "The only one left in the county." He smiled thinly and offered his hand. "I'm Dom."

"Sister Mary Theresa. How do you do, Dom?" I turned to the woman. "And how do you do? I'm Sister Mary Theresa."

"Hi," she responded, still linebacker-faced. She held a dog-eared placard of a bloody fetus in her lap.

"What a lovely jacket," I said.

That got a little smile from her. "Oh! Thank you! I got it in Dayton when I went to visit my—"

"Are you a nun, then?" said Dengel.

"Yes, with the Little Sisters of the Catechism. Our mother house is in Green Bay."

"Oh!"

I saw comprehension in the faces of Dom and his companion, a shadow of understanding: *Yes, this is how plainclothes nuns look. Yes, this is a nun.*

"I'm traveling around, to write a book of true stories. True stories about heroic Christians like you."

The woman, whose name I decided had to be something like Sherri, just stared into space; Dengel, though, looked uncomfortable.

"Well, Sister," he said, "that's nice, but I'm not really religious."

I smiled in wonder and awe. "Why, how could you say that, Dom, when you're doing the Lord's work?"

A car pulled into the parking lot across the street and a scrawny girl of about sixteen got out from the passenger side. Instantly, Dengel and Sherri moved to the edge of the curb and began shouting, "Murder! Bloody murder! Shame! Shame!" Sherri waved her placard.

The girl walked stiffly to the door, eyes down. Whoever had driven her was staying in the car.

Dengel and Sherri, still yelling, glanced my way.

Oh, right. "Jesus loves you!" I called out. "He really does!"

As the girl yanked open the clinic door she shrieked over her shoulder, "Fuck you! I'm just getting a Pap test!"

Dengel turned away as she disappeared inside. "That's what they all say."

"I gotta go pick up Tyler," Sherri said.

I said, "We took in one of those girls once at the convent."

"Disaster, right?" said Dengel.

"Bless us, we didn't realize how—well, how 'street' she was."

"Anything that wasn't nailed down, right?" Dengel shook his head wisely. "Those situations always turn out wrong. Never take one in. Never take one in."

"I am so fed up," I said. "I just get so fed up, you know?"

"Wait a second." Dengel went over to a derelict Chrysler Imperial parked nearby and got another folding chair out of the trunk. He carried it over for me.

"Thank you so much, Dom."

"See, Sister," he said, sitting carefully down, "I'm pretty much of an atheist. I'm just against the murder of little kids."

"I see. Well, then, we actually have a great deal in common, you and me." I smiled sadly. "Do you mind if I ask how you came to be atheist?"

He looked down silently.

"Dom, you know—" I stopped when he looked up at me, his eyes searching mine. A car went by and honked, and without looking over he raised his hand in acknowledgment.

"Bad things happened to me," he finally said, "that destroyed what little faith I ever had."

"I'm very sorry, Dom. Sometimes I wonder…"

"What?"

"If there's a place in this world after all for people like

you and me. What I mean is, oh"—I pressed my fingers to my temples—"I just don't feel like I fit in."

"Over at the convent?"

"Most times, I agree, you know, the church says we should be loving all the time, turn the other cheek, but sometimes I get so mad—"

"Yeah?"

He was suspicious of me, I felt it, but his drive to tell his story to a virgin audience would win out over his reservations about a stranger. I don't know how it came to me, but I have a knack for getting people to tell me things. I've never fully understood it, but there it is.

I said, "I get so mad that I want to do things."

"Yeah?"

"Thoughts come into my head, and I get so darned angry…"

He watched me closely, breathless.

I closed my eyes. Softly, I said, "I want to kill these people. I want them to beg for their lives, and then I want them to die screaming, and I want them to descend into hell. I know it's wrong, but sometimes it seems…so right. So very right. I don't suppose you can relate to that."

"Well, I—"

"Sometimes I feel my faith slipping. That's why I'm writing this book."

"Mm-hmm. Yeah! I've heard of these rogue nuns. So you're a rogue nun, huh?"

"I learned that a brave soul bombed this clinic once." I smiled a little tiny smile, a halfway kind of smile from beneath my eyelashes.

"Well," said Dengel, "see where that siding looks different around that window?"

"Yes, yes, I do."

"Well, that's where the bomb went in and then blew it out, that place there. They patched it. You can still see a little soot up high, see, by the rain gutter?"

"Oh, my dear. What did—do you know what was used?"

Sherri reaffirmed, "I gotta go pick up Tyler, and then Gary's taking us for pizza."

Dengel ignored her. "Let's just say there are people around here who know things about explosives."

"Yet the clinic still stands."

"The device should've been more incendiary. The problem is, the more fire you want, the bigger and heavier the bomb has to be. The more there needs to be in it, you know?"

"Oh."

The afternoon was growing chillier. A few buzzards circled high beyond the rooftops, out over the prairie. It was a quiet time in East Horton.

"Dom, tell me something—"

"I'm on disability."

"Huh?"

"I had cancer. Before that, the thing was—"

"Dom, did someone hurt you?"

He looked into my eyes deep, real deep. "Sister, it's like you know me. Usually, a woman needs to give me a massage before she can really know me."

I suppressed a shudder.

"Sister, sister—uh, I'm sorry?"

"Theresa. Mary Theresa."

"Sister Theresa, I was hurt bad. It happened when I was too young to know how to protect myself. I'm the kind of man who loves kids. I'm the kind of man who wants to be a father. I think about a lot of things when I'm sitting out here. I'm a very competitive person. When I do something, I do it to win."

"Was it a girl? Someone you loved very much?"

"How do you know?"

"Dom, I might be a nun, but I wasn't born yesterday."

He chuckled gratefully.

I said, "It was a girl, then, and it was about a child you wanted."

"Yeah. I'd have a son today if she hadn't—"

"Killed it, right? I see. Where is this girl—woman now?"

He snorted. "You'd never believe it. Never in a million years."

He was spilling it, so easy and purely.

I assured him, "I have all the time in the world."

"We both came from the same shithole on this prairie—pardon my French—and what do you think? She's big. She's a big star. Wealthy. Very wealthy. She got out and left me here."

"A movie star?"

"Not exactly. I'm not—I can't—let me put it this way." He leaned close to my ear. Sherri was just sitting there nearby; I judged she must have heard all of this, but somehow he wanted a measure of privacy, if only for show. "I'm going to pay her a visit real soon. It's time she remembered me. She thinks everything's over, done. But I'm not going to stand by and let her ruin my life."

"Do you have friends who help you, sometimes?"

"I do. That I do. You'd be surprised how far and wide my friends reach."

"And they help you in return for..."

"I help them with information."

"Like, how to do certain things?"

"Yeah."

"Dom, I want to know, could you—have you ever loved anyone else?"

"Love's got nothing to do with it. Not anymore. I got cancer. I got cancer in the you-know-where—pardon my French again—and I can't have any kids anymore. I used to think, big deal. But now I know different. Now I know what it means to give your name to a new generation. I learned."

"He wants to get inseminated," Sherri said.

"What?" I said.

"That isn't it," Dengel said. "It's that I saved some of my sperm, you know—they saved it for me, and I can still have a kid if I can find somebody to, you know, get impregnated. Who'll agree to do it."

Involuntarily, I glanced over at Sherri. She quickly stared at the cracked pavement.

"It costs money, see, to get somebody to do it, who doesn't know you. Not like somebody who would just want to do it out of...out of—"

I said, "Love? Or idealism?"

"Yeah." He shot a dirty look at Sherri.

She leaned forward in her lawn chair, grunted, and got up. "I gotta go pick up Tyler."

"See ya tomorrow."

"See ya tomorrow."

"Nice to meet you," I chimed.

She looked back at me with a totally fake smile.

"It's expensive," said Dengel, "and I'm on disability. I used to have a good job. I ran an equipment place."

"Oh. And if you can get some money from the one who hurt you—"

"It's caring, not money." Suddenly, his eyes narrowed and his whole body tensed. "I'm the last of the Dengels! Sister, do you have any idea of what that means to a man? My old man said, 'Son, you've got to carry on the family name. You've got four sisters! *I had four sisters!* Don't let me down!' On his deathbed he told me that. Now what am I supposed to do? I'd have married her! I loved her! I'd have offered to marry her if I knew she was gonna—or if I knew I was gonna get cancer, I'd have married her!"

Genie Dengel. I shook my head sadly.

Dengel went on, "I mean, money is a sidelight of caring. If she cared, she'd spring loose a little money, or she'd do it herself."

"Do it? You mean get inseminated with your—"

"Yeah. I bet I could convince her, given the..."

"The?"

"The right situation. You know?"

22

After leaving Dengel with a promise to keep in touch, I stopped at a gas station and used the pay phone to call Dr. Fischell's office.

"My husband," I told the friendly receptionist, "was a patient of Dr. Fischell's before we moved to Cicero—uh, that would be fifteen years ago. Sixteen years. He never bothered to ask Dr. Fischell to send on his records, but now he's got cancer and—"

"Oh, no!" The receptionist was the sweetest old thing. I pictured her with honestly gray hair, a partial bridge, and her glasses on a chain around her neck. This receptionist kept a cardigan sweater handy, to drape over her shoulders when she got chilly.

"Yes, and the oncology doctors want to see his records—I

don't know what for. Can you send them right to me? Because we're flying next week to the Mayo Clinic."

"Oh, absolutely, Mrs.—?"

"I'm Mrs. Kenneth Johnston—t-o-n. Do you keep records for so long, then?"

"Oh, we absolutely do! We—"

"And you have them right in the office?"

"Oh, absolutely! Dr. Fischell has every file on every patient, from the first day he opened his office after the war. I'm sure I can find them quickly. Let me just..."

I wondered which war she meant. After giving her a fake address I drove out of town to the office, which, as described by Skip Doots, was miles from nowhere. I was lucky; it was getting close to five o'clock. The building was a small, neat brick one. I pulled in to the gravel parking lot and popped in just for a sec.

Using a high little voice, I told the receptionist, "I'm trying to find Pearl Center, and I think I'm badly lost."

"Oh, you're not lost at all! Not the least bit!" Her smile was overwhelmingly reassuring, as though she just had all this good will pent up inside her. She wore her glasses on a chain around her neck; her cardigan was neatly folded on a shelf behind her. I am so good.

"It's such a lonesome road," I whined.

"Oh, you poor thing! You're almost there! Eight miles, right straight on. You'll go through East Horton first, and you'll see a sign? Class D hockey champs. Then you'll go over some railroad tracks, then..."

She gave me deluxe directions as I cased the joint. No alarm system at all, it appeared. I saw no control panel, no sensors. Just a stout front door and a good lock.

Back in the car, I circled the building before peeling out,

and I noticed a rear door and a few side windows. The building was flanked by a bed of low evergreen shrubs set off by a cobblestone border. Stubble fields stretched off in both directions along the road; woods grew up to the doctor's property from behind. Across the road were a few snarly acres of brush; a farmhouse sagged, weather-beaten and abandoned, amidst them.

I really started to hold my breath at this point, because now everything depended on what I'd find in that office.

I drove southeast toward Chicago, as the afternoon waned. I was hungry. I saw a McDonald's sign and reflexively turned off, then decided to keep going a little ways. Eventually, I stopped at a Szechuan restaurant. The cashew chicken I ordered was good, and so was the hot tea; I took my time.

When I came out it was seven o'clock and dark, but not late enough yet. In the car in the darkened parking lot, I changed back into my jeans, sweater, and pea coat, also my Weejuns. It felt good to put on my old red sweater again. Sister Mary Theresa got dumped into the trash bin at McDonald's. I drove around Chicagoland for a while, taking the I-290 all the way downtown, then picking up the Kennedy to the Edens. Then I cut west again somewhere around Waukegan. Déjà vu set in as I remembered driving around just like this in Detroit, settling my nerves before a task just like this, some few years back. That break-in had been dangerous from the get-go—highly dangerous—but this one ought to be a slice of pie: No homicidal maniacs were out to get me, no would-be paramour was stalking me. Still, it gets your nerves when you're planning to break the law, when you're planning to go creeping around a strange place in the dark.

All I needed to think about, though, was Genie Maychild: Wondrous, beautiful, unsurpassed sexpot of the LPGA Tour, she was all I needed to calm right down. I thought of her hands, so easy and sensitive, caressing me; I thought of the glade of golden down in the hollow of her back, stirring in subtle, delicious response to my breath. I thought of all her parts, and a serenity came over me, and a longing. *Ah, my darling, I'll take care of everything. You can count on me. After this weekend I will be your love slave forever, and you will be my goddess, except for once in a while taking a turn as love slave.*

The country G.P.'s office was deserted and dark, and the road was even more lonesome than in the daytime. The afternoon overcast had thickened into a velvety black night.

I drove off the gravel lot onto a patch of half-frozen lawn on the side of the building away from the road. My headlights picked up an opossum moseying along the edge of the woods. It looked into my beams with those red eyes.

Turning off the motor but leaving the car door ajar, I moved fast. I yanked on my leather gloves, kicked loose a cobble from the shrubbery border, strode up to the lowest window, whose sill was about knee-high, and broke it out. I could see well enough by the glow of the car's dome light.

Tossing the cobble aside, I carefully stepped in, finding myself in the doctor's private office. Nice mahogany desk, leather swivel chair, hat rack—nice. I heard no alarm, and, walking quickly to the reception area, saw no blinking lights, no silent alarm that I'd missed earlier. The air smelled cool and antiseptic.

My Weejuns patting on the clean floor, I pulled out my trusty Mag-lite and went to the bank of sliding drawers behind the receptionist's desk. This was an old country doc's office all right. The very feel of the place was comforting to me, the burglar. The braided rug in the waiting room, the sheaf of magazines expertly fanned out on the coffee table. All around me were the symbols of cleanliness and kindness. Isn't it funny? But I felt it.

I doubted I'd find Genie Wickers's file right in with the active ones; likely, the doctor stored old files in a more remote space. But it was so easy. I'd already rejected the possibility that she'd used a fake name; it just wasn't Genie. My fingers flicked along, Walciski, Warrell, Westphal, Weyandson, Wickers.

WICKERS, GENIE. I lifted out the thin folder.

The file consisted of just one sheet, a printed form with Genie's medical history on one side, and notes about an examination on the other.

"Patient requests Rx for birth control. Pt. complains of 'a tennis ball moving in my tummy.' Pt: 'I'm afraid I might have cancer.' "

Then the pelvic examination. "Cervix long & closed... Fundal ht. 25 cm... Fetal heart tones heard. Rate 122 per min. Fetal movement noted. Gestation around 24 weeks based on LMP... Diagnosis: probable hidden pregnancy. Patient & partner very surprised at diagnosis. Recommended prenatal care ASAP, possible counseling."

I read it over a couple of times more. I heard my own breathing in the silence that suddenly pressed around me. *Now what the hell?*

I expected to break into this office and find a record of an examination, then of an abortion, both of which I'd steal and destroy. Because Dom Dengel was threatening Genie with revealing this illegitimate pregnancy and abortion. But without the actual medical file, there'd be no proof of any pregnancy, no proof of any abortion. The doctor's own memory? Would he remember Genie from fifteen years ago? Would it even matter? Medical files are confidential, aren't they? Stealing the abortion file was only part of my overall plan, but it was a key part. If no evidence was available to Dengel, even if *he* was intending to steal it, Genie could dismiss his threats.

I stood there for another minute, knowing I had to leave, yet rooted, stunned.

She'd been six months pregnant.

You've come for the file; now take it.

I creased the folder with its single sheet into quarters and tucked it inside my sweater. I found a sheet of the doctor's letterhead and a ballpoint pen and took them into the doctor's private office. Holding my light in my teeth, I printed: "TO HELP PAY FOR THE WINDOW. I'M SORRY. I BROKE INTO THE WRONG PLACE."

I placed the note in the center of the doctor's desk pad and laid a twenty-dollar bill on top of it, then weighted it down with his pencil cup. I climbed out the window and drove away.

23

I just made it on the last United flight from O'Hare to Los Angeles. As I hurried into the Jetway, I almost got run over by a sprinting executive hissing into her cell phone.

"That is not acceptable! If the jury believes her even a little bit, we could be totally—" She slowed down after jostling me. "Tell him to try again. Tell him—no, go up ten thousand."

We were the last passengers on. As the executive, or lawyer, and I made our way down the aisle, she apologized for bumping me. "Things turn to chaos sometimes."

"Don't I know it," I said over my shoulder. "That's all right. Looks like we're seat mates, then."

I helped her hoist her garment bag into the overhead bin, as the flight attendants were urging us to get settled.

"Hey, this one's not full at all," said the executive, moving over to an empty row. "Give us both more room."

"Thanks."

Having a row to myself again made me happy in spite of the baffling situation I was in. I settled down with my thoughts and my notebook and wished for a drink.

When the plane got to cruising altitude, I bought a Scotch on the rocks, even though it almost killed me to pay four dollars for it.

So here we are. Nothing in my experience made me think there could have been any way a healthy girl could've gotten a doctor to abort a six-month pregnancy. What happened to that baby? Dengel thought it had been aborted. Could Genie have given it up for adoption without anybody knowing? What was the deal with the baby?

The threat of Dom Dengel, I felt, was both pressing and not pressing. He was a weirdo, all right, a nasty son of a bitch, but he seemed listless, almost passive, sitting there in his lawn chair, talking big.

But who, then, had broken into Dewey O'Connor's house and scared the hell out of us that night? Who had left the note on the car? Well, I'd gotten Dengel to admit that he had friends who helped him.

I leaned over from my aisle seat to peer out the airplane window into the blackness below, into the invisible grandeur of the North American continent. Fairylands below—towns and cities and their lights—little tiny fairylands.

Genie and I needed to have a talk. But somehow I had to hold off doing it until this weekend was over.

A terrible thought rose up in my mind. It jumped out at me from the jumble of my day on the Illinois prairie, but it was so terrible that I shut it away instantly. *No. There's an explanation, and I'm going to get it sooner or later.*

The whisky made me feel warm and cozy inside my sweater and jeans.

With the time difference, the flight would come into L.A. around one in the morning, then I'd have the ninety-minute drive out to the house. I wondered how Genie had scored that day in the tournament. Earlier, I'd lucklessly fiddled with the car radio, trying to find a sports report that mentioned it.

Even with my coat over me, I wanted to be warmer. I asked a most attractive flight attendant for a pillow and blanket. During the twenty seconds it took her to fetch them, I fantasized that she would compassionately tuck me in, as the advertisements encourage you to expect. But she wordlessly handed them to the passenger in the row ahead of me.

"Oh!" said the passenger.

As I popped up and stepped forward to claim my bedding, she, the passenger, perceiving my face, said "Oh!" again.

And my heart plummeted through the floor into the baggage compartment and I said nothing to coach Marian Handistock, who in her aisle seat, looked very different than she had in the afternoon. Her face was drawn, yes, but that wasn't all.

She said nothing to me, and I couldn't think of anything to say to her. She glared at me with utter coldness, utter contempt. Having surely seen me board, she wasn't surprised. She had that look ready for me. Distracted by my hurry and talking with the stranger, I hadn't spotted her. There was nothing to say, anyway.

I sat down in an icy sweat. Coach Handy suddenly had a thorough-going furtiveness about her. What else had caught my attention? For one thing, I'd noticed that her hands looked terrible. They were red; they looked sore. Several knuckles were covered with Band-Aids.

Her legs were crossed, and one foot stuck slightly into the aisle. I studied her shoe, noticing that it had gotten terribly muddy very recently. Mud had been scraped off the sides and the sole. The remaining mud hadn't had a chance to start to flake away yet. There was mud, too, on her pant cuff.

A stone of dread began to grow in my stomach.

There was nothing for me to do but settle back in my seat and get my pulse under control. I hoisted my coat collar around my neck and forced my eyes closed. Incredibly, I must have fallen asleep, because I practically had a heart attack when someone's hand clamped over my shoulder. If I hadn't been wearing my seat belt, I'd have hit the call button with my eye. It was just an unsteady guy on his way to the toilet.

When we landed, Coach Handy didn't look my way as she left her seat. I lingered, wanting her to get far ahead of me, wanting not to bump into her as I made my way to the parking shuttle.

The last few passengers filed past my row up the aisle. One man, in jeans and a tattered sweatshirt, caught my attention.

No. Lord, no.

I carefully watched for his profile as he exited into the Jetway.

It was Dengel.

He must not have seen me, must not have recognized me as I'd boarded, had he even been looking. That was part of the purpose of my nun ruse. Somebody would say, "Oh, yeah, that woman—she was wearing a funny scarf and a really ugly sweater." Not: "Oh, yeah—she was about five foot ten with a mole on her right cheek."

I picked up the car and drove to Mission Hills like a maniac, blasting through the night, thinking. My main goal was to get Genie through the weekend without anything dreadful happening. Figuring out what the hell was going on would have to wait.

It was the desert again, Southern California; it was hot. I'd stripped off my coat and sweater as I hustled to the car, breathing in that LAX jet-fuel air.

It was about three in the morning when I let myself into the house at Mission Hills with the key Genie had given me. I thought I'd slip quietly into bed beside her. I listened for Todd, expecting him to come bumping right over to me, as was his custom. Then I went looking for him, first stepping out of my shoes. I heard nothing.

Todd wasn't in the den, he wasn't anywhere. I went to the bedroom door, beneath which a seam of light showed, and listened. I realized that if I opened the door now, I'd scare the bejesus out of both of them.

Softly, I said, "Genie, it's Lillian." I opened the door. She was sitting on the bed in her kimono, hugging her knees, her inhaler in her hand, Todd at her side. He jumped off the bed and came to me, enthusiastically sniffing. I squatted to pet him. Looking up, I saw that Genie's eyes were big.

"Why are you up so late?" I asked.

"Hold me."

I obliged gladly. As I breathed deep from the back of her neck, a tremor ran through her. Somehow she felt more angular to me. I brushed her hair out of her eyes and inspected her face. What did I see? Fear? Confusion? There was a depth in her eyes, a depth that seemed to just keep going. I looked for the bottom and didn't find it.

She murmured, "I need you so much."

"Has something happened? Tell me."

"I'm one shot out of the lead. And I'm scared."

I waited, holding her head against my heart, stroking her hair. Needless to say, I was scared, too, but wasn't about to reveal it.

"Genie, dear—"

"He wants to destroy me."

I held her tighter and tried to get her to talk more, but she wouldn't. So I played my mandolin and eased all three of us to sleep until we had to face a new day.

24

I felt I was occupying some kind of netherworld, a separate reality of my own making. Genie and I, awake at dawn, didn't talk much at breakfast. I told her I'd spent some quality time with Truby. She knew I was lying, I think, but didn't care. The tournament was her focus, and it was going to stay that way.

So there was this huge unspoken thing in the air between us, and I felt both of us fighting the tension it created. Finally, after I cleared the table—she'd hardly eaten—I took her into my arms and said, "You know, I'm trying to help you."

She nodded into my breasts, but she didn't appear comforted. A miserable groan rattled up from her throat. After a minute she whispered, "I want you with me today."

"You'll have me. It's just that right now..."

She looked up. "Right now what?"

"Well, I'm going out for just a while."

"No." Her eyes hardened.

"You're not teeing off until, what, ten o'clock?"

"That's right, and you're not going anywhere until we leave. We're holing up here until the car comes, and you're riding in with me."

"But Genie—"

"No!" The tiny shards of emerald in her eyes caught me and held me in a rush of fury. "You don't understand!" she cried. "None of it is important! Nothing counts! Nothing counts except—"

"Except that trophy."

"Yes. Yes. Yes! I will not be forgotten! Genie Maychild will not be forgotten! No one but me knows that my career is just *beginning*. Lillian, I've found a way to focus that I never had before. I'm going to win this one, you know? And the next and the next. I think you do know it. I know it."

"Tell me about your focus."

"Not yet." She riffled her hand through her perfect sun-kissed hair.

"Well, I don't doubt you in the slightest."

"You don't doubt me?"

"No," I assured her.

"You believe in me all the way?"

"Yes. Yes, I certainly do, my darling, my most darlingest. I've never known anyone even remotely like you. I've never known anyone as strong as you. As intense as you. I'm trying not to totally give in to your spell—have you felt it?"

"Yes. Oh, Lillian, give in! Surrender to me. Surrender your whole self to me. You won't be sorry. You said you believe in me?"

"Yes. Oh, God, let me kiss you."

"You'll stay—mmph—with me now? Mmph. Mwa."

"Mmp. Yes. All right."

"Nothing can touch me now."

Smooching sounds filled the kitchen, and Todd hopped around to where he could get a good look at what was going on. It wasn't that he was a voyeur, just curious.

I watched Genie come out of her upset. I watched her smile, her lips with their little downturned corners so easy and her body so alive, so alert.

I'd thought I'd be able to temporarily neutralize the threat of Dengel, perhaps by getting to Coco Nash and asking her to keep her security people, or whatever they were, on Genie for the duration, buying me some time until the tournament was over. Now, I'd just have to shadow her all around the course and hope for the best.

Dengel, I figured, would approach her at some point, either at the course in public, or at the house for a little private pow-wow. He needed not just an opportunity to frighten her; he needed an opportunity to coerce her. He needed time, and if he was serious about wanting her to agree to get injected with his sperm, he'd have to make nice with her. In whatever horrible way.

I kept expecting Coach Handy to call or show up, but she didn't. Genie and I cuddled on the couch with Todd until the courtesy car pulled up out front.

The driver was a hardy lass named Stacy, who looked as though she might teach a little gym herself. She wore a bright red golf cap and a hulking brace on one knee.

"Very glad to help out," she said briskly, when Genie thanked her. "You're my last pickup. I'm looking forward to watching you play today. I've got my vantage points all picked out."

I asked, "Even on that bad leg? What happened?"

"Oh, it's way better, I can walk okay. I slid into second and tore my ACL."

"Oh, no," Genie said, "my nightmare."

"As soon as you're through," said Stacy, "I'll be ready to take you back."

Peaches was on the spot with Genie's bag when she came out of the locker room looking like a million bucks. I'd never known anyone who could wear clothes like Genie did. She'd chosen a silky, featherweight shirt in a clear fawn shade, and a pair of gorgeous pale-blue shorts. Her hair caught the sun like gold, and she'd put on some pink lip gloss. Everything looked just right, down to her broken-in but polished saddle shoes.

Peaches Oshinsky didn't appear too shabby himself. He was the kind of guy who could look good in a greasy under-shirt, but he had on a neat polo shirt and shorts beneath his spanking white official caddie jumpsuit. His eyes were bright, and his teeth shone out from his beautiful flawless face.

"I bet your wife's missing you," I said.

He just smiled as he fastened the front of his suit.

I looked down at my own frayed golf shirt, rumpled shorts, and black sneakers, and decided I ought to get at least a minimum-wage job.

I trailed along to the practice range and stood quietly, watching not Genie and Peaches, but the other people near-by, like Secret Service guys do. Dewey O'Connor wasn't around. Genie said she'd sent him home; he'd helped her enough, she felt.

Truby found us and stood behind the ropes. I went over to her. She began, "Thank God you didn't get yourself—"

"Truby, I need your help today. I need you to hang around Genie's group with me. I'm looking for a guy in the crowd, and if I see him, I want you to help me watch him. I'll give you a sign if I see him."

She gave me a long hard look. "All right. Lillian, why are you talking to me instead of a cop?"

"It's not that serious."

"Oh. Really." She folded her arms. "You went to Chicago?"

"Yeah." I tried to make it sound casual. "Don't worry."

"And?"

"I gotta go. Oh. Have you—?"

"Not." She blew out a breath, shook her head, then laughed softly. "You need my help today. Fine. But I still need *your* help. Okay, so the world's hanging in the balance or something, for this golfer of yours."

"She's Genie Maychild."

"I know. But what do I do if my best prospect for sex only wants to cuddle?"

"Oh, Jesus, Trube, I can hardly think. Hey, cuddling's great. I just spent a nice morning doing it."

"But that's not all you've been doing."

"No."

"I thought if I cuddled her enough, she'd make love with me. You know, eventually." Truby's brow lifted and her expression softened. "So I cuddled her. I mean, like, I cuddled my ass off, I cuddled her until the embroidery wore off her pajamas—"

"*Her pajamas?*"

"I know."

"Oh, hon."

"They have cats on them," she said helplessly.

"Hell," I said. "Well, you've got one more night."

"Tonight's the night, baby."

"I gotta go. See you on the first tee."

"Lillian."

"What?"

"*Please* don't do anything stupid. *Please.*"

If it wasn't for the hell I was trying to deal with, I'd be having a great time. The sun was shining, the mood was festive—everybody's but the golfers', of course; they had their game faces on. The TV towers made everything feel important and exciting. Well, it *was* important and exciting. I kept checking my watch; Genie's tee time was nine-fifty; we had about fifteen minutes.

Looking around, I saw the spectacle in all its glorious bits and pieces. The former champion Judy Rankin, now an announcer for television, walked briskly toward the clubhouse. A course marshal held up his sunburned arms on the first tee, signaling for quiet as Maria DiCenzo, the outstanding amateur from Italy, smacked her drive. A chubby, happy fan with a curly perm stood transfixed at the sight of Coco Nash applying Chap Stick. The fairways looked as though you could sew a prom dress from them.

I realized Coco was teeing off in the group immediately ahead of Genie's. In that case, her security people wouldn't be far off.

On the men's tour, they go off in pairs. The women, in order to accommodate TV schedules built around other events, must play in threesomes, to compress the air time they take up.

Genie's partners in this round were Janet Anson and

Sally Trent; they were a shot behind Genie, who in turn, was a shot out of the three-way lead held by the veterans Lois Underwood, Rosa Garcia, and Valerie Klamm.

Peaches and Genie went over to the on-deck area. He helped her double-check her equipment, as they did before every round. He counted her clubs, touching each one, counting softly, "Twelve, thirteen, fourteen. One dozen balls with your mark." Genie's mark was a cluster of three penciled dots above the logo; Peaches marked a fresh dozen every night for her. "New pack of tees, sunscreen tube half full, Band-Aids—"

"Did you get that glue stuff off, that residue off the grip of my five-iron?"

"Yeah, Mike helped me, over in the equipment trailer—he had this stuff that took it right off. Where's your inhaler? Remember, you threw away the old one?"

"Oh!" She looked up. She slapped her pockets, then panicked. "I didn't have it in the locker room. It must have fallen out of my spare socks in the car. Lillian, remember, I had my clean socks and my inhaler?"

"I'll go find it," I said quickly. I looked around and luckily spotted the red cap of our driver.

"Hey, Stacy! We left something in the car. Is it locked? Give me the keys, okay? I gotta run and get it."

She tossed them, saying, "It's in the members' lot, left side as you come around to it."

But Peaches picked the keys out of the air in front of my cupped hand. "I'll go with you," he said with a challenging grin. "I bet I can get back faster."

"Four minutes!" Genie called apprehensively.

Peaches and I took off, leaping over shrubs and dodging around spectators. I kept up with him; my juices were flowing. It felt good to run and jump, felt good to burn off some energy.

"Which one is it?" he said, when we came to the lot.

"Blue Volvo," I panted, "I think it's that one over there, see, way at the end."

He turned on his real speed and was at the car before I'd even started down that row. I saw him get the passenger's door open, then bend down into the car.

Somehow, right then, I became aware of everything, everything in the world.

The sky was the prettiest, widest sky, and the ancient rocks of the mountains that ringed the valley were seamed with black: riven, mysterious. I was aware of the husky little buzz of a hummingbird overhead and of the quiet hubbub of people going in and out of the swanky clubhouse. I was aware of the bigness of the earth and the smallness of this instant, aware of the desires that had brought me here, aware of the flimsiness of life and of the treachery that lies in wait beneath cleanliness and order and safety.

The explosion was not a large one. It tore the air—yes, with a *bang!*—and it lifted the car slightly before it bounced down on its tires, yes, and it shot smoke and fragments outward. Yes. But there was no fireball, no echoing blast, no destruction save for part of the Volvo, and the windows in the neighboring cars, and Peaches Oshinsky, who, by the time I reached him, had opened his mouth and begun to scream.

25

Not that he could have known what hit him. He had been turned into something raw and terrible. He had been thrown out of the car, and was lying on his back on the asphalt between the Volvo and the next car.

I knew help was already coming; there's always an ambulance on hand at big events like this.

I edged between the cars and crouched over him. *Dear God—oh, my dear God.* The flesh of his face had been blasted apart, outward and away. His eye sockets were pools of blood, filling and running over, and he had no nose. His mouth was open in agony, his jaw badly askew, and the screams he was screaming made me wish we were both dead. His hair was bloody, and his chest was bloody, and he began to thrash.

"Peaches," I said, low, "it's Lillian. Lie still. Lie still."

He screamed once more, then made a gurgling sound; lying on his back as he was, he was beginning to drown in his own blood. "Peaches, I'm turning your head so you won't choke." *Christ, I hope his spine's not broken.*

The air around us was still blue from the blast. Burnt gunpowder smell filled my nose.

"We need help here!" I hollered. I heard footsteps rushing toward us.

Peaches extended his hand toward the sound of my voice, and I took it with both of mine. He gurgled again, loudly. His hand convulsed, and I tried to hold it tighter, but it squirted out of my hands like a fish. I saw then that it was as mangled and bloody as his face. The force of my grip had caused one of his fingers to come all the way off; it dropped from my knee to the ground and then rolled a little way under the Volvo. I reached across his chest and retrieved it. His other hand, I then noticed, was missing completely.

I was gripped by the shoulders and pulled away: the paramedics. I handed the finger to one of them.

Someone took my arm, saying, "Lillian, Lillian," and led me, stumbling, to a patch of grass. A ring of people had formed around the scene.

It was only an hour later that the decision was made to go on with the day's round. The police had gathered; some of them stood looking at the Volvo, waiting for lab people to come along with experts on arson and explosives. Another medical team was summoned to check me over because I had so much blood on me, I suppose. All of it was Peaches's, though.

Barely alive, he was rushed off.

The cops had sealed the gates for the time being and were asking everybody questions, starting with me. It took me a while to pull myself together. Truby was at my side, keeping calm, and so was Genie. I wanted a chance to wash up. There was a little flurry of confusion as more cops arrived; Genie took the opportunity to hustle me into the locker room. We were alone.

It was very clear to me what had just happened. It was as plain as anything.

Peaches hadn't seen the inhaler on the seat, so he'd bent to look on the floor, placing one hand on the mat in the footwell. Beneath the mat was where the explosive had been placed, with some kind of pressure trigger. The violence was intended for Genie, of course. It was intended for her lower body, and it was intended to maim her, not kill her.

It was the work of a clever monster. Clever to think of such a horrible payback and monstrous to set it up, but a complete fuckup to not have anticipated that it could work perfectly but fail to harm Genie.

Deep inside one of the vicious caverns of my imagination I could see Dengel's fantasy: Genie in her wheelchair, pregnant, spinning around the kitchen fixing him a steak dinner, planning on giving him a king's blow job later.

After I'd taken a few deep breaths, I turned from the sink and said, "Genie, I know who it is, and you know who it is."

"I can handle it." Her voice was very quiet, and I pitched mine accordingly, uncomfortable with doing so, but doing it anyway.

"You're insane."

"I don't want you talking to the police."

"Genie!"

Her nostrils flared, and she took me by the shoulders. "Don't. Say. Anything. I'm going to let Meredith handle this."

"Meredith?"

"She's getting in touch with my lawyer. And Donna'll take it from there."

"Yeah, but..." I shrugged off her hands. Something was making my ears ring, as if the explosion were still echoing.

"I'm not going to say a blessed word to them, and I'm telling you you shouldn't either. Look, it's not going to matter what you say, anyway."

"What do you mean?"

"Donna will advise you, too. She'll make sure this gets handled right."

I shook my head and wiped my face with a towel. "I must be—"

"Look, Lillian. You can talk to the police all you want. After the tournament. All right?"

"After the—? Aren't you going to withdraw?"

"I can't do anything for Peaches now, can I? I can't do anything but win this thing and dedicate it to him."

I looked at her, my jaw hanging open.

"I know what you're thinking," she said. "But will you give me that? Can you do that much for me—and Peaches?"

"What about his wife?"

"Meredith'll call her."

I now knew what people meant when, after going through a shock, they said they were numb. I'd always thought it had to do with emotional numbness. But I felt numb physically, specifically. I turned my clean hands over and looked at them. They did not appear to be mine. Someone could have driven a spike through my hand—or my arm, or my head—and I'm sure I wouldn't have felt it. It was the oddest thing.

"Genie, I don't like this," I told her.

"It doesn't matter what you like right now. Do you understand?"

"I guess it doesn't."

"Do this for me. Please, Lillian. Please. You've got to trust me on this."

There was that depth in her eyes, that bottomless look, that made me just want to fall in and not have to think.

"All right."

As we returned to the group of cops, I heard Stacy telling one that a woman had approached her in the parking lot and asked whether she'd be taking Genie home.

"And I told her yes, and I asked why, but she just patted my arm and went away."

"In which direction?" asked the cop.

"The clubhouse. I just figured she was a fan and was maybe going to try to ambush Genie for an autograph."

"What'd she look like?"

"Well, she—I don't know, she was—"

"Was she white or black or—"

"She was white. Um, brown hair, I think."

"What was she wearing?"

"Like a—a, well, she had a funny dress on, like a tennis dress or something. And a sweater, like a lightweight sweater. And a hat. A sunhat."

"How old, how tall?"

"Oh. Maybe forty? Thirty? I don't know...she was kinda husky."

The cop kept asking questions, and two other cops got hold of me.

I told them only what I'd seen, what had happened. I volunteered nothing else. They were just beginning to get themselves organized. Everybody figured it was a crazed fan, you know, a Monica Seles–type thing. The police gave Genie a hard time for not cooperating, but it didn't faze her. She expected them to understand that she needed to keep her mind focused on golf.

The public and the other golfers were informed only that there had been a terrible accident involving a caddie. The tournament people consulted with Genie and the other golfers yet to tee off. Given the choice, most athletes, primed for a contest, want to go forward. And that's what they all said: *Yes. Let's go. Let's do it. I'm ready.*

After the cops wrote down where we were staying and gave Genie some more hostile hassle, she told me they were going ahead with the tournament.

"Uh-huh," I said.

"ABC will tape it."

"Uh—"

"We can finish before dark. Come on."

"We?"

"Lillian, listen. You're going to caddie for me."

"*What?*"

"I need you to caddie for me. You can do it."

"Are you—are you—"

"Lillian!"

I accompanied her back to the first tee. Truby, pale and bewildered, looked on.

"I am up for this round," Genie announced. "This one's

for Peaches. All right, now—" She looked around and called, "Where're some coveralls for my caddie?"

"We're getting them," someone answered.

In a minute I had on the bright white jumpsuit with the tournament logo on it and a blank space on the back where MAYCHILD was on Peaches's jumpsuit. Everything looked and sounded and felt completely wrong. Sounds were muffled. I felt shrunk down, somehow, as if I were hiding inside a bale of cotton.

"I'll tell you everything to do," said Genie, standing her bag and me to the side of the tee box. "I'll choose my own clubs. You know how to wipe dirt off. Get her a towel, please—thanks—and just look after my divots. You know how to handle the pin."

"Peaches has your yardage book in his pocket."

"I got it." She handed me the small spiral notebook, filled with notations for each hole on the distances of every hazard, every safe landing spot, the height of trees. It was still damp from Peaches's sweat.

"You—"

"I got it while they were lifting him. I explained it was mine."

"Oh."

"All right?"

The starter announced her.

I don't remember much more about that day. I did get through it. I toted Genie's monstrous bag down the fairways and up to the tee boxes. I fetched divots and stomped them back in. I avoided the curious eyes of the fans, and I made hushed small talk with the two other caddies in our group. I raked bunkers. I gazed, during pauses, at the grass and the sky and the trees and the mountains. I picked Genie's birdie putts out of many cups. I watched her beautiful liquid swing over and over again, and I heard her tell me she was in the lead by a shot over Coco Nash as we were leaving the club and the sky was going slowly purple.

I must have done all those things, had to have, but I don't really remember.

26

Genie slept deeply that night; I know because I barely did. I got up and talked to Todd in the den, then played Mad Scramble with him and talked to him some more. We dozed together for a while, on the nice carpet in there, then I went back to lie in bed. My shoulders and back ached from carrying Genie's heavy leather golf bag.

By morning I was feeling more solid, more in control of my emotions. The bloody image of Peaches had faded somewhat; we'd gotten word that he'd been given a fifty-fifty chance of making it, which was more than I would have thought. I couldn't let myself think about his suffering, and I couldn't let myself think about what would lie ahead of him if he did make it.

Genie was in the zone. Man, she was hyper-there, hyper-Genie, but wrapped in a cloak of serenity. Dreamily, she told me, "I played out of my mind yesterday." She did her stretches and got herself ready for the day with placid determination, and I puttered around and thought.

By the end of yesterday, the word had gotten around that what had happened to Peaches wasn't an accident. I wondered what Coco Nash was thinking. I wondered what Marian Handistock was thinking, knowing that she had to have seen me caddying for Genie. I wondered what Dengel was thinking—and where he was.

And I tried to put myself into their heads.

I remembered Coco telling me, when the subject of Peaches came up, "I'd love to take him away from her." She wanted the championship trophy as much as anyone. Maybe I'd misjudged her. Maybe I'd been too generous.

The look that Coach Handy had given me on the airplane kept coming back to me.

Dengel wouldn't be stopped by repeated failure, I was certain.

It felt to me that today, Sunday, the final round of the most sought-after trophy in women's professional golf, would be the day when everybody would grab for their own personal brass ring, their own heart's desire. And it was plain to see how high the stakes were—for all of us.

Incredibly, Genie wanted me on her bag again.

"Oh, Genie, no. Didn't you ask the club to find you a caddie, a professional? My God, hon, for a day like today, you need somebody who knows what the hell they're—"

"Lillian, you're it." Not only that, but, "I want Todd along, too."

Since there could be no reasonable response to that, I just looked at her.

"I mean it," she said.

"What?" I countered.

"Yes."

"Todd is not coming onto the golf course."

She took my hand and led me to the living room, where she made herself comfortable on a couch. I perched on its arm.

"It's time for me to explain something to you," she began. "You wanted to know about my new source of... special focus."

"Yes."

"Well, it's you."

I hadn't expected that; I had not. I twisted a strand of my hair into a knot and kept listening.

"I don't know how," she said, "but since I picked you out I've felt...I saw you and I knew. If I talk about it too much, I'll ruin it. When you're around me, I feel like—like there's more of me. I feel unafraid. Golf feels effortless. Life feels effortless. Do you have any idea what that's like to me?"

She took my head in her hands. "What is it like to be inside Lillian Byrd? To *be* Lillian Byrd?"

I said nothing, feeling her hands caressing my head—such fine hands, such good hands.

"You might think it's a very funny joke for me to want Todd along today."

"I don't."

"He's your touchstone. You get energy from him. And you are my touchstone, I get energy—and courage!—from you. The two of you together are magical. I don't know how or why I brought you into my life. I do know that I can't ever let you go."

"Do you want Truby to carry Todd along with us? That's just no good. He'd get too nervous—"

"No, I want you to carry him in my bag."

"Genie."

She waited.

I said, "I'll carry your bag, and you can pay for my hernia operation later, but I'm not carrying Todd, too."

"Yes, I want you to carry him in the bag. In the big pocket on the front."

"It's too hot. He'd overheat."

"Not if you keep a cold bottle of water in there with him. Rabbits like small spaces, don't they?"

I had to admit they seemed to feel safe that way. Do magicians still pull rabbits out of hats? The reason they use rabbits is that they're quiet animals; they keep silent and still in dark, close places.

But I protested, "Carrying Todd around all day—what if the bag falls over with him in it, Genie? He could get hurt! He could die! What if he panics? What if—"

"No!" She snapped her head emphatically. As it did when she whacked a golf ball, her hair flew into a golden halo, then settled into a perfect thatch. "The two of you together are magical. You'll look after him. Nothing will happen to him. I know it. Lillian, I've got to pull out all the stops today. I'm leading by one."

"And Nash is at your heels. Genie, not that I want to— oh, hell! Golf is just a *game*! All right? It's a game! And Peaches—oh, God! This is ridiculous, Genie. And I'm sorry, but there's something unhealthy about it."

It is the measure of me that I allowed Genie to bully me into doing exactly as she wished. I rationalized it to myself: I *could* use Todd's energy, his friendship, at my side today.

This day. He was a patient, good rabbit who'd always been there for me. If he could understand what was going on, he'd want to help me.

A Mission Hills security car picked us up and took us to the course. Genie's bag was stored in the club's bag room. Carrying Todd in a canvas tote, I used the caddie credential I'd been given the day before to claim the golf bag.

I carried it into a corner and slipped an icy bottle of water into the bottom pocket, then Todd, murmuring to him over and over what a blessed bunny he was, and what a goddamn idiot I was. I zipped the pocket almost shut.

All I could think of was Genie, my true love. After dinner last night and before she had fallen asleep, she'd taken me totally by surprise with a tempest of lovemaking. Yes. If I'd been paying attention, I would've noticed her desire building, her passion rising up out of the horror of the day.

It's true: In the face of death, some people want to make love. A way of forcing back the terror, I guess it is, a way of showing grief who's boss.

Until she touched me, I would've doubted I could even become aroused that night. But boy, she took me there. Never had I experienced such excitement, never such sustained pleasure, never such thorough release. She allowed me to reciprocate, then she took me there again, then we slept like logs.

Now she was in the clubhouse having a conference with Meredith who, I guessed, was keeping the media at bay. They were there, though. They were massing. I'd brushed past a few reporters already; they wanted to talk to me, find out who I was, find out what I knew about what happened yesterday.

I ducked around the back of the building and threaded through the throng near the members' pro shop. Todd added about six pounds to the bag. "It's gonna be a long day," I muttered. I wanted to find a piece of shade until I needed to meet Genie at the practice range.

"Hey," came a tight voice at my shoulder.

I glanced over and kept walking. "Finally," I said.

Coach Marian Handistock followed me to a quiet spot at the north side of the building. Shade from an overhang made it slightly less blistering there than in the direct sun. I set Genie's bag upright against the wall, and coach Handy and I talked across it. Her face sagged in the heat, but her body was tense. I saw the muscles in her forearms twitch.

She said, "I don't like you."

I folded my arms.

"I don't want you fucking around with her."

I said, "Is that what you think's going on?"

"You want something from her."

I didn't deny it.

"What's your real name, anyway?"

I showed her my credential. She murmured, "Lillian Byrd," as if she'd been expecting the name to tell her something.

I said, "Have you asked Genie about me?"

"No. She doesn't know I'm here."

"Why not?"

She thrust her aggressive chin at me. "I pegged you for a rat the first minute I saw you. She doesn't need you. The last thing she needs is you."

"Why are you wasting your time on me? How come you're not—"

"Because you're just as dangerous to her, and she doesn't know it." Searchingly, she asked, "Do you...care for her?"

"What do you think?"

"I think you pretend to, but all you really want is to drain her dry. You—you—all you want is to suck the life out of her. Look at you." She bared her teeth contemptuously. "You're the kind of person who doesn't bother to make your own way in the world. You just want to ride somebody else's coattails. A parasite. If you care anything for her, if you really care, you'll leave right now. Go back to wherever. Find somebody else to feed on."

It was with tremendous effort that I refrained from punching her as hard as I could. She could've taken me anyway, I'm afraid.

Instead, I chose to obtain information.

Cracking my knuckles, I said, "I know what you did after we talked in your kitchen."

Her breath caught in her throat. I heard it, like a match being struck. She couldn't speak. I saw her mind working, her eyes staring straight out at me, desperate.

I waited.

"It had to be done," she finally said.

Boy, did I nail it.

"Genie called on you," I said, "and you took care of it. And now she's safe."

"Not yet."

Coach Handy began to fondle the black plush clubhead covers sticking up from Genie's bag. She stroked them as if they were alive.

"Dengel doesn't know what you went out and dug up, does he?"

She glared at me. "Get away from Genie."

"Did you know before—"

"No. I didn't."

"And it doesn't matter to you that—"

Coach Handy stepped around the golf bag, shoved me against the wall with her own solid belly, and twisted a fistful of my white coveralls.

"You listen," she hissed into my face, "you *nobody,* you, you *nothing.* I created Genie Maychild. She is mine, more than anything in the world. I dreamed her. I dreamed her up, don't you see? No one's going to hurt her. Not you. Not anybody. I gave her the clothes off my back. I gave her—everything."

"You loved her."

"Yes, I loved her," she breathed, still clutching the front of my coveralls, her face inches from mine. Her eyes were hot and hard. "I loved that girl."

Deliberately, I said, "But she didn't love you."

"She...she..."

"She never loved you."

That was cruel, but I tell you, I was feeling pretty goddamn ornery right then.

If there had been a button labeled PUSH TO VAPORIZE LILLIAN BYRD, she would have jumped on it with both feet.

Instead she jerked me sideways, then rammed me against the wall. My head bounced off the masonry.

As she turned away from me, all she said was, "I've waited for her all my life."

I've said it was a hot day; the thermometer was reading, I believe, ninety-four. But watching Marian Handistock walk away, I felt a sudden cold wind down my neck.

27

I lugged Genie's bag over to the practice tee. She wasn't
in sight yet; I stood the bag at the right-hand end of the
hitting area, her favorite spot.

"Need anything?" asked the range boss.

"Yeah, a couple of towels, please."

Even though Genie's clubs looked perfectly clean, I
dampened a towel and went over them, rubbing the faces
and wiping the grips. The practice tee wasn't busy, since
most of the golfers were on the course already.

I thought about those golfers, the ones who were out of
contention for the win. Their tee times were early and,
ignored by the TV cameras, they were out there grinding
out a tenth-place, or a thirty-something place, or a last-
place finish, working on their stats, hoping for a decent

check, glad they at least made the Friday cut. If you're a journey-woman golfer, one who's just good enough to stay on the tour, well, you've got to deal with dentist bills and oil changes and termites like everybody else, and you're not thinking all the time about glory: You need the dough.

The right-hand end of the range was Genie's favorite because, if you swing right-handed, you don't see the other golfers: Your back is to them, so there's a feeling of privacy there. Nobody else's swing gets flashed onto your brain cells while you're working hard on yours.

I fiddled around. I checked on Todd, I kept an eye out for Truby, and for Dengel.

An extremely natty guy, one of those combed-back Aqua Velva types, came up to me, wanting to talk. He had on a golf shirt with the embroidered logo of one of the big equipment manufacturers over the heart, khaki shorts with a razor crease, and anklets. Men in anklets make me nervous, no matter how good their legs look. But this guy had a very reassuring smile.

"Jeff Evans," he introduced himself, "Ace-Tek."

"Lillian Byrd. How do you do?"

"Fantastic! I haven't seen you around before. Before yesterday, anyway."

"No, I'm new."

"Well, I wanted to make a point of wishing you well in the final round!" Jeff tilted his head and squinted at me. "Looks like you got some sun!"

In fact, I'd gotten slightly fried yesterday afternoon, having neglected to replenish my sunscreen after getting on the course with Genie. I only had one summer hat, my Vietnam surplus hat, but I hadn't thought to pack it. My cheeks and nose were pretty pink.

"Well, I have a little present for you!" said Jeff, reaching into his shoulder bag.

I stiffened, waiting for an assassin's bullet, but he pulled out a brand-new sun visor and held it out to me. It was a beauty, high quality and bright white, nice terry-cloth sweatband. The main feature, of course, was the logo of Ace-Tek with its famous pouncing rooster. They made clubs for half the men's pro tour, I guessed, and maybe a third of the women's. Big company. Genie played Ace-Tek. I'd always considered their logo ridiculous, this rooster jumping on a golf ball. You had to figure they'd tested it thoroughly on focus groups, though.

"Uh, no, thank you," I said. "I'll remember my sunscreen today. Thanks just the same."

"Would you prefer a cap? I've got one in here…"

"Really, thank you, but I'll be fine. Hats give me a headache sometimes."

He laughed heartily, then leaned closer. "See, Lillian, I'd like to make you an offer. Doing my job here. How does five hundred dollars sound?"

"If it's in nickels, it sounds like jingle, jingle, jingle."

His laugh rang sudden and free. "Oh, I like you!" he cried. "Whew! Lillian, here's the deal: You wear our visor during today's round, and we give you five hundred bucks. Simple as that."

"Because people'll see the logo on TV?"

"Yep!"

"Well…I still have to say no, thank you."

He clutched his chest. "Lillian! You make my work tough! What'll it take here?"

I was thinking about a quick five hundred. I'd spent a bundle, coming out to see Truby, then the Chicago trip. I hadn't had time to wonder how I was going to pay down my credit card bill.

Jeff Evans said, "*One thousand dollars,* Lillian! Going once, going—"

"All right," I said. "When do I get the money?"

He whipped out a clipboard and a pen. "Sign right here. This is a one-page contract: very simple, dated today, dealing only with today." He filled in "$1,000" next to where AMOUNT was printed.

I read it in half a minute—it looked all right—and I signed it.

"I'll catch up with you after the round, and I'll have the check with me. How does that sound?" Jeff clapped the visor on my head.

"Wow. Okay." I took it off to adjust the band, and he waited until I put it back on.

"Wear it nice and straight," he said. He looked me over. "Too bad we can't do anything about those shoes."

I looked down at my feet. My black Chuck Taylor sneakers were homely, but damn it to hell, why should anybody care?

"I don't give a shit," I said.

"Well, good luck!"

Genie didn't notice my new visor, nor anything else, save the task ahead of her. She warmed up in her tunnel of concentration, murmuring to herself once in a while. She looked solid, solid as anything. Her swing repeated perfectly and effortlessly, it appeared to me. After practicing her middle and long irons and her woods, she chipped a few balls, pitched a few, and then we moved over to the putting green. She didn't ask about Todd.

Truby came by, not much less worried and bewildered than she'd been after the explosion yesterday. I went over to her.

"I can't believe any of this," she said. "I can't believe you haven't gotten away from this. I don't even know what the fuck—God! You're not telling me what the fuck is going on. I have no idea, and here you are, still involved in this bizarre—"

"Truby, I'm not arguing that this isn't bizarre. Okay? I need you to be around today, just like yesterday. Please be calm, okay? Life is weird sometimes. We can deal with it."

We stood for a minute, watching Genie practicing her putting stroke with no ball, just making the pendulum swing with the club and her arms.

Truby looked at me again. "Where did you get that?"

"Believe it or not, I'm getting paid to wear it."

"A pasta strainer would be more attractive."

"I'm not arguing with that either."

We watched Genie some more, then Truby hooked her thumbs in her waistband and said, "Not that it's the slightest bit important right now, but—"

"You got laid."

"Yes."

"And?"

"I have to talk to you. Will you be able to spend any time at all with me after this is over?"

"Yes. Yes, hon, I will. I've got a lot to sort out."

"Yeah, so have I."

As I followed Genie over to the first tee, I caught sight of Meredith listening intently to a woman wearing a press pass, who was talking low into her ear. She dropped her head, then turned away looking at nothing. I veered over to her.

"Meredith."

She looked at me. "Peaches died an hour ago."

I took a deep breath and, looking skyward, sent up an arrow of prayer.

Meredith said, "Don't tell Genie."

"No."

"I'll talk to her after. I'm sorry I told you. Now—"

"It's all right."

Oh, God, I thought. *Oh, Peaches.*

The crowd was the biggest of the week. Ten thousand? Twenty thousand? Fans were trooping along next to their favorites, rustling their programs, lining up to buy pop and beer and hot dogs, ducking in and out of the porta-pots, adjusting their belt packs, murmuring admiration for the strength and composure of the best players in women's golf.

Gay women were enjoying themselves everywhere. All week I'd noticed this twinning thing going on. For example, one couple who walked by was wearing matching anodized rainbow necklaces, Ray-Ban sunglasses, khaki shorts, and Adidas running shoes. I saw lots of matching jewelry, earrings and such. Rings, of course. It made me happy to see matching rings. However, I thought the rest of the twinning signified lack of imagination.

Marshals and monitors kept everybody neatly behind the ropes; lots of police officers strolled and stood watching, their gold badges winking in the sun.

And at number one, Coco Nash was on the tee, Genie Maychild was on the tee, Lona Chatwin was on the tee, and I was there with the two other caddies, and the starter was peering into the distance watching the last approach shot of the group ahead, and we all had one more minute to gather ourselves.

28

If you've been around the game of golf at all, you've met that most ubiquitous of bores, the shot-by-shot raconteur. You know, the one who comes into the snack bar, or the kitchen at home, smelling agreeably enough of fresh air and crushed grass, but then he holds you at vocal gunpoint for forty-five minutes.

If it's a classic, the story starts well in the past: "Well, you know, Claude's wife had that operation last week, so he called me up and he's, like, 'There's no way I can get out on Sunday,' so I'm, like, 'Great.' So I had to sit on my neck to get somebody, because if you don't have a foursome they always stick somebody in there with you, and it's always some guy nobody else wants to play with for whatever reason, and finally I thought of Larry—remember Larry? He's

Ignacio's accountant, and he can hit the ball but he's wild—
remember at that charity thing for the Prostate Society?
When he got lost in that marsh looking for his ball, remember I told you about that and what his pants looked like for
the rest of the day, but he's a good guy, so I called him up."

If you're lucky, you've got something monotonous that
needs doing while you're listening to the story, like shelling
peas for a big church supper, or sanding down a pair of
bookcases.

"So I was like, 'Okay, I'm using a new ball over this
water hazard if it kills me,' and wouldn't you know it—
there's this rock about two feet from shore…so my second
shot I'm, like, trying to remember how to aim for a down-
hill-sidehill lie, and I'm standing there, and finally I just go,
'Man, hit the goddamn thing,' and I swear I just looked at
that pin and then I swung, and it was, like, perfect. It hit the
fringe, and there was a little upslope, so that took something off it, but if that upslope hadn't been there, I woulda
been right at the pin…"

Well. I am not one of those bores—no, not even when
the round concerns the play of champions. I will tell you
what happened, and I will recount certain shots, but
beyond that you'll want the videotape.

Here is what happened Sunday.

Genie got a solid start, smacking a nice drive on the first,
making a good, wide, smooth swing that gave me every
confidence in her that day. It was clear to me that she would
allow herself to play up to her potential, ready to reach, but
not beyond herself.

When both Coco's and Lona's tee shots found trouble, I
relaxed a fraction and took stock of things.

Coco and I had made eye contact on the tee but hadn't

had a chance to speak. Her eyes were serious, but she took me in with a shade of amusement. Was it my visor? It was as if she were trying to reassure me. *Yes, this is really only a game, Lillian, and it is up to you and me not to forget it.*

But as we all headed down the fairway, she gave me a sidelong look and a shrug that said, *And trouble could come to us today.*

I hoped it would be nice for Genie to have Lona Chatwin in the final group; they were friends but not rivals. You'd often see Lona's name in the top twenty or twenty-five, once in a while in the top ten. She'd won a few times on tour, no majors. After a lackluster Thursday, she'd put together a couple of terrific rounds on Friday and Saturday, and there she was, in contention.

She and Coco began the day two under, and Genie was a stroke ahead at three under. Any one of that trio had the game to win it. And as our round got underway, we saw on the leaderboards that the others had fallen back, had fallen prey to some of the devilish hazards on the Dinah Shore course, and most likely to some of the equally devilish hazards within themselves.

Except for shaking hands with Coco on the first tee and muttering "Good luck," Genie ignored her. She ignored Lona, too. I sensed this bothered Lona, who was used to being friendly during a round, you know. She liked to chat with her playing partners and the gallery. I believe it was her way of dissipating the tension.

Coco and Lona saved par on the first, despite their poor drives. Genie nearly made birdie with a beautifully judged twenty-footer that missed by an inch.

I told myself I should feel quite safe today: Two police officers were walking along with us behind the ropes, and I knew that Coco Nash's security detail had to be around close. And there was Truby faithfully tagging along, albeit looking as if she needed a drink. Todd was at my side. I looked overhead: There was the Met Life blimp, Snoopy at the controls, floating benevolently over all. Yes, I should be feeling quite safe indeed.

But I wasn't.

The job of caddie is one you have to get your head into; inattention can cost your golfer a stroke or worse, say, if you don't spot her drive carefully and it gets lost in the macaroni back from the fairway. Or if you miscalculate yardage or if you accidentally switch balls on her. Lucky for me, Genie wasn't counting on me to help her with club selection or reading greens. She knew those greens pretty well.

And she was in such a zone that I guessed she could use a shovel to play every shot and still dominate the course this day.

I was careful and worked hard to anticipate what she'd want, but in moments when I could, I scanned the crowd, which was thick around our group. I decided that if anything happened, I'd jump on top of Genie, shielding her with my body until the cops could get control of the situation.

Genie played the first six holes steadily—pure USGA golf: hitting all the fairways and greens in regulation, giving herself chances for birdies. She even had a putt for eagle on the second hole; it was a twelve-footer that looked good all the way, but it rimmed the cup and she tapped in for her birdie.

After easily navigating the treacherous sixth hole with its serpentine water hazard, she got into trouble on the seventh, the short par-four. Maybe she let down a little bit, or maybe something spooked her from inside, but whatever it was she executed the most hideous hook I'd ever seen a professional hit. The ball somehow tore through a line of trees, dribbled through the rough, and out of bounds. We weren't sure it really was out, because the course marshal assigned to that spot was hurrying back from the porta-pot, so we had to hike down to see for ourselves.

It was close, but it was out, so we trudged back to the tee for Genie to take her stroke-and-distance penalty. As we began the trip back to the tee I caught a glimpse of coach Handy strolling through the bunches of fans on the opposite side of the fairway, walking right in tandem with us, but not looking over at us.

Genie hit another drive, this one perfect and long. After sticking her pitch right next to the pin, she came out of it with only a bogey.

Two birdies had put her at five under, and the bogey brought her back to four under, but Coco and Lona had remained at two under, playing the first seven holes in even par.

I took advantage of a brief wait on the par-three eighth to check discreetly on Todd and, for the second time, exchange the water bottle with a new cold one. He appeared to be fine, sitting quietly in his mobile home, not thumping, not scrabbling. Just calm old Todd. I put my hand inside and stroked him and murmured to him.

When I looked up I saw Coco holding her finish after hitting a six-iron that arced gorgeously against the sky, bounced in front of the pin twice, and rolled in for an ace. The crowd erupted. Holy everloving shit! A hole-in-one in the final round of a major championship! Incredible, absolutely incredible. All of us, including Genie, slapped hands with Coco. What a moment. It took the crowd five minutes to begin to calm down. Now Coco was tied with Genie.

Right then, the tournament became the head-to-head everybody had been hoping for. Lona's putter started to misfire, and she would three-putt that green and four-putt the next.

As we made the turn into the back nine, Genie and Coco were still tied at four under, the TV cameras were all over us, the crowd was alternating between hushed reverence and wild cheering, the wind was starting to kick up, and I realized that my period was starting. You know that feeling. You're thinking, *Hmm, is that a gas pain? Did I eat something funny?* Then you remember, *Oh, shit, it's time for cramps, and here they come.* Can you blame me for having forgotten my cycle?

I don't usually get bad cramps, I just bleed like an elephant. Rooting through Genie's bag on the eleventh tee, I came up with a tampon and raced into a porta-pot to install it—just in time. It was only a regular, though, and I knew it wouldn't hold me more than an hour, what with the strain of carrying Genie's bag. I thought about my snow-white caddie jumpsuit, and I thought about color TV.

As we marched down the fairway I muttered to Genie, "Do you usually keep more tampons in here?"

"Oh!" she said. "Uh, I don't know." She was in a tunnel.

At the twelfth tee, I hustled over to the ropes, where the crowd pressed up to see their heroines take their mightiest swings.

I didn't see Truby right then, though I knew she was sticking close. Cupping a hand to my mouth, I leaned toward a concentration of women, all but one of whom leaned eagerly in toward me, and softly said, "Anybody have a tampon? Super?"

The first woman I happened to make eye contact with drew away instead of forward; she sort of recoiled, in fact. She was wearing sunglasses, but I saw her eyes through them. She flipped her gaze away instantly, as I found a nosegay of tampons thrust eagerly my way. I plucked three supers from the bunch, giving solemn, quick thanks. Everyone understood my gratitude; you could see it in their faces.

The woman who'd looked away melted into the crowd, and I lost sight of her. Something about her was off. She'd appeared surprised when I asked for a tampon, or frightened, or something. I replayed the tape of her in my mind's eye. Plastic sunglasses, a bad hairdo—a mousy tangle that hung down beneath a wide-brimmed hat: sort of a low-budget Garbo. I didn't know.

29

I managed to change my tampon and wash my hands in a john before Genie teed off. The tension of the whole damned day was getting to me, and I wasn't even playing. At one point I snatched a quick word with Truby, described Garbo to her, and went back to hoping for the best.

As Genie and Coco matched each other stroke for stroke through the fifteenth hole, now battling the wind as well as each other, the crowds grew more silent. Lona fell back to three over, and began to lose her composure over her long shots, spraying them all over the place. She had fallen prey to the pressure of being in contention on Sunday: *My first major title, maybe. Oh, God, I could win it. Please don't let me blow it.*

I kept shifting my awareness between my caddie duties and watching the crowd.

The sixteenth hole is a bitch. A long par-four with a sharp right-hand dogleg, it rewards a perfect drive, but if you give it anything less, you're in big trouble: trees, fairway bunkers, screwy slopes. Most players hit a three-metal here, leaving the driver in the bag, so as to easier land the ball in the narrow, safe throat of the fairway.

Here Genie got in trouble again, pushing her drive badly right, giving herself an impossible shot to the green. When we got to the ball, we saw that the gigantic eucalyptus tree in the right rough was exactly on the line between her ball and the pin.

That was one big honking tree. You know eucalyptus? They grow real, real tall and dense, like enormous drum major hats.

"Ah, shit," I muttered involuntarily when I saw the situation.

Genie walked up. "I either need to start it left and bend it around that tree or…" She gnawed her lip.

"Think you could just hit it straight and land it on the right edge?"

Squinting, my boss said, "The angle's not that good. I'd be in the bunker or worse. Remember how wide that bunker is?" She laughed softly. "Dewey said I don't need to work the ball. Well, I always knew he was full of it. I've got to work it now, and I hope he's watching on TV."

Coco's drive had landed exactly where she wanted, in the left-center of the narrow fairway throat. She'd allowed herself a half-smile as everybody watched it float down and roll into perfect position for a safe approach to the green. I thought about that sprinkler head I'd watched her look for that night, and I'm pretty sure she winked at me as she pocketed her tee.

I stood watching Genie make the mental calculations and go through the physics—or metaphysics, more accurately—of the shot she wanted to make. I could see her seeing it in her mind's eye, feeling the swing in her little inner Genie. The marshals had pushed the fans back, and stood holding the ropes against a row of stomachs.

I saw Garbo again, standing with her arms folded, watching Genie from thirty yards up. I looked at her hard, but it was like looking at a discarded mannequin. I noticed she was wearing a white dress, grayed with age, in a dated a-line shape.

Perhaps it's needless to say, but Genie hit the shot of the tournament right then. She tucked her head down and swung, and the ball took off like a quail, on a rising angle, skimmed past the eucalyptus, and, with the spin she'd put on it, curved gracefully to the right, coming to rest at the front edge of the green.

She'd barely talked to me since the first tee, but several times she'd made a point of touching me more than necessary whenever I handed her a ball or a drink of water. Her hand would linger at mine, her fingers on my skin, or she would use two hands, cupping my hand briefly in hers. Then she'd take a nice relaxed breath.

I knew when she hit that shot there would be no stopping her today at all. This day would be hers. She parred sixteen, and Coco did, too.

I studied Coco for any cracks. There were none: no perspiration on the upper lip, no fiddling with club shafts, no telltale dive into a porta-pot to cope with nervous bowels.

Still, one of them had to beat the other. One of them had to make a birdie or a bogie. Something had to happen.

And it did on the seventeenth, the pretty par-three,

where Coco's supporters chanted for her to make another hole-in-one. She nearly did, too: Her shot landed softly a foot from the cup and rolled five feet past. She made the birdie.

Genie's ball went into the deep left-side bunker, from which she blasted a beautiful recovery, but it needed to go in, and it didn't. She made par, and now, at the eighteenth, Coco Nash was in front by a shot.

Genie was totally serene. The wind, which now verged on a gale, ruffled her hair, but that was the only part of her that was ruffled, I'm quite sure.

She had to gain a stroke on her opponent on this final hole to tie and send them both into a playoff, and she needed to gain two to win it outright. If she eagled and Coco made par, she would win.

If you're a fan, you know the eighteenth is a very tough hole to gain a stroke on, let alone two. It's the signature hole of the Dinah Shore course, the killer par-five, long and hazardous, with an island green. To make it onto the green in two shots is very rewarding—and very rare; only the longest hitters can do it. Most golfers play it safe, laying up their second shot to set up an easy wedge over the water to the pin. If you make your putt, you've got your birdie. But if you go for the green in two and find the water, you're lucky to make par; bogies are the usual result of such a pride-fueled fiasco.

I'd loved that eighteenth hole for years, watching on television. Damn, that second shot to the dance floor is the most daring shot in women's golf, and it comes on the last hole of the biggest major. Oh, yeah.

And now, being here, watching the contest I was watching, I thought I'd wet my pants.

Genie, however, stood looking down that fairway as if she were about to drive a motor scooter to the green. She was tranquil, she was confident, she knew she could do it, had done it before, would do it ten times in a row if she had to.

Coco had the honors, by dint of her birdie on seventeen. She stepped up and sent off a rocket straight and true, the ball landing in one more perfect spot, exactly at the bend in the dogleg, sitting on the close-cropped fairway grass that felt like velvet beneath our feet.

Genie went next, with as smooth a swing as any she'd made in her life. She hit it so hard, it ran through the fairway, past the bunkers on the right, and rolled to a stop in the first cut of rough.

I made a sound, but Genie took my arm and murmured, "If it's sitting up, it'll be easier to hit it off there than the fairway."

I understood: A close lie, even on the fairway, gives you little margin for error, as you attempt to sweep your ball away with a fast-moving fairway metal. But a ball sitting up nicely in a fluffy bit of grass is almost like hitting from a tee: A professional can catch the ball very slightly on an upswing, thus adding to the height of the shot and to the chances of the ball holding the green when it comes down again.

Lona, whom everyone had by now forgotten about, bunted a safe short drive down the fairway.

This tournament happened to be the swan song for the Texas legend Deborah Wolsey, who had announced that she would retire at the end of this season. Old as she was, she'd played an outstanding tournament, making it onto the leaderboard after the second round, and into the next-to-last group today.

There'd been a tremendous ovation when Deborah's group approached the eighteenth green, quite a deservedly long one, and that caused a delay in play as she acknowledged the crowd's tribute. The fans really loved that woman, especially the old-timers who easily remembered her playing in the very first Dinah and all of them since then. Finally, she had to ask the crowd in the big grandstand to hush down so that her group could putt out.

Our group strung itself across the fairway at Lona's ball, waiting.

And as we stood there, I felt a new dread enter my heart, such as I'd never known. For I saw plainly that if there was to be a cataclysm, this was the moment for it.

It was a dazzling moment. The contest was reaching its climax, and all the witnesses were ready to see something they'd never forget. There was the whole tableau of competition, the whole dream; everybody's brass ring lying out there in the afternoon desert sun, lying there for the taking beneath the eyes of God and ABC Sports.

30

I was scanning the crowd ahead and to the right when I saw my low-budget Garbo duck beneath the rope and charge onto the course toward us. My blood pressure doubled. I looked for a weapon in her hands but saw none, at first.

It took her maybe four seconds to cover the ground to where Genie and I were standing. Genie was gazing at the ground, gathering all her fibers for the perfect shot to the green she needed to make.

Hoisting Genie's bag to chest level, like a tackling dummy, I stepped into the woman's path just as she reached us. Her hand was held high, ready to strike with something. What was it—a rock, a grenade? A bottle? She was clutching something. She ran into me as if I weren't there, but I was braced, the bag with its fourteen clubs and unusual payload giving me extra weight. She more or less bounced off. The pocket Todd was in was on my side of the bag, and I was sure he hadn't gotten crunched.

By this time Genie had leaped away, behind me, putting maybe three yards between us, moving more on instinct than from a clear sense of what was going on.

There was a confused gasp from the nearby portion of the gallery.

The two police officers assigned to us had been talking together, some distance back in the fairway, but now noticed the trouble and began to react.

Coco Nash had been leaning on her two-iron, near her ball and caddie on the other side of the fairway. Instantly, she started toward Garbo, raising her club.

The woman threw herself against me again, but I managed to stand my ground. She bobbed one way, then another, trying to get a clear path to Genie. She grabbed one of the bag's straps and, with frightening strength, snatched it away from me one-handed and flung it to the ground. She was still holding her weapon, and I saw, to my total bafflement, that it was a lightbulb. Genie had stepped closer, staring at this woman, as if trying to make sense of what was happening. Now very close to Genie, the woman cocked her arm with the lightbulb, preparing to smash it into Genie's face. All this took only instants, but to me it happened in slow motion.

Rage flared inside me against this bizarre assailant, and I forgot my plan of jumping on Genie. I lunged for the lightbulb, got hold of her wrist, and hung on, trying to twist it. We both crashed to the ground. I saw liquid sloshing in the bulb—its screw end was covered with duct tape—and realized then what kind of damage she intended to do. She grabbed my throat with her free hand and squeezed hard.

Coco Nash, using all her strength and skill, slammed the forged blade of her two-iron squarely into Garbo's hand holding the lightbulb. She missed my arm by a millimeter.

I heard the crunch of bone, and Garbo let out a roar, a full-chested baritone bellow right in my face, and I saw that this was no lady—it was Dom Dengel in a disguise that was as pathetic as it had been effective. I was close enough now to see his stubble; his sunglasses and hat had fallen off, and the wig was slipping to one side. Along with the bones in his hand, the lightbulb shattered, too, and the shards flew as the liquid within splashed on the two of us.

Dengel screamed then, as he felt the searing pain of the acid on his face. Whatever kind it was, it was strong. I could smell it and see it: The sour, harsh liquid was turning his face red in blotches already. He let go of my neck, and I rolled off him to the grass. The cops had seen the acid flying, realized what it was, and were reluctant to grab hold of him with their bare hands. They stood uncertainly over him as, his hands to his face, he screamed. One cop fumbled for some latex gloves from his equipment belt.

I got to my feet, not feeling anything, and saw Genie flanked protectively by a pair of tough-looking women with mullet haircuts who had followed our group. They were Coco Nash's muscle, I realized. They'd hustled Genie about fifty yards back up the fairway, and were watching to see what would happen next. A third mullet had materialized next to Coco and had her in a bodyguard hold, her arm linked through Coco's, her hands gripping for good measure.

Dengel screamed through his pain, "Yeah, arrest me!"

He struggled to his knees as the cops fumbled with their equipment saying, "Shit! Shit!"

The wig fell off and there he was, wearing some kind of waitress dress, looking like Sluggo in drag.

The cops got one cuff on him as he squinted and struggled and sobbed. The red marks covered most of his face and one eye. Something was happening to his flesh: Was it starting to melt?

Everyone was staring, rooted, dumbfounded, as Dengel pointed up the fairway to Genie with his yet-free hand and yelled, "She's the killer! Genie fucking Maychild is the killer! Right there, right there! Now you have to deal with me, Genie!"

He reached into the pocket of his dress and pulled out a little white card. "Here's his fingerprints! See? See?" He kept struggling, and I saw more cops coming running. "His name was Nick!" Dengel screamed. They finally got both cuffs on him. The white card fluttered to the ground. The cops were now holding him gingerly, one on each arm, right next to Genie's bag, when the bag lurched and Todd came shooting out like a champagne cork. He leaped straight into the air, right in the cops' and Dengel's faces, and hit the ground running as fast as his bunny legs would go. I perceived that, fed up with all this nonsense, he'd gnawed his way out.

The cops were so startled they lost hold of Dengel, who seized the advantage and bolted toward Genie. I knew Coco's thugs wouldn't let him reach her. And the cops, now half a dozen strong, were thundering after him, and I began to think everything would be all right, after a fashion, when Coach Marian Handistock emerged from a spot directly behind Genie and did what I should have known she would do.

Beating the police to Dengel, she set herself and, with both hands, rammed the blade of a commando-style knife straight into his chest. She sawed it back and forth for good measure, his blood surging onto her arms.

Yes, I should have known that if Dengel tried anything with Genie, Handy would kill him, and somehow I even should have known she'd find the right knife to do it with.

A collective scream rose from every throat, and the shadow of the blimp passed over.

Dengel was dead before the end of the first commercial ABC hastily cut to.

Coach Handy turned and gave Genie one long clear look, then stepped bloody and empty-handed into the arms of the police.

Todd had disappeared up the fairway, seeking a safe place, which, he'd concluded, wasn't anywhere near me.

I picked up the white card Dengel had dropped. On it were two rows of five tiny black smudges. That was all. A cop plucked the card from my hand.

Truby appeared at my side shouting, "Water! Pour water on her! Water, everybody, come on!"

I reached up to my face, suddenly feeling a hot spot on my jaw and another on my forearm.

"Don't touch it! Lillian, sit down on the ground. Here, here, gimme!"

Surrounded now by a small crowd, I felt my head and arm being showered with cooling water. I coughed for air. The water ran off pink, and Truby said, "You've been cut, too. Son of a bitch! More water!"

"I'm a medic," said a voice at my arm. "She'll be all right."

If this was just a made-up story, you would surely not believe that the tournament eventually resumed that very day, and that the sporting finale everybody wanted to see was, in fact, given them. But maybe you watched on television, so you know, or maybe you saw it with your own eyes from any of the thousands of vantage points overlooking the eighteenth hole that afternoon.

31

A cool hand patted my shoulder and a cheerful voice said, "Honey, you're in the best place in the world to get your face fixed. After all, this is Palm Springs. People come from all over the world."

It was true.

I could see only white, and smell only cleanliness, beneath the drape the emergency room nurse had placed over my eyes, in preparation for the plastic surgeon.

"Oh, he's the best," said the nurse. "Believe me, this is nothing. Now let's see that arm again. There."

An hour later I had five stitches in one cheek, five more near my ear, and a small patch of raw skin on my jaw. My whole face felt numb.

"Don't get up yet," the doctor said. "The acid didn't

go through all your skin layers. Your friend here acted fast and did the right thing. How did you know to flush the area with water?"

"I had a boyfriend who had a car battery explode one time," said Truby, who was sitting next to me on a straight chair.

"Blot your stitches with a little hydrogen peroxide once a day," said the doctor. "See a doctor when you get home. Once the cuts heal, the scars shouldn't be noticeable at all. I'm putting some gauze on your arm to protect it, but you can take it off tomorrow. I think I got all the glass out, but don't be surprised if a sliver works its way out in a month or two. Better stay lying down for a few more minutes. I'll be back."

"I have to go find Todd," I said to Truby.

"I'll find Todd, Starmate. Relax."

"No! He might not come out for you. I have to go and call him. He can't be far from that spot. He knows my voice, I'm sure he's waiting for me." I sat up. "I'm really fine. See?"

"Oh, Lillian."

"We're going. Let's go. Think they take credit cards here?"

"I've paid for it."

When we walked onto the course at Mission Hills, the shadows were long and deep, and tournament week was over.

The grandstands were deserted, the trash baskets were full, the pins had been gathered, and the course was going to rest overnight before the food stands and toilets and souvenir tents were taken away.

It was striking how still the place was, how fatigued the

course appeared. The very air felt spent, burned up. I could almost smell the brimstone. The blistering heat of the day was dissipating into the evening sky.

It was peaceful.

One of the tournament directors sat perched on the railing of the footbridge to the eighteenth green, drinking a glass of wine. She looked at me with a dazed expression.

"I'm here to find my rabbit," I said.

"Whatever," she said.

"Who won?"

She told me, and I thanked her.

There was no trace of the disaster on the fairway. The acid had soaked right down; Dengel's blood had soaked right down.

Truby followed me quietly as I searched for Todd.

I went in the direction he'd gone, softly calling his name. I skirted clumps of greenery and little rocky places. He was hiding, resting, maybe eating. I was worried that he'd eat something bad for him. I was disgusted with myself to the bone for having put him through such trauma—and such risk.

I knew I'd find him, though. I saw tracks going straight through one of the bunkers on seventeen, and I followed their trajectory to some shrubs near a house off the fairway.

"Todd."

He bumped out to meet me, and I sat down on the ground and petted him and held him. He looked fine.

"Man, I'm an idiot," I murmured.

"You're always an idiot when you're in love," Truby reminded me. "I've told you and told you. Wait here."

It was the most beautiful evening the desert could possibly offer. Oh, it was a soft, relaxed evening. The air was like a warm bath, and the breeze was shifting and dying as night came on.

Truby returned, walking over the cropped championship grass, carrying two glasses of wine, a bag of peanuts, and a carrot stick.

"I don't know if it's any good, but it's red," she said, hunkering in the soft grass. We were in a little hollow, the three of us, comfortable together, looking out at the blackening palm trees and the grass.

We drank our wine and ate the peanuts. Todd gobbled up the carrot stick, then rubbed his chin on Truby's shoes.

"Well," I said.

"That was rather a day," she said.

We laughed, God help us, and we began to talk. We talked as the stars appeared and the night covered us with its velvet. It was good to sit and talk with my friend in the dark, as we used to do whenever the power company cut us off back in our apartment on Prentis Street.

We talked for a long time.

Finally she said, "What are you going to do?"

"I'm going to go and talk to her."

"Then what?"

"Then we'll see."

We watched the stars.

Truby asked, "Do you know any constellations besides the Big Dipper?"

"No."

"Me neither."

"You saved me from becoming the Phantom of the Opera's little sister. Is there a Phantom of the Opera constellation?"

"I don't think so."

I reached out for her arm. "Anyway, thank you."

"Mention it again and I'll throw Diet Pepsi on you."

"Anything but that."

I said, "So, my dear," after we'd sat quiet for another while, "you had a breakthrough last night."

"I sure did."

"Tell me," I prompted.

"She was a babe, Lillian."

"Yeah?"

Truby rocked on her haunches. "And she was experienced."

"Oh, boy."

"We really meshed, you know?"

"Awright!"

"And she couldn't make me come."

I inclined my head for more.

"Well?" said Truby.

"Well what?" I said. "Sometimes that happens. First time and all. First date. Jeepers, Trube."

"What the hell do you mean?"

"What do you mean, what do I mean? Did you get *her* to come?"

"No."

"Well, don't feel bad."

"It wasn't easy, Lillian!"

I laughed. "Nothing worth learning ever is."

"I thought it'd be like, you know..."

"You thought it'd be automatic? Like, just start messing with each others' vulvas and watch the fireworks?"

"Well...yeah! I thought it was supposed to be beautiful and smashing, and *satisfying* and *wonderful*!"

"Oh, Truby."

"Her body was gorgeous, and it was exciting, but somehow the experience fell short. It was a lot harder to come than I expected." She shook her head in the dark. "I guess I had a preconception about it."

"I can't believe it. I could have disabused you of that in a second. My God. Didn't you ever *listen* to me when I talked about my affairs?"

"Yes, but..."

We sighed together. Beneath my hand, Todd sat between us quietly.

Truby said, "Why didn't you tell me about technique?"

"You didn't ask! I thought you wanted discover the joys of lesbian sex all by yourself."

"Shit."

"Truby. Look. I sense your experiment has come to an end. You're not really into women, are you?"

"Don't hate me."

"Shut up. Come on, hon. If you were a lesbian at heart, the orgasm-on-the-first-night thing wouldn't matter."

"Yeah, I know."

"You wanted to find something out, and you did. It's irrelevant to me who you sleep with."

"I might not sleep with anybody for a long, long time."

"Get a rabbit. They're warm and—"

"Lillian."

I shut up.

Truby said, "Now I have a sense of what Theo went through. You know, what it was like for him."

"Well, it's not *that* hard. Never mind. Think you'll try to get him back?"

"Oh, God, no."

"I always thought he was a little prissy."

"You never met him!"

"He *sounded* prissy."

She paused. "Well, he was."

We looked at the stars a while longer. The moon was coming up, what was left of it.

I was able to make out the face of my watch. "It's getting late," I said.

"You going over there?"

"Yeah, I'll walk over."

"What if she's not there?"

"She'll be there."

32

It was past eleven when I clambered over the patio bushes, Todd under my arm, and walked into the house on the sixteenth fairway. The lights were on, and Genie was alone, sitting in the largest leather chair in the living room, her feet up on a hassock, a mug of coffee in her hand. She was wearing her blue kimono and a comfortable smile.

"Meredith and everybody just left," she said.

To be accurate, she wasn't alone, not really alone at all; the championship trophy was there with her. A tall, classic loving cup, it gleamed from its place at the center of the coffee table. No, no, it didn't merely gleam; there in the fine lamplight in that fine room, it shone; it took light and did something splendid with it, amplified it, as expertly wrought silver does. Genie's name was now engraved on it a second time. The trophy was keeping her excellent company.

With tenderness and joy in her voice, she said, "Come here. Are you all right now?"

"I'm going to fix Todd up first," I said, walking through the room.

"There's fresh coffee," she said, still smiling. "Hello, Todd!"

After I'd seen to his food and water and newspapers, I poured myself some coffee. Used glasses and hors d'oeuvre dishes had been stacked around the sink. I returned to the living room.

"Would you be a dear," Genie asked, extending her mug to me, "and fill me up?"

I took a seat on the couch and stretched out my legs.

"Lillian?" her smile faltered. "Do you see that over there?"

"Yes. Congratulations."

"You know, Meredith was worried about you, but I wasn't. Not in the slightest. I knew you'd be just fine—and Todd, too. I knew everything would be fine."

She rose, and stepping carefully around the coffee table, came to the couch. "Let me see you." She eased down into the cushions. "Oh, you've got stitches! But you're as lovely as ever to me." She tried to nestle in for a kiss, but I nudged her away.

"Not yet," I said. "Genie—"

"You're tired, aren't you? But did you hear—oh, did you hear about it?"

I didn't reply.

She took my arm and kissed the bandage, and stroked it gently. She turned her face up to mine. "*I nearly holed out on my second shot.* Oh, Lillian, you should have seen it. Coco and Lona and I insisted that we be allowed to finish, and Meredith leaned hard on the tournament people, she really did, and we played in, oh, maybe just half an hour after...after everything calmed down. Oh, my dear. You should have seen me. Well, I'll get the tape from ABC."

Her eyes were hot glittering ingots. "Coco folded, she absolutely crumpled. Seeing my shot, she had to go for the green in two, and she put it in the water, and that was the end of her. Guess that'll shut her up. Oh, you should've seen her face. She could barely bring herself to shake my hand." She pumped her fist as I watched her, sipping my coffee.

"I *tapped in* for my eagle, which I didn't even need anymore because she bogeyed. I tapped in from eight inches. Now! How about a kiss?"

She leaned in and I let her.

"Hm. You *are* tired. I love your lips. I love-love-love your lips. Lillian, thank you for today. Thank you, thank you, thank you. I want to sweep you away somewhere for a—for everything! I'm taking next week off. Let's go to—where would you like to go? Let's go to New York and buy you a new wardrobe! How would you like that? I want to buy you some jewelry. Look at that poor little watch you've got. You can have anything you want! A car! Do you like that Jaguar? Let's look for a house together. Let's get a house in Florida—we'll get a big one!—and one in Italy. Wouldn't you like Italy? In the off season?"

She breathed deeply, luxuriously. "I'm free. I feel so free; I feel so fresh. Like I could beat them all again! I can beat anybody, and I will beat anybody. With you in my life—

maybe this sounds crazy, Lillian, but it's not, it's not!—with you in my life, I am invincible."

"Genie."

"Oh, if you could've been there. They cleared off—they cleared everything away, and we hit our shots, and I carried my own bag to the green. Look what I got!"

She held out a crumpled, stained rag.

"What's that?"

"Look, look, it's yours!"

Then it looked familiar. "Is that one of my handkerchiefs?"

"Your friend had it, she was dabbing your face with it, and I took it from her and put it in my pocket."

"It must be the one I lent her the first night I came to town. She must have intended to give it back to me. And you wanted some of my blood to carry along with you?"

"I felt you with me every step of the way. And it's over, and I'm safe. Aren't you going to ask if I took the jump?"

It was a tradition, a screwy one, for the champion of the Dinah to dive, or wade, into the water hazard before receiving the trophy. *I* wouldn't, boy. That water didn't look any too clean to me, although they'd dyed it blue for TV. Golf course water never does look clean, because of the fertilizer runoff, plus most hazards aren't part of a natural waterway, so the water is slow-moving to the point of stagnation. I'd overheard a marshal on seventeen say, "They had to use about three gallons of Aqua-Shade this year."

I sat silent.

Genie said, "Well, I did! A nice belly flop, I did, and it felt great! I can look anywhere now, and see the future. It's so beautiful. *I'm the best ever*—do you realize that?

I'm going to set records no one will ever break. The history of golf belongs to me. The history of sports! No one will forget me."

"Aren't you grateful to Coco Nash for smacking Dengel?"

"What?"

"Genie. Didn't you see her break Dengel's hand while I had him on the ground? She cracked him with her two-iron and broke the acid all over him."

"Oh. She did?"

"You were being carried up the fairway by her security women. I would judge that precise hit on Dengel took something out of her. For all you know, she broke her own hand doing it, slamming her club into something like that. For all you know, she used up everything she had, defending you. I'm not surprised her second shot found the water."

"Well, who knows, right? You know, I have so much more to talk to you about."

"Yes, Genie, you do."

"Lillian." She brushed my hair back from my eyes and peered in. "What's wrong with you? Aren't you happy? Aren't you happy for me? For us?"

"You know that Peaches died today."

Her eyes shifted away, and she nodded.

I said, "He died this morning."

"Seems like a week ago, doesn't it?"

I closed my eyes.

"I'm going to, ah, set up a fund," she said, "like a caddie scholarship, in his name."

"Are you going to go see his wife? And the baby?"

"Uh...I don't really know her."

Looking at her, I said, "Genie. You need to shut up and listen to me. Okay? I'm going to tell you a story. It's a story that's very important to me, and it's important to you. It happened a long time ago. I don't know how—I need to know how it ended. Then maybe we can go on together."

She stared hard at me, her mouth tight.

"A girl and a boy are in love," I began. "It's puppy love at most, I guess. They fool around and she gets pregnant, only they're so dumb they don't know she's pregnant. These two kids, they're on their own. They're trash; they're nobodies that nobody gives a shit about. And they've found each other, and they think, *Well, this is something. This is love.* She thinks, *My God, this boy loves me.* She's an overweight slob, her mother's a drunk, her father's a shit-ass, and she doesn't give a damn about anything except being loved."

Genie's eyes moved to the trophy. She looked at me again, and a veil came over her eyes. She eased away from me on the couch, her back against its fat leather arm.

"Let's see," I went on, "the boy had a car. And that was their private place, the one place they had to themselves. And after a while she notices that her periods have stopped, and they're having sex more often, and it occurs to them that they should have birth control. And she's worried about this thing that's moving around in her stomach. And the kindly country doctor says, *'Honey, you're going to have a baby. A baby!'*"

Genie's face was blank, her eyes dull now; not even the shine of the trophy showed in them.

I kept talking. "The kindly doctor is very concerned. *'Would you like help giving this baby up for adoption?'* *'Oh, no, thank you, Doctor. You won't tell, will you?' 'No, child. But you must go home and tell your mother right away.' 'Oh, yes, I will.'* They're confused, and they're dumb, and maybe they don't really believe a baby will come along after all. She ignores the pregnancy. And since everybody ignores her, nobody notices. She's fat and unfriendly, and nobody notices that she's gotten fatter and maybe a little unfriendlier. She wears—let's see, she wears big sweatshirts to school. Big jeans and big floppy sweatshirts, and the baby kicks in the middle of the fall of the Romanovs and it kicks during calisthenics and it kicks while X squared plus Y squared is equaling Z squared. And she wonders what will happen."

Genie turned her face away from me and held herself rigidly against the arm of the couch.

"They try to decide what to do. *'Let's not tell anyone yet. We can always tell, but we can never un-tell.'* Her mother yells at her for eating too much. When her stomach starts to hurt, he gets hold of his dad's credit card, and they go to a motel. She gives birth there, with him running for more towels, scared shitless. It's a bloody scene, but there is a baby, there in the middle of all that blood, and whoa, here comes the afterbirth—my God, what kind of a freak gives birth to something like *that,* so soon after a regular baby?"

I could see I was nailing it all pretty well, so far.

"Were you happy when the baby came?" I asked.

Genie sat as motionless as her trophy. She murmured, "It hurt. It hurt so bad. I felt so bad."

"Was Dom happy? Dom was happy, wasn't he?"

"Dom..."

I waited, then pressed on. "The next day, Genie, he goes out to buy some things."

"The baby needed milk. He went to buy milk for the baby."

"And when he comes back…" I waited again. "Look at me, Genie. Come on and look at me."

Genie turned her face to me, her eyes empty, and said, "When he comes back…"

"Tell me, Genie, when he comes back, the baby is dead. Isn't that right?"

"The baby is dead."

"But it wasn't born dead. It was born alive, wasn't it?"

"He was excited. He wanted to buy a stroller. He went out to buy milk and a stroller. I needed Kotex."

"What happened to the baby, Genie?"

"Somehow…it died."

"How?"

"It was crying."

"The baby cried—"

"And I was scared. It cried. It didn't even look at me when it cried."

"What made him stop crying?"

"A pillow."

"A pillow made him stop crying."

"We were in a motel."

"And there were pillows," I said. "The baby was crying, and there was a pillow. And Dom—"

"And Dom went out."

"Why did you smother the baby, Genie?"

"I was afraid…"

"What were you afraid of?"

"I was afraid it didn't love me."

"Oh, my dear God."

"Dom was angry when he came back."

"Did you love the baby?"

Genie's gaze was utterly blank.

I asked, "Where's the baby now?"

"I don't know."

"You don't know now, but you did know."

"I wrapped it in a towel. Dom had a box. He wanted a funeral."

"What did you tell Dom?"

"That the baby died."

"He didn't believe it died by itself, did he?"

"I don't know. I might not have been the one.... He wanted a funeral, so we made a funeral. I thought he'd be happy then."

"Dom had a box—what kind of box?"

"For tools."

"It was a metal box?"

"A box, a hard red box, and he dug a hole—we went down to the river and he dug a hole, and I put the baby in the box, and he put it in the hole and buried it."

"And he marked the grave somehow?"

"At the end of the fence."

"The grave was at the end of the fence?"

"Where it comes out from the parking lot. We sang a song."

"What did you sing?"

" 'Puff, the Magic Dragon.' It was May. It was a pretty night."

"You buried the baby at night."

"I had a candle. It was May."

"The child was your May child. You had your May child, and you killed it, and you took its name. Genie Maychild."

"I buried..."

"Yes?"

"Myself."

"Yes. Yes. Did you know that Dom took the baby's fingerprints? That he marked ink from a pen onto his fingers, and pressed them down one by one onto a piece of paper?"

"No."

"It doesn't matter, does it?"

"No."

"The two of you buried that baby, and you buried yourselves, and you split up."

"He said he wanted to marry me."

"But you didn't want that. And you didn't want a baby."

"There was... Somewhere, there was more for me."

" 'More.' And you found it. Coach Handy—she helped you find it."

Genie nodded slowly. "That's right."

"And after you made it, and after he got cancer, Dengel showed up again. Wanting help from you. Wanting money."

"But..."

"But you refused, and he began to terrorize you. He showed up in that dead bloody baby costume at Handy's retirement."

"Yes, that was him."

"Then he threatened to tell about the baby. He threatened to dig it up."

"Unless..."

"Unless you helped him. And he got people out here in California, those people in their little anti-abortion terror societies, to bug you, to harass you. And then he came out to get to you himself."

We didn't speak for a while. Little sounds came to my

ears: the refrigerator motor, a crinkle of newspaper from Todd's room.

Gradually, Genie came out of the past, back to herself. Back to Genie Maychild right now.

She said, softly, "Lillian, you've got to try to understand."

"I helped you, and Coco helped you, and Coach Handy helped you. She's in jail now. She's your little Jack Ruby."

"No, no. She might have to stay overnight, but she'll be out tomorrow. My lawyer's taking care of her. They're not going to charge a sixty-six-year-old woman with murder. She won't ever tell anybody anything, and she won't go to jail."

"You called on her, and she got a shovel and dug up that box and moved it to another place."

"It wasn't safe where it was."

"*You* weren't safe with the box where it was."

"Lillian. Marian understands. You've got to understand, too."

It was some time before I spoke again. "How do you justify it to yourself?"

"I was young and I didn't know. How much different is it from an abortion? You understand getting an abortion, don't you?"

"Actually, I have a hard time with that one. An abortion's a brutal thing to do—there's no way anybody can say it isn't. But I guess a woman ought to be able to do what she wants, when it's her body. But when there's a baby, Genie, a breathing baby you've given birth to, that smells like you and came right from you and survived its first night on earth…that's murder."

"I'm not saying it isn't."

"Oh."

"I'm saying you've got to understand. It's not a simple thing."

"From the baby's viewpoint it is. And from the law's viewpoint, too."

"Can we stop talking about this?"

"And just move on?"

"Yes!"

"No."

"I can't believe this."

"Genie, you know you're going to have to live with this, with all of this."

She looked at me impatiently. "I do live with it."

"How?"

She had no answer.

33

The shuttle doors banged shut, and it lurched away. My car was just as I'd left it, albeit covered with a grimy film. I'd always taken good care of my geriatric Caprice, a former cop car, but at this point in its life I always held my breath when starting it after it'd sat parked for more than two days. But the old girl chugged right into action.

The engine warmed up while I loaded in Todd and my mandolin and suitcase, and breathed deeply of the western Wayne County air, hanging there beneath a ragged cloud cover. Spring had come.

Yes, you could smell it for sure, that loamy wet fragrance, little seeds and roots and whatnot shifting in the soil, the earthworms poking out and rubbing their eyes, saying, *Hey, it's sort of warm!*

Was there a skim of green on the bare branches yet? Maybe not, but I could feel that photosynthesis would not long be denied hereabouts.

"Ah!" I said, settling behind the wheel. I rolled down the window, and Todd lifted his nose as we peeled out and headed for home.

Going up Middlebelt I had to swerve to avoid a streaking squirrel. Here and there, furry carcasses littered the shoulder.

Springtime in Detroit is squirrel-carnage time. Every year the squirrels emerge from their nests up in the trees, where they've hidden all winter, venturing out only to scrape around for the caches of acorns they absentmindedly buried last fall, and as we know, they're not terribly adept at it. So come spring, thin and excited, they climb down to the thawing ground and start running around looking for new things to eat. They're crazy with relief, and it takes them a while to get focused. On top of that, during the long winter they've forgotten what roads are and what cars are. Don't they tell stories up in those nests during those long winter nights? Don't they have legends? What do they talk about? They appear to pass on no lore whatsoever to their young.

All this results in much needless loss of squirrel life.

Mrs. McVittie was on the porch digging into a flowerpot with a trowel when I pulled up. I saw Mr. McVittie up the driveway near the garage, rinsing the winter's worth of accumulated salt from the undercarriage and wheel wells of their station wagon. He'd made a special nozzle for the job from some PVC pipe and one of Mrs. McVittie's support stockings.

"I'll do yours next!" he hollered as I came up to the house.

"All right! Thank you!" I shouted back, in deference to his deafness.

"Trip go okay?"

"Yeah! Did you catch some fish up north?"

"Hell yes, I caught fish! Me and the boys—" He peered at me. "Lillian, did you get in a fight?"

"Yeah. But you should see the other guy."

After I unpacked and hooked up my little washing machine in my kitchen, I smelled gingerbread baking in the kitchen below. I set my stovetop percolator to boil with a basketful of nice fresh Sumatran.

Fifteen minutes later I heard Mrs. McVittie coming up the stairs in her hesitant, light-footed way. I opened the door for her. She carried a plate of the steaming spicy cake, and I asked her to join me for some coffee.

Being diabetic, she couldn't eat the gingerbread, but she enjoyed watching me eat it, and she enjoyed her coffee.

"It sure is good to be home," I said with satisfaction. I'd stood a while on my balcony surveying the neighborhood and looking for Monty. You remember Mrs. Gagnon's dog, Monty.

"Did you see the crocuses in the backyard, dear?"

"No! Are they up?"

"Yes, and just as pretty as ever."

"This gingerbread is the whip, Mrs. McVittie." Somehow I never could call her "Mildred," nor Mr. McVittie "Emmett."

"Oh, it's a pleasure, isn't it? I just love how it smells." She shifted in her chair and looked my face over carefully. "Did you get in trouble with the police in California?"

"No, no, I just got into a little—it was more of an accident than anything. I'm just fine."

"Well, did you have a nice time, aside from that?"

"I did have a bit of fun, yes. I spent some time in Los Angeles."

"Los Angeles is an interesting place."

"Yes, it is."

"Then where did you go?"

"Oh, the desert area, you know."

"Oh. I bet it was nice there."

"Yes, very good weather."

Mr. and Mrs. McVittie were not golf fans, which I was glad for.

I asked, "Have you gotten out on your bike yet?" She liked to ride that three-wheeler to hell and gone, making friends everywhere.

"As a matter of fact, yes, dear, I have gotten out. And I think you'll be glad to know something." Her thin hand shook just a little as she lifted her cup to her lips.

"Yeah? What's that?"

"I think that Monty won't be bothering Todd and you anymore."

"Really? What happened? I didn't see him outside. Would you like some more coffee?"

"Yes, dear, it's delicious. I can't get mine to taste like this." She drank it black, as I did. "Well, I was riding up and down the streets—you know how I do. And I thought— well, you know how dogs love rotten meat."

"I sure do." I set the pot back on the stove.

"Well, I took a plastic bag along with me the other day— spring came so fast! Doesn't the air feel wonderful?"

"Yes, it does. It feels swell."

"I expect we'll get one more flurry before the warm weather sets in for good."

"Mm-hmm."

"And I had my plastic bag, and I picked up three dead squirrels—you know how they're all over the place now..."

"Yes!"

"I picked up the rottenest ones I could find, with lots of maggots and ants, and also I got one little raccoon, too, although come to think of it, it might have been a cat—"

"Yes!"

"And I put them in a crate Emmett had, a plastic crate that he didn't want anymore?"

"Yes!"

"It's more of a tub. Anyway I dragged it out front, and Monty ran right over—"

"Yes!"

"And he jumped into that crate, and oh, dear, he had a wonderful time! Rolling back and forth in those rotten squirrels."

"Was Mrs. Gagnon—"

"Oh, yes, Dolly was out planting petunias in her box, you know, yes. She saw him come over, but she couldn't see what was in the crate. I pretended to shoo Monty away, and of course she just laughed, and Monty kept rolling and chewing and sniffing in that crate for the longest time. Then she held her door open and called him to come in, and I gave him—well, I gave him a little kick, and he ran right across the street and into the house, and I haven't seen either of them since."

I looked at her, and she looked at me, and an atomic bomb couldn't have set our smiles askew.

"Mrs. McVittie," I said, "you are a true friend."

"I bet she'll keep Monty in the backyard from now on."

"I bet she will."

The next day as I was looking over my accumulated bills, it occurred to me that I hadn't received my thousand dollars for wearing Ace-Tek's chicken visor. For the hell of it, I called the company and actually got Jeff Evans on the line.

"Hey!" he said on a falling note. "I'm really sorry, but the deal was you'd wear our visor for the whole round. Eighteen holes."

"But Jeff—"

"Not seventeen and a half holes. That was the agreement you signed. I'm really sorry, but—"

Cursing myself, I hung up on him as hard as I could.

That night I received a phone call I hadn't been expecting but was glad to get.

"I am sorry I finaled out on you," said Coco Nash. I'd tried without success to get a hold of her before flying back home.

I said, "Never mind. Are you all right?"

"I will be. You?"

"I'm fine. What do you mean, you will be?"

"I jerked up my wrist some on that two-iron to the metacarpals."

"I thought so. Is it broken?"

"No."

"You're getting therapy for it, then?"

"Yes, I have the most righteous of therapists—infrared, everything."

"You know, Coco, Genie probably will never thank you, but I will. You saved me as much as you saved her. Thank you, Cornelia Nash."

"You are welcome."

"I wish there was something I could do for you."

Her voice went husky. "It would be nice to see you again."

"Oh! Uh, Coco. Whew, boy, um."

The line was silent.

At last I said, "I hope you can understand that I kind of need to—"

"You need to keep to yourself for now."

"Yes."

"So I believe you read some Bible to Genie."

"I did, and she didn't like it."

"And when you left—"

"She *really* didn't like it."

"Well. I do not know everything I would like to know."

"Coco, I think you're plenty hep to all of it. You do know. Hey, I'll be watching you on TV next tournament, okay?"

"That swings."

I went for a drive a few early brights later, taking along Todd, my mandolin, and a picnic lunch. I thought we'd ride around the Irish Hills, take in the sunny soft breezes and just have a good time.

But I found myself forgetting the exits off I-94 and just driving through, past Ypsilanti, through Ann Arbor, Jackson, Albion.

Me: You're going out there, aren't you?

Me: Maybe.

Me: Why?

Me: I just want to.

There was a good oldies station on the radio in western Michigan, but I turned it off as I kept the pedal down and talked to Todd about happiness and about achievement and about love.

What the hell did I want? What the hell did I ever want? Who the hell cares?

Truby wanted to know a certain score, and she found it out. At least she learned as much as she needed to know now. When we'd said so long at LAX, she was looking a good bit better than she had when I'd seen her at the baggage claim a week and a half earlier. And I looked the worse, but no matter.

I thought about Genie. Three people dead in her wake. The baby. Peaches. Dengel. I guessed I was lucky. I didn't feel lucky, though.

Was I a chump? I'd always seen trouble coming. But this time trouble saw me first, sneaked up behind me, and sapped me but good. Did I have it coming?

After my talk with Coco on the phone, I got out one of her scrapbooks on Genie and leafed through it. Yes: I'd stuffed it into my suitcase and brought it home. Looking at the pictures, I thought, *If only you'd done it differently.* Don't think I'm going soft, though. That scrapbook might be worth a bundle someday.

It wasn't all right with me that Genie was who she was. I understood that the making of Genie Maychild was the suffocation of her son, while she believed that the making of Genie Maychild was putting the killing behind her. And she was going to go on being who she was, and there wasn't a thing I could do about it. I could rent a billboard calling her poison and a murderer, and nothing would come of it, except possibly a libel suit.

It was late afternoon when I hit the Pearl Center town line, having stopped outside of Benton Harbor to eat lunch and exercise Todd. The Illinois prairie sky was mottled with gray clouds that were moving ahead of a westerly wind. I took the river road and parked the Caprice on the bluff overlooking the small series of rapids west of town. I watched the water for a while, then I walked the fence line to the end, where it jutted out from the oiled parking lot.

The earth there had been disturbed. I saw loose clods, and spade marks on the wooden fence post. The hole had been carelessly filled in and stomped down, and the dirt had already sunk a few inches. I tried to make out footprints, but it had rained enough to obliterate any that had been there.

I drove over to Coach Handy's street and cruised down it slowly. The public works department had finished its job: The sewer line or water line, or whatever had needed fixing, was fixed and the trench was filled, the broken concrete hauled away and new concrete poured.

I pulled over and stared at that new concrete.

Full many a flower is born to blush unseen
And waste its sweetness on the desert air.

Those lines, from Gray's *Elegy Written in a Country Churchyard,* came to me then.

"One of those wreaths." I pointed into the cooler, and the flower shop lady smiled.

"That's a lovely one," she said. "Are you going over to the cemetery?"

"Uh...how much do I owe you?"

I fought with myself as I drove past the office of the Pearl Center *Bugle.* If I could've driven past it with my eyes shut, I would have. When I returned to the coach's street, I noticed that her house had a Century 21 sign out front: FOR SALE. A cardinal lighted on the yellow crossbar and pecked it experimentally.

I shut off the engine and said a Hail Mary. I carried the wreath, made of lilies, carnations, ribbons, down the street, walking beside the wide strip of new concrete. I didn't know where to put it. It would be ridiculous to leave it in the street.

I returned to the Caprice, muttering to Todd, and drove back to the river as twilight came on.

The air at the river smelled fresh and healthy. I stood on the bluff. The water swirled around the rocks below, not far below. It splashed and caught itself and raced on, and it played that music everyone likes to hear, the music of cleanliness and no troubles. I slung my mandolin around and joined in, slowly playing "Bury Me Beneath the Willow" and "Were You There?" I put the pick in my pocket and watched the tips of the trees tossing in the breeze. The sky had cleared. Its blue deepened as I watched.

One by one, then in handfuls, I plucked the flowers from the wreath's backing and tossed them into the water. They bobbed along prettily, pink and white and yellow.

When it grew too dark to see the river anymore, I stood and listened. Then it was time to go.

ABOUT THE AUTHOR

RANDALL LAMB

Elizabeth Sims is also the author of *Holy Hell*, the first book in the Lillian Byrd Crime Story series. She holds degrees from Michigan State University and Wayne State University, where she won the Tompkins Award for fiction. An experienced reporter and bookseller, she has written about the book business for *LOGOS: Journal of the World Book Community,* and book reviews for the *Detroit Free Press*. For more information, visit www.elizabethsims.com.